Bahamas
N.C.BACCHUS
M. D.
Harbour
Eleuthera

DO NO HARM

Cliff Bacchus

Do No Harm

ISBN: 978-1-4582-0096-9 (sc)
ISBN: 978-1-4582-0095-2 (e)
ISBN: 978-1-4582-0097-6 (hc)

Library of Congress Control Number: 2011919522

Abbott Press books may be ordered through booksellers or by contacting:

Abbott Press
1663 Liberty Drive
Bloomington, IN 47403
www.abbottpress.com
Phone: 1-866-697-5310

Printed in the United States of America

Abbott Press rev. date: 11/11/2011

DEDICATION

To Olga, Angelika, Melinda, Jason, Yanni, and Moanna

First, do no harm.
—Hippocrates

God heals, and the doctor takes the fees.
—Benjamin Franklin

CHAPTER 1

Atlantic Isle, Bahamas

"In the name of peace, I'll—I'll fight him to the end." Dr. Al Chandler shuddered, and his body tensed. "No matter what it takes." He couldn't get the image of Obi Falconer out of his mind.

Chandler worked hard. He sweated at the hospital's ER but, in truth, he was committed to being a warrior. Life excited him. He came to earth to be bold, and he would be. Adventure was his life.

He washed his hands and stepped outside. The warmth of the afternoon sun blazing in the western sky felt good on his skin. He looked at the horizon, where thunderclouds were building. The sky's threat to burst open aroused no fear—unlike the somber secret that haunted his soul.

He hurried to the park. Pandora expected him home for dinner in thirty minutes. He felt obligated to get there on time and pressed the gas in Pandora's Swiss Jaguar Daimler. The 363 Hp high-end car, with burr walnut, leather interior, and GPS navigator, responded immediately, sending him to sixty miles an hour in seconds. He negotiated a curve, relishing the screech of the tires on the roadway. The police car that suddenly loomed in his rear view and then sped ahead of him crushed his euphoria.

"Pigs!"

He slowed down. He owned the Jaguar, but still felt uneasy accepting the car as a dowry. "American men don't do that." With the police now way ahead of him, he whipped up speed.

A glance at his wristwatch showed six fifteen. Pandora loved her meals fresh and hot, and he was late. That could mean trouble.

But she wasn't there.

"Pandora?" No response.

He opened the kitchen door. No smell of food met his nostrils. No one was around. The dinner table was bare. He grabbed a beer, gulped it, and went from room to room. No Pandora anywhere. He scratched his head and paced the floor. Bemused, he rubbed his blond close-cut beard.

"Game's finished!" He finally called out. "You won. I'm really hungry."

He heard nothing as he eyed the hall. She was nowhere to be seen.

Baraka howled outside.

"Ah! I know where you are."

He ran out onto the stretch of green lawn. Wind gusted against his skin and swayed the coconut palms. A battery of lightning raked the sky, honing the trees into black skeletons. Thunder clapped, and exploded in his ears.

"Shit!" His voice echoed. "I'm getting bad vibes here." He moved back a step. An urge told him to run to the house for cover. "Feels weird." He stared into the distance as the dog barked. He moved to the pond, zeroing in on an object by the water's edge, next to a cluster of palm trees. "A piece of weather-washed driftwood?" He jerked his head around. Nothing, nobody. He cursed the wood. "Damn!"

A voice echoed in his head. "Pandora."

"This is absurd!" He slouched off.

Ducks huddled and quacked. The caws of a flock of black carrion crows echoed eerily. His fear was now palpable; he shrugged it off and sprinted to the pool.

"Hello!"

His footing wavered as a burst of thunderclaps shook the ground, temporarily overwhelming the whine of his German shepherd. Chandler stepped away from the pond. He must go back to the house. She had to be in one of the rooms.

"But I checked the house."

He stepped back, and his heel hit the dry branch. He fell backward. Slowly, the color faded from his world.

"Oh my gosh!"

Pandora lay face down, naked, a gunshot wound at the back of her head. His breath caught in his throat. He stared into space. His breath, finally released, now matched the rapid rhythm of his heart hitting against his breastbone. Her body showed black and blue spots. He touched her.

No pulse. No heartbeat.

No movement but for the Swiss Audemars Piguet she wore: the minute hand continued to tick.

"She's dead!"

Coral Springs, Florida
20 January 2009 One month earlier

"O-o-h-h-m-m." Chandler meditated. He was glad he lived far enough from the Everglades that its reptile denizens did not invade his red, Spanish-roofed house. The thought of reptiles sliding across his straw mat during his meditation made his skin crawl. No, the one-story off-blue building with columns was safely tucked away in the Pelican Isles gated community, guarded by lines of Royal Palm Trees along the streets. He could lie on the polished floor of his sky-lit den, on his straw mat, without worry. He shut his eyes. Four minutes more to wait. "Oooh—"

"*Woof.*"

Chandler sprang up and squatted on the mat. "Baraka!" He put his index finger to his lips. "I was meditating."

"*Woof,*" the dumb animal repeated.

"Hush! I'm a hippie. Bite the yuppies."

Baraka whined, circled him, and squatted. His paws inched closer to his master.

Chandler gripped the dog's ears and let his own nose touch the dog's cold snout. He stripped off his colors: a Levi's jacket without sleeves. He took off his blue crocheted tam with wooden beads and slipped on a purple bandanna.

Baraka ran from him. "*Woof-woof-woof.*"

"Yap as much as you want." Chandler stood. His red Zippo lighter flared as he lit a joint. He discarded his hemp shoes, choosing instead the sturdy rope sandals. The half-mug of home-brew beer on the coffee table still retained a frosting of ice. Its cold fizz flowed delightfully down his throat. He licked the last bit of foam from his lips.

"That was good. I need another," he said to the dog.

His fridge yielded a second bottle. The contents soon joined the first mugful. The ice-cold liquid chilled his stomach and he belched. He had two minutes more to go.

"I'm proud of my new leader."

Toying with the amber birthstone on his hemp chain, he focused his attention on his sixty-five-inch flat-screen Sharp TV. One and a half minutes more. A thrill went down his spine as the White House came into view. Millions of people were gathered. *Ten-nine-eight-seven-six-five-four-three-two-one!* African-American President Abraham King began his inaugural speech.

"He's an orator." Again Chandler reveled in the man's sincerity, motivation, and focus on the grassroots. The massive, chanting crowd clearly shared Chandler's hero worship.

He clapped and chuckled. "A dream has come true! Sure, my president, you inherited a financial mess. You have an economic crisis on your hands. This planet has never had anyone like you—or me!" His vain words struck him as humorous, and he laughed.

Chandler continued to watch. The TV screen was now somewhat obscured by marijuana smoke. *The nirvana is different now,* he thought. *My president reigns.*

He believed in the president's vision. He wondered about a world rife with poverty, disease, illiteracy, terrorism, and war. The more fortunate people bullied the ill-fated ones. Doctors maltreated the sick and did harm. He mused. *Same damage all over the world. Human tragedy!*

He glued his eyes to the TV, distracted only occasionally by the joint, the third beer, or the dog that needed patting. At the end of the broadcast, he offered up a short prayer for his president friend and then spoke directly to the TV. "You can perform miracles. Make Hailey Clint your secretary of state."

He sucked on his joint. "Organize, deputize, and supervise! Stop the war in Afghanistan. Bring home the troops from Iraq. Lift the economic blockade against Cuba."

He shot up, marched around the sofa, and pointed at the skylight. "The sky is the limit. Go with passion, sir! You'll be president again."

King wanted to change the status quo of greed in America. Chandler shared those feelings: The fraud and malpractice in medicine must stop.

The four-legged shepherd whined. Chandler opened another beer, dropped onto the sofa, and sipped the liquid gold. The wetness of a tear coursed down his cheek as his feelings for King's success now rose to the surface. He empathized with the new president for the crises he was about to face. Drawing in on his marijuana, he floated in space. He stubbed his joint in an ashtray. "I quit smoking now. We would stop wars, drink beers, and uplift spirits." He raised his beer bottle. "Dig my crazy old kicks!"

Baraka scratched on the floor. "*Woof.*"

"Hush." He stared at the shepherd and made faces at the dog. *He understands that my discreet mustache matches my beard. The silver-tone beaded peace sign earring on my left ear means calm for him. He thinks I'm not all there.*

Baraka whined and nodded. Chandler cupped the animal's head in his hands and kissed his forehead.

Chandler stood for peace. On his twelfth birthday in Chicago, his friends had chosen a lonely spot by a sewer for him to fight. A boy bashed his nose until it bled. He ran from them. Rain poured and lightning sparked in the sky. He didn't know where to go. A thud of thunder scared him. "Run to your mom, stupid." He shot home. Pain pulsed in his head.

"Son, we love you." His mother had consoled him and nursed his wounds. "You're like our own. We believe you're at an age when you—"

"What? What?"

That was when they had told him. He was lost in a maze. Even now, twenty-six years later, he still cringed at his mother's candor.

Colic suddenly gripped his abdomen. He rushed into the washroom and vomited. Streaks of blood came out.

Baraka ran in, and put his paws on the sink. "*Yap.*"

Chandler held his stomach. He ruffled Baraka's ears. The pain eased, flashed back, and died off. He heard his mother's voice: "You're an orphan born in Kenya of English residents who died in a road traffic accident."

He went to his study and sat before his desktop computer. A blurb caught his attention. Dr. Obi Falconer, Falconer General Hospital, Atlantic Isle, Caribbean. Falconer declared, "I am black, but no black man can ever lead America."

Impatience crept into his voice. "Strange dude."

All day, he followed the comments from leading political analysts for and against his president. Joy filled him. His watch showed five p.m. He scanned the channels and settled on CNN. Crickets chirped outside, heralding dusk. He got into hemp pajamas, switched off the bedroom lights, and tucked himself in. He had to go to work early in the morning. He closed his eyes and willed himself to sleep.

The telephone rang. So late—only in an emergency would it ring at this hour. *Did someone assassinate my president?* He switched the lights on and grabbed the receiver.

"Whoever you are, say a bedtime prayer. Thank you, good night."

"Hello, Al!"

"Who the hell's calling?" Chandler demanded.

"Al Chandler! Is that you?"

He recognized King's voice. "Oops! Sorry, Mr. President." His brain chilled from the surprise. "You're supposed to be celebrating."

"I am, but a call to you adds to the joy."

"You're kind, Mr. President. I congratulate you on a great first speech."

"Hear me out, Al. You like people. You're outspoken. You give them strong handshakes. You reach out to American voters."

"I learned many fine traits from you."

"You can read minds."

Chandler faked an Indian accent. "Your fate and sun lines show a good future, and a helpful mother-in-law."

"You'd make an ace test pilot. You were an A-1 campaign adviser. We won Florida. I admire your stance on healthcare. I want you to be my secretary of health."

"Mr. President, I—"

"You're saying no?"

He fidgeted with his pajamas button and collar. "My place is in the hospital. I prefer Florida to Washington."

"I have an early morning briefing."

"Uneasy lies the head that wears a White House, Mr. President!"

He killed the dimmer. He regretted disappointing the president, but he had to do his mind's bidding. Sleep evaded him, and he tossed and turned. He arose and again turned on the lights. The wall clock chimed three a.m. His priorities in life were medicine, politics, and love, in that order. "Let me finish some personal business."

He went to the fridge, poured yet another homemade beer, and ambled into his study. He reclined on a leather chair covered with a knitted hemp throw. He logged in to the Luna Matching Website chat room. A webcam gave him a photo of a woman. She was slim, with a white, Irish face and small, round hazel eyes. She had a chiseled nose, inelegant mouth, and fair hair. Her height was five feet six, and she weighed a hundred and ten pounds. "Great Basic Metabolic Index. Not sleeping either." The logo ID read: Atlantic Isle, Caribbean. Ninety miles from Florida.

America had beautiful women. He could choose one, marry her, move to Washington, and live the life. He drank the beer and spat out a grain of hop. He bit his lip and typed *Peace!*

Pandora: Where were you?

Chandler: Busy working the presidential campaign. Still more bread to collect for postelection business.

Pandora: What's bread?

Chandler: "Money," in hippie dialect.

Pandora: Congratulations! Again, where in Florida is Coral Springs?

Chandler: Broward County, twenty miles northwest of Fort Lauderdale. Population 127,000. Different from hometown Chicago.

Pandora: How many springs in Coral Springs?

Chandler: No springs. Maybe I'm the only one.

Pandora: Carry on.

Chandler: I'm in a group. We protect the reefs, the ecosystem. We talk about global warming, pollution, and overfishing. I'll simplify the environment to make the world more manageable.

Pandora: Swell! You meet ugly American women there, too.

Chandler: May I come to visit you? ☺

Pandora: Proposing again?

Chandler: Let's go down Kasbah.

Pandora: What's Kasbah?

Chandler: "Lover's lane." Marry me and I'll never gaze at another Pandora ... Can I get a job there?

Pandora: You're a typical man. Our prime minister Gray is my brother. I'll get you citizenship. You can work in ER, at Falconer's Hospital. A vacancy exists. Reverend and Mrs. Chandler worked at our hospital. They served as chaplains. They're your parents, right?

Chandler: Mom and Dad adopted me when I was three.

Pandora: What nationality is Reverend Sam Chandler?

Chandler: He's Irish-American.

Pandora: Mrs. Amelia Chandler?

Chandler: She's Irish. I'll visit you later.

Pandora: I remember some Irish jokes. LOL. Handsome photo of you here. Still love you although you're American.

Chandler: American men are great lovers.

Pandora: Do you want to marry me, American boy?

Chandler: I suppose I do.

Pandora: Yes!

Chandler: Start making plans. You're a challenge. I'm liking you. You're scaring me.

Pandora: LOL! Switch to Facebook.

He disconnected the website and finished off his beer. He signed in. She sent him photos of hospital consultants. "My friends go gaga over me. My men fight to dance with me at parties. Every one of them wants me to be his wife. LOL! You'll love the island."

He scratched his head and paced the study. He dropped into his chair and reconnected to their chat. "Do you have national health care?"

Pandora: No socialism, please. We're capitalists. We think like the American Republican party. My family owns the private health insurance.

Chandler: Give me six months there, and I'll change the system.

Pandora: Crap!

Chandler: What d'you know about famous people living on your island?

Pandora: The Shah of Iran hid here. Howard Hughes lived on Atlantic

Isle. Sean Connery resides on the Isle. Anna Nicole's body rests in peace in a cemetery. This is the place to be.

Chandler: Blab about the doctor-in-charge of the big hospital.

Pandora: Dr. Falconer.

Chandler: Go ahead.

Pandora: He's a secret order member, and the only man here who stands seven feet tall. He has the ego of an alpha wolf. Scary! At Christmas, Falconer gave $1,000 worth of gifts for a Kiwanis Club children's party.

Chandler: I love children.

Pandora: I don't.

Chandler: If I can't have any of my own, I'll adopt.

Pandora: A desperate measure! Early January, Falconer donated $2,000 for a blood bank drive. He also donated $1,000 each to the leading churches, Catholic, Anglican, and Baptist. He's a giving man, but a wolf.

Chandler: A friendly dude!

Pandora: A mystery man. Gambles a lot. Supports the Day of Pardon.

Chandler: What's the Day of Pardon?

Pandora: The head of state pardons prisoners. Falconer and I advise on convicts to release.

Chandler: That's cool.

Pandora: Everything's calm here. Like, we believe in dowry.

Chandler: What do I offer you?

Pandora: The woman's side gives.

Chandler: What do I get?

Pandora: My house, my car, and my bed.

Chandler: LOL. Peace! ☺

He killed the lights at 5:30 and went to bed. He prayed for help to decide what to do. Sleep eluded him. The slices of slumber he got gave him nightmares. In one, he ran around the New Orleans cemetery. A hand from the grave pulled him in. People danced a Junkanoo slave dance and trampled him. A witch cast a voodoo spell and transformed him into dust. She turned him into a wizard.

He sprang up, panting. Like a lightning bolt, he decided on his plan. "I'll do it now."

His personal nurse shook her head, almost crying. "Please don't go."

His ER hospital staff, the local politicians, and his hippie friends gathered at his house. He smiled at the crowd and announced, "I'm leaving the hospital here to work in Atlantic Isle."

A doctor stepped up to him. "Congratulations!"

A politician raised a hand. "Poise and personality are your admirable attributes."

"The island wants me, now!"

They partied all night. Disco lights flashed in rhythm to the music. Chandler swilled beer and Campari. The DJ played *The Star-Spangled Banner*. Chandler led the singing, "Oh, say, can you see, by the dawn's early light …"

The farewell party was swinging, and the music drowned out the ringing telephone. The hospital receptionist ran and picked up the phone.

"Al, President King's calling for you."

The line clicked several times and King came on. "Congratulations on your new venture abroad, Al. Hope we meet again."

"My heart goes out to a man who cares."

"I'm the president, you're my friend. I had my staff do some quick research on your future home. You'll bump into cutthroats and a few people with lowered motives. You'll encounter someone who is power-hungry and greedy. He's going to tyrannize you. I get your way of thinking. You strategize well. You know the liberal plan for the grassroots. The big boys will crush you."

"Good research, sir."

"You're an honest man, and you embrace the American people. You're different. You fight temptation and rise above. You can foresee a problem and respond before anyone suffers. Clear the jungle and, if you can, introduce government health reform with non-government participation. Whatever conflict you take on, awaken the higher nature in you. The year has just begun. Best wishes to you. Life can be slow overseas. Take six months off."

"Is that a deadline?"

"That's a good sign. You're already thinking ahead." He signed off.

Chandler still held the phone in his hand. He swallowed drily. The prospects didn't appear good. He was plunging into a quagmire. His head spun. Campaign photographs with King and him flashed before his eyes. "You lend force to me, Mr. President. All the strength I need." He belched beer and Campari. His mind traveled far away, to New Orleans, and to the slave dance at the graveyard. He danced until the DJ stopped the music. To the crowd he announced, "An American chick with fourteen children lives in a small home. I'll give them the house."

The local newspapers highlighted his exodus: "America Loses a Hero Doctor." He gained overnight media fame. He loved King and America. King disliked Falconer.

Two days later, he put on a yellow rhythm shirt, desert-sand hemp cargo pants, and a white bandanna, and left Fort Lauderdale on Bahamas Air. The flight was fifty-five minutes late. He agonized about Pandora having to wait at the airport. Somehow, he couldn't connect with her on his cell. She might just leave. He sat by the window. He pressed his right foot to the floor and willed the plane to go faster. It knifed through the fluffy white cumulus clouds. He worried about abandoning his president. The American national anthem echoed in his ears. He sighed and decided, *my inner make-up dictates.* Suppose he introduced King's healthcare plan to the island? Later, he could spread it to the entire Caribbean and South America. Then, he recommends it to King. Falconer's Internet blog played in his mind.

They approached Atlantic Isle. The pilot announced, "Traffic is heavy. We expect a thirty-five-minute delay."

He fretted more.

In less than half an hour the pilot announced, "We're cleared for landing. Enjoy your holidays."

He arrived at the international terminal. A calypso band blared in the air-conditioned immigration hall. It eased his worry. "Life as it should be." He tapped his foot to the music as he waited in line. He heard a voice in his head, *Tap your feet to the rhythm of* The Star-Spangled Banner, *American boy.*

Pandora Gray stood in the reception room by the newsstand. She was talking to an immigration officer.

Chandler shuffled around. He didn't see Pandora as she sneaked up behind him. He strode off. If Pandora were a phony, he'd return to Florida the following day. He walked up to the tourism information booth.

The eighty-degree January temperature and humidity made him sweat. His sinuses congested. He looked at the guide's nametag. "Pam, do you know—"

"Interesting clothes you're wearing," said a woman with a robust voice.

He twisted around and sighed. His lips grew parched.

"You're classy. Piercing bottle-green eyes. Wow! Wow! Wow!" She sucked in air. "I'm Pandora Gray." She hugged him.

He managed to get a word in. "Thanks."

She was about five-nine and 175 pounds. She had a different Facebook photo. He raised an eyebrow. She sported an Air Strip shirt and Cardiff stretch pants. He sensed her coconut-and-lime skin lotion. Something about her reminded him of his biological mother, and it pleased him. The instinct would change his life.

Baraka wore a bright red hemp collar. He lolled in a cage on a trolley.

"Meet my Baraka." He packed his luggage and the cage into her Jaguar. He sat in the backseat.

"I let you sit in the back. D'you know why?"

"I was wondering."

"Most of the traffic casualties result in death of the front seat passengers. That's what the hospital chief of staff says."

She sped off. Her tires skidded against the curb. "I have to see my hairdresser in twenty minutes. Takes forty-five minutes to get to my castle." She increased her speed, and lightened up. "I'm sorry, I recant, and I apologize. You stay at my place."

He sensed her commanding nature. "My dog stays, too."

"I'll tolerate him. Welcome to Atlantic Isle. Warm, tropical sun, and blue sky." She went faster.

Baraka reclined in his cage in the rear and whined.

Chandler gazed at the speedometer: seventy mph. "What's the speed limit?"

"Fifty-five, but who cares. The police know who I am." She laughed with a sharp edge.

A Mack truck approached. He grew numb. He gripped the seat in front. She swerved away and laughed.

His neck bones cracked. "Mercy!"

The speedometer went up to eighty miles per hour.

He gasped and held on to his seat. "Slow down, could you?"

"Will you shut up?" She opened the throttle. Eighty-five miles an hour.

"You're speeding."

She burst out laughing. "I use high-grade cocaine, buddy."

His breath quickened. "I—I—I'll go to a hotel. Or to my parents."

"Hell, no!" She dropped to sixty-five mph.

"As long as you're fair to Baraka, thanks for your hospitality."

"Baraka?" She grimaced, and upped the speed again to eighty mph. "Dogs stink like skunks." She negotiated a turn. The brakes screeched. The Jaguar leaned to the side.

She's an Amazon! His skin grew clammy with fear. He was facing his first challenge. He was returning that night. *Damn!* She slowed down to fifty-five mph.

A red Spanish-tiled roof gave Pandora's castle a rich, foreign air. Something a queen dwelled in. A house a witch lingered in.

"Come right in." She walked ahead. "I don't have much time." She hustled into a room.

He stepped in and waited for her. Five minutes passed. "Pandora?"

She laughed somewhere beyond the walls.

He anchored his feet at the center of the room on a red Persian carpet. A huge crystal chandelier hung above him. A vice behind him suddenly gripped his arms. "*Uh!*" He swung around, and gasped.

Pandora hugged him, laughed, and slid off his bandanna. She opened a box, took out a yellow diamond-studded bandanna, and put it on him.

"Great pad you have here."

"The better to love you in." She squeezed him. "Let me take you on a house tour."

From every room, her home boasted a clear view of the Atlantic Ocean.

"I'm running to my hairdresser. Will return in an hour. I need a tint." She hustled out.

In the sitting room, a panoramic canvas displayed a painting of the

Swiss Alps. The house had an aboveground basement and garage. It boasted a main and second floor with balustrades and hurricane-proof sliding glass doors. He was beginning to appreciate her.

The time passed. She wasn't back. Two hours, three hours, three hours and eleven minutes.

"Like my tint?" She rushed in and panted.

"Your home is the peak."

Her mood changed. Her lips and eyes teased him. "You're my man. You have the license to my body."

He chuckled.

"You're funny." She leered, glancing below his belt. "Got bones in your pants?"

In the den, they sipped cocktails. She ate conch fritters and spicy conch salad. She gave him American jalapeno peppers with beer-battered cheese.

"We leave in ten minutes."

"Where're we going?"

His eye caught a collection of miniature flags of Switzerland on a wall stand.

"Why Swiss?"

"I go skiing in Switzerland. I own a chalet, and a sex slave in the village."

"Boyfriend?"

"Don't be foolish. You're the best. He's a male escort. I just use men. He's my accountant. My brother has a big account in the Swiss bank, too. You know, politicians launder money."

He fidgeted, but volunteered nothing.

"I keep a Jaguar there, too. Convenient. D'you like Jaguars? This island is where I'm going to be because you're here."

The ocean stood at complete surrender to him. He was lord of the fishes, the whales, the octopuses, and the sharks. He wasn't sure he was master in the castle with a human shark around.

"I'll show you the town. Let's go."

The couple rode on a two-seat honeymoon surrey. The driver made small talk and joked. Passersby stopped and waved. Chandler was the lord—America's chief executive.

"Speed up, taxi man. Got to go to dinner soon." She played the tour guide. "Sir Tony O'Reilly's home. He was a media tycoon. Lady Chryss Goulandris. She was a shipping heiress. Joseph Lewis, British billionaire. Peter Nygard, fashion executive."

"Let's talk about us."

"Our life is not trotting away from us."

The surrey cantered on.

She touched the driver on the shoulder, "Tell the horses to put on a show."

"*Ho-ho.*" The driver pulled the reins. The animals galloped.

Chandler held his temples. "I want to clock out."

"No!"

"I can't take this!"

She goaded him. "Horse rider, keep moving."

"Stop!"

The driver pulled on the reins. The horses slowed down.

She hugged him and laughed aloud. "Just whipping up an appetite ... for you."

They passed by a familiar site. Chandler played the guide. "At last, Pandora Gray's palace!"

"You learn fast. It's soon yours by dowry."

His heart shrank.

He and Pandora dined at the Atlantic Isle restaurant. The atmosphere was a little posh for him. He and King believed in a more modest, grassroots setting.

She said, "I asked Obi Falconer to join us."

"Swell."

The server came. "Dr. Falconer called to say he was busy in surgery. He'll pop in soon."

In less than ten minutes, Falconer rushed in. He kissed Pandora on both cheeks. He shook Chandler's hand. "Sorry, Dr. Chandler. I was busy. I have to go back for an appendectomy—son of a resident celebrity."

"I understand, sir."

"Just wanted to meet you and welcome you to Atlantic Isle."

"Thanks."

"You're in good company. A handsome man like you deserves it." He chuckled. "I must go." He turned to leave. "Oh, I forgot." He took out something from his jacket pocket. "Here, Dr. Chandler. This is a welcome gift. Any friend of Pandora is a friend of mine."

"What is it?"

"Open it."

Chandler opened a purple velvet cloth. Nestled inside was a key chain with a conch pineapple pendant that said "Welcome." He got up, embraced Falconer, who returned the greeting, and mumbled, "You're too good for her. She's more like for me." He shook his head and left.

"Contrary to what I thought, Falconer is not a threat to me or anyone."

"He loves my friends."

They had filet mignon and asparagus, and shared a slice of coconut cheesecake.

She nudged him. "This food makes you sexy."

They drank red French wine.

He missed his homemade beer. "Life's groovy."

"I'm a sport, too. I'm an island woman. Billionaire investor Sir John Templeton lived here. Bestselling author Arthur Hailey and Charles Lazarus, founder of Toys "R" Us made their homes on the Isle. They know me."

"Any celebrity friends?"

"What d'you mean?"

"Like sleeping with them?"

They laughed off the joke.

"You're a joker, Al. More gossip later."

"I can't wait."

She jabbed him in the back. "Let's walk through the casino, stake a few thousand, and clear our minds."

"I don't gamble."

"That's not sexy. Be a sport. Money is no problem." She grabbed his hand.

Doctor and socialite strolled down to the gaming house.

Casino Atlantic Isle was a palace. People in casual wear played craps and shouted.

"The chaos here is giving me a headache."

The gamblers roared. She embraced him around his waist. They passed the baccarat table and noticed Dr. Falconer. Falconer gave a wad of paper money to the croupier.

She squeezed him. "Dr. Falconer's working the high-roller table."

Falconer pushed up his gray-tinted horn-rimmed glasses. Chandler estimated his age to be seventy. He bore a body close to two hundred pounds. His height made him resemble a basketball player.

"Let me go and say hello to him."

She held him back. "Never disturb Falconer when he's wagering. His world wraps around gambling like a child in a merry-go-round. He blows everything he makes on baccarat. His whole bloody life!"

"Why is he so compulsive?"

"You'll learn." She checked her watch. "Time. Let's go."

"Where?"

"Now."

"What? Why?"

"My hormones are seething, baby. You get me? I'll tell you some bedtime stories. Let's run."

Early the next morning, he phoned his parents. Gossip spreads in small islands. He cracked his knuckles. He expected them to tell him off for attaching himself to Pandora. She was taking a shower.

"I'll be out soon, baby. Allow me another hour." She hummed a song.

He covered the mouthpiece. "Take your time, dear." In a shy tone, he spoke to his father.

"Hi, son. You'll visit us sometime."

He closed his eyes and mused on the word *son*.

Pandora floated in, her steps as light as air.

"Be-be-before I leave, may I ask your opinion on something? I ..." Chandler eased his eyelids open. Stunned in her presence, he grinned and covered the phone. "Hi, Pandora! Didn't you say an hour?"

"Time goes by so fast with you around, honey."

Changing the subject, he spoke into the phone. "Dad, what d'you think about medical malpractice?"

"Jesus Christ, our Savior! A bunch of yes-men doing the bidding of one man. Or a woman."

"I get to whom you're referring. You bet *no* would always be my answer to him. I'm seeing greed." Disgusted, he shook his head. "Glad you're both doing well."

"We'll talk."

"Soon."

"That would be later." Pandora interrupted. "We're going to the Marina Restaurant."

"Y-You finished showering? Restaurant? When?"

"In a minute or two."

He inclined his head. "I can't go like this."

"Put on clothes. Now! You crazy men!"

"Waiter!" beckoned Pandora.

Soft music played from ceiling pipes. The waiters bowed to Pandora, and even the male cleaners shouted hello to her.

"You're popular."

"I'm beautiful." She nudged him. "Are you jealous? Hardcore green-eyed, are you?"

The server came.

"I'm a busy woman. Got my nails to do. Pedicure, and so on. Get us some food, and quick. Tell the chef who's here."

She had barbecue lobster. He ate marinated grilled flank steak. She sipped a Cuban mojito and adjusted a hibiscus in her hair. She regarded him with a lofty expression. Ice slipped into her throat, and she choked on her liquor. He hit her in the stomach from behind her, and the ice pitched out.

"Try the mojito. Hemingway drank it in Havana. My friends and I drink the booze."

"I'll stick to Campari or American beer."

"Waiter, one double mojito for the gentleman."

"No!"

"Don't *no* me, boy!"

A chill stirred in his stomach. The drink came. He sniffed the liquor and made faces. "Rum and cane sugar."

"Take the smirk off your face. Be a man. You quaff a mojito." She chinked her glass against his.

"To sweet, sweet Pandora!" He tasted the lime and mint in the rum. "Not a bad mix."

"To Al Chandler! Let's swig to your entry into the club. I'll do everything to make you happy."

"I'll do more." He finished his mojito.

"Waiter! More booze for my man."

"I'll take a rain check."

"When the rain pours." She winked at him and chuckled. "One of our cultural events in summer is the annual regatta on a sister island. I'll go with you one day."

"I'm easing up."

"Only a wimp slows down in my company. I ignored Falconer for wanting to lose momentum on me."

He didn't argue. He ran his hand over hers. "Sounds groovy. I'm game for a treat anytime."

She raised her eyelids. "More mojito!"

"Sure." The barman mixed the drinks in no time.

The liquor came and they drank. The alcohol clouded his senses. The island was a magic kingdom. The islanders hailed tourists. He loved the life after the mojitos. The time limit was melting away.

She squeezed his chin. "I have to marry you, darling?"

He was in another world with his rum mix. His head spun.

He pulled back and hiccupped. He swigged mojito and coughed.

"This country is a tourist destination. Like in Las Vegas, we can marry in a day. Las Vegas, baby! Ooooh!" She sang, *"I'm getting married."*

"You are?"

"We are."

"When?"

"Sooner than you think, baby."

He tasted the drink and raised an unsteady hand. He licked his lips. "I-I- do."

"I do, too," she sang. *"I do, I do, I do."*

He communed with the spirits. He wasn't leaving the Isle anymore. He was flying in New Jerusalem. "Falconer's land!"

She creased her forehead.

"My screen is blank," he drawled, giddy with drink. "Project your thoughts."

She rolled her eyeballs.

Tipsy, he giggled.

The following morning, a drizzle wet the grass and flowers. The late January weather brought a cold front from Canada. The sun hid behind gray clouds. The mojito withdrawal gave him a splitting headache. He popped two aspirins and prayed for health and happiness. He returned to bed.

"Al? Where are you?"

"I'm here in bed."

"I got you some hot chocolate and microwave doughnuts."

"Later." He buried his head in the pillow.

"The drink will get cold. Come right now."

"I'm on my way."

The chocolate was too sweet. He ate one doughnut. She ate six. They were rancid, but he kept quiet.

"Al, I'll go outside and pick some flowers for the kitchen table." She flashed him a grin and left with scissors and gloves. "Be back in thirty minutes. I'm doing my usual routine in the sun."

He phoned his parents again. "Dad, may I tell you about our wedding?" He backed up to the latticed bay window.

Sam snapped, "Your what?"

Pandora leaned by the grill in the yard.

"I've decided to marry Pandora."

"Al ...?"

"Talk, I see her. She's outside."

"Son, I don't want to run your life." He stressed his words. "If you marry Pandora, your entire life will be doomed.

They say she cares only for herself."

"I'll look after her."

"She cons men in her search for fame and fortune."

He picked his words carefully. "Dad. I have a soft spot for her. Something tells me she reminds me of my Kenyan mother."

"You're marrying for the wrong reason." Sam's voice exploded. "Good heavens! She'll tell you off and won't care. She'll outsmart you. She speaks the devil's language."

A thought flickered deep in Al's mind. He clasped and unclasped his hand. He was mute.

"I'll put you on with Amelia."

Amelia was listening. She came on. "Al?" She sobbed. "Listen to me. I nurtured you. I cared for you."

"You've got a point."

"We'll support you, but Dad knows better."

"You have to understand the relationship, Mom."

"Pandora is a sex kitten."

"Mom!"

"She's a ragamuffin."

"Pandora is?"

Her voice became high and hysterical, giving him a headache. "Her rich status fools you. Be smart, my boy. Avoid her."

His skin crawled with the fear his mother instilled. "You've been my angel, but you both are acting selfish."

Someone huffed into his free ear. He swung around. "Pandora!"

She carried a bouquet of bougainvillea and gardenias in her hands.

He stammered, "Gee, Mom—I … I—Pandora says hello."

Her eyes narrowed.

"My mom and dad are checking to make sure we're fine. I told Mom you're a hip host. Mom and Dad understand."

"Don't spit bullshit."

"Their house has only one bedroom. Can't go there. They pray all day. I won't disturb them."

"Daddy Sam is an asshole," said Pandora. "Mommy Amelia is a bitch. Obi also thinks so of them. Cut off ties with them."

Rain poured and added to Chandler's anguish. He had to pander to Pandora. They snacked on Domino's Pizza for lunch. For supper, she ordered a home delivery of baked swordfish and arugula salad. He lost his appetite. His world was becoming psychotic.

She forked a piece of onion and chewed it.

"About my parents—"

"Go to them and worship all day. Devils pray, too.

You're a flippin' mother's boy."

"Stop the bad words."

"*Uh*! I'll hit you hard."

"A woman should not strike a man."

"American! Abuse!" She stomped away from the table.

Frustrated, he squatted in the den late in the night and watched TV. She retired to her soft, canopied, queen-size bed. He drained beer down his throat and sipped Campari and grapefruit juice until he dozed off on the sofa. He woke up determined to leave the island. He tiptoed into the guest room, packed his suitcase, picked his way to the den, and snoozed.

His earlobe stung. He bounced up from his sleep. He grabbed his ear and gripped Pandora's hand.

She stood before him in her duster. "Good morning, sunshine." She didn't comment on his sleeping outside. "I treat you like shit. Did you kill some American woman?"

"Yes, yes, yes."

"I've unpacked your suitcase."

"I understand you well. Why?"

"You're not going anywhere."

"Never?"

"We got plans, right?"

He developed a nasty headache.

Cameras flashed, and three DVD cameras with portable floodlights panned the area. The sun shone above the western horizon as guests gathered for the wedding. Chandler's life soared. The sun bore witness, but the forecast promised rain.

Pandora's brother, Gray, a short nimble man in his sixties, gave Pandora away. A justice of the peace married them on the steps of the Coliseum. The white columns reminded Chandler of the Greek Coliseum, a symbol of strength and long life. Pandora sported a scoop neckline aquamarine dress. He was a lord, dressed in a white mandarin jacket, raindrop cotton shirt, and white corduroy pants.

Pandora behaved like a megastar. She nodded and waved to people. She hugged them, kissed the men, and lip-kissed the most handsome ones. Sparkling with an all-powerful grin, she sang, "*Today I'm queen of the jungle.*"

Amelia wept throughout the ceremony. Tension and anger on her face, she shuffled her feet. She was so short her chubby shoulders were at her husband's slim waist. The hospital consultants and Falconer attended. Falconer's beady eyes, bald head, and seven-foot stature stood out. The guests gave glowing speeches and toasted with Cristal champagne.

"To our most beautiful bride."

"We will miss her late-night parties."

"She's a cuddly, warm, and loving woman."

"I could have made a better husband."

The doctors' speeches weakened Chandler's knees. Sweat trickled down his armpits. He had to move on and prove himself.

His parents left early without saying good-bye. He wanted to go and bring them back.

"Don't be stupid, Al," huffed Pandora. "Today is your day. I'm yours."

"S-s-sure you are." His soul refused him comfort.

The sun hit the horizon and painted the ocean yellow and red. The crowd moved to the beach. The skyline was silhouetted against a dirty orange sunset. Chandler felt dirty from the union, but he got married to the woman he loved the best—his mother's image. Soon a full moon glowed in a star-studded sky. Three yachts sailed on the distant horizon. A huge cedar bonfire blazed and fought with the wind. Boom boxes blared disco music.

At midnight, Pandora was nowhere around. Someone tapped his shoulder.

He turned to see Pandora smiling at him as she danced cheek-to-cheek in Falconer's arms. "Pandora!"

She danced cheek-to-cheek in Falconer's arms.

"Dude, I'm cutting in," said Chandler.

"Right, young man."

He stepped between them, and slipped his arm around Pandora's waist. "Dr. Falconer, she needs a macho man."

Falconer said to one of his consultants, "He's Hercules." He burst out in a snigger.

"She's mine." Chandler pressed his cheek against Pandora's.

"I'm beginning to like you, Chandler. You're gutsy. I suggest you redirect your energy. When on the island, do as the islanders do."

"I accept the advice of a learned woman."

"You're in-depth and spiritual."

"You think well."

Chandler lifted Pandora off her feet, kissed her, and danced with her. "You had too much to drink."

"I didn't."

He drew her closer to him. "Stick by me."

"Al!"

Her words confused him. "Pandora, you love cavorting with Obi."

"With you, too." She leaned against him. Her eyelids closed and she mumbled, "I pity him. He tells me his sad story."

"Can you share the tale?"

"I shouldn't."

"Snitch, and make me happy."

"His father's behavior was schizoid. He drank no water, only hard liquor, and changed jobs often. He abused his wife and flogged Obi for the slightest mistake he made." She hiccupped, eyes still shut. "Many times Obi had to run from home."

"That's horrible."

She leaned back on his shoulder. "His mother worked the streets." Her eyelids flipped open. "She was only alluring to the horny American tourists—when we had American tourists."

"'Twas a tough life."

"Obi worked on Saturdays and Sundays and after school every day. He cleaned people's yards, mowed lawns, and removed garbage. His friends laughed at him and his self-esteem went down. He labored and sweated. Falconer is coming this way. Keep dancing."

He shuffled away. Falconer passed by and moved away.

"The mother tolerated his labor. He started to steal, pick-pocketed tourists. He quit his job and stuck to stealing. One day the police caught him and flogged him. His only friend was a white rabbit."

"*Sheesh*!"

"What?"

"Keep quiet, would you?"

Falconer's two consultants cavorted close by.

He whirled away from them.

"Obi's a psycho. He keeps the rabbit with him." She picked her words. "Shit! He can cuss you, and the rumor is he slaps his dates. Jackass! He likes to rule people. He loves power, but I'll control him."

"I will, too." He moved a step and swung her to the left in rhythm to the music.

"You're making me dizzy and horny." She ground her hip into his. "You're well endowed."

"Let's go home and make children."

She stopped dancing. "Hell, no!" She pushed him. "Flippin' little bastards."

"They're kids, family, offspring."

"I hate those buggers!" She withdrew from him, and lumbered away.

Falconer came up.

"Pandora!" Chandler moved closer and gripped her shoulders.

"Listen to the woman, Chandler," Falconer said.

"Obi!" She pointed a finger at Falconer. "You get the hell away from me!"

"If you say so, boss." Falconer moved away.

Chandler squeezed her arms.

"I'm a career person," she said.

He stepped back and glared at her.

"Go ahead, call me a bitch!" Pandora snapped.

A soft gasp escaped his lips. "You're a hellcat."

Chandler woke up the following morning and promised Pandora breakfast by eight. He peered through the French windows. Their wooden mansion boasted an artificial pond, filled with Victoria Regia water lilies. They added up-country class to the land. He had eaten lily nuts in Africa. Ducks swam, played, and quacked. He was only three when he left Africa, but he felt a sweet nostalgia from the scene. A lonely almond tree stood barren.

He made a meal of spicy hash browns and over-easy eggs, Texas toast and salsa, and coffee. "Pandora? Breakfast is ready."

"You're twenty minutes late." She swiped her plate off the table. "I hate this shit."

"Take it easy. I'll make you something else."

"Toast and coffee." She held her forehead. "I just remembered. Soccer practice this morning. I eat with gusto and keep fit. I eat on time."

He cringed inside. "I was trying—"

She snapped, "Then I'm a silver-dollar bitch."

"No, no, no." He gripped her arm.

She stared and cried. "Al, you're a handsome man." She adjusted the straps on her silk duster and let her hand fall to her breast. "I'm closing my law firm."

"Oh? When?"

"Now."

"Y-y-you'll stay home?" He held her hand, and swallowed hard. "I-I-I'll tend to you."

She peered down her nose with airs. "Oh, you will. I'll call my brother. You'll work at Falconer's Hospital."

He kissed her and felt she gave herself to the passion of his kiss. "I trust you." He scratched his earlobe. "I have a secret."

"Let me get this straight." She shifted in her seat. "What?"

"Never mind."

"Spill it, boy!"

He bit his lip and said nothing.

"Al, I'm not ashamed of my secrets. I'll tell you sometime."

"How about now?" he said.

"I abused heroin and cocaine," she replied. "I flippin' smoked marijuana, too. Still use them now and again. I sold drugs, too. Just for kicks."

He was struggling, in a maze and shaking inside. "You never told me. Heroin will kill you, Pandora."

"Stop the crybaby stuff. I eat and sleep like a stuffed horse. I pop megadoses of vitamins. Let me worry about me, Al. Cough up your skeleton." She rubbed a finger over his lips.

"I-I can't talk now."

"Al! You're playing unfair to me. Want me to misbehave?"

Her pupils zeroed in on him. "Go right ahead."

He gaped at her. "Just after senior high, I vacationed on this island with a few friends. I met a chick."

"Native girl?" Her pupils constricted. "A flippin' whore?"

"She came from Switzerland. Her name was Astrid Wagner."

"Little Swiss hellcat."

"She was a tall, blonde model."

"Sure, they're all models! You stupid men! Hurry up with your thesis."

"We drank to excess by the seashore, by the same beach where we had the bonfire. Boys collected turtle eggs and trapped the mother turtles. Animal abuse is another story. Three sailboats anchored in the bay."

"Disgusting! *Huh*!" She grabbed a plate and crashed it against the wall. "Whore!"

"She wasn't. We both consented." He released his fingers off her hands. "She decided to go swimming in the ocean. I stayed back. She went alone. I drowsed on the pink sand, half-drunk." His voice lowered to a childish whimper. "I woke up. She was nowhere, and she never returned."

She threw more plates. "What did I get myself into? Keep talking because, if you don't, I might use my hand."

He raced through his words. "I imbibed liquor to extreme. I was young. I explained the disappearance to my friends. They betrayed me and reported the crime. Jealousy, I guess. The pigs arrested me for murder."

"Did I marry a murderer?" Another plate exploded on the wall. "A good-for-nothin' killer!"

"They detained me for three months. My father came. No evidence to convict. They released me, and I went back to Florida."

She squinted at him.

"No files, no body, no case, no crime," he explained.

"Happens on our island. You're lucky to have escaped death row."

"The newspapers and the TV here and in Florida flashed breaking news about my raping Astrid. They claimed I dumped her into the ocean. The headlines said 'Killer!' 'Rapist!' I never raped her! I lived with emotional baggage and false guilt. No one to talk to. I cried day and night."

She shook her head and gawked. "I can't say anything. Not a flippin' word. Get to the end."

"I consulted a Dr. Filo, a TV psychologist. He relieved me of the mental pain. Something told me I had to return to this country. I had to find a bride. I was human again." He ran up to her and hugged her from behind. "Many thanks, Pandora."

She showed no emotion. "I'm speechless. I'm your flippin' end? Maybe you were looking for your mother."

At age thirty-eight, Chandler became the island's first consulting emergency doctor of a hospital. A money-crazy hospital chief ran it. Chandler wore a black T-shirt under his white coat and kept his neck chain on. He was proud of his identity.

Unknown to him, Falconer walked into the ER.

Chandler attended a male patient.

"He sustained an electric shock." An intern breathed hard. "We're losing him, Dr. Chandler."

He applied advanced life support and spoke to the intern. "What's your opinion of Dr. Falconer?"

"*Shh*! He's here."

"Oh!"

Falconer's double chin, boxer's nose, and bleached dentures made him favor a villain in appearance. Chandler found his guttural voice annoying. "I'm Dr. Obi Falconer, chief surgeon and hospital head. Welcome to this fine institution. Let Mr. Powers live. We're buddies at the casino."

"I understand, sir."

"You dress otherwise. Looks smart. So, your black president is a Communist."

"He's Democrat and president. The position speaks volumes."

"Volumes of poor healthcare. I sense you won't try any bureaucratic health reform here. I like you, son." He tramped off. "Save Powers' life, okay?"

The man died.

The radiologist ran in. He pushed a portable X-ray unit. He headed to another casualty whom Chandler was checking for rib cracks.

Something about the radiologist seemed familiar: the sorrel-brown bug eyes, rosacea-affected nose, and ginger complexion, the diminutive size. "Wait a minute, I recognize you." Chandler goggled at the midget. "You studied at the University of Miami." He ripped off his mask.

"I'm Arnold Kennedy." The man spoke in a cackling voice. His eyes focused on him as he set up his X-ray unit. "You're Chandler, Al Chandler!"

"Right!" He ripped off his gloves. They exchanged handshakes. "I attended the University, too. Never liked you."

"You were a yuppie or a hippie," Kennedy said.

"I was a yo-yo." Chandler chuckled and pointed a finger. "Hippie professional."

Kennedy took the X-rays. "The blue-and-green peace symbol tattoo on your right hand. I like it. I stand for that." He unplugged the X-ray unit. "Tell the chief of staff about peace."

"He's salty," Chandler said.

"I didn't get you."

Chandler checked the X-rays. "He's rude."

"You married into the big-shot family. I wasn't at the wedding. No one invites midgets. Had an interesting life after you graduated?"

"I did a thesis on medical misconduct," Chandler said. "Ran the ER at a hospital there and investigated malpractice cases in the state of Florida."

Kennedy brushed aside his carrot-colored Moe-cut hair.

Chandler studied an X-ray. "Multiple fractures of the ribs. Possible pneumothorax developing. Nurses, pulmonary tray, please!"

The nurses dashed in with the instruments.

He applied a tube to the patient's chest and connected it to a bottle. "Busy life after medical school, Arnold?"

"A master's degree in political science." Kennedy stroked his pointed beard. "I had a girlfriend on the faculty."

"Prepare this patient for surgery, stat!"

"I loved her. She was a midget, too. We had to split."

"Might be a blessing."

They shook hands. Chandler's spirit took to the man.

Kennedy had a glint in his eyes. "The chief is mad at you. He was talking to the nurses outside."

"Why?"

"You just killed his friend."

The intern tapped his fingers on his thighs. "The patient is ready in Theater One."

"Got to go." Kennedy wheeled his machine away. "Just watch out for the boss."

In thirty minutes, Chandler came out of Theater One.

Kennedy stopped his portable X-ray unit. "Did another X-ray. Let's run down to the cafeteria for a quick bite and a chat."

Still with their white coats on, Kennedy and Chandler wended their way to the diner. They had coffee and croissants.

The wall clock chimed. Kennedy filled his mouth with the pastry. "You know something?"

"What?" Chandler asked.

"Falconer comes down here for his breakfast about now."

"Let's be quick," Chandler said.

Kennedy ran his words quickly. "The hospital stinks with medical foul play and insurance fraud."

"Malpractice and scams I won't stand."

"Someone's got to nail him," Kennedy told him.

"Who?" Chandler looked for the boss.

"Your chief of staff is coming." Kennedy spoke with a whole croissant in his mouth. "Pandora often goes to Falconer's office."

"Why?" Chandler asked.

"She handled his legal matters." Kennedy raised his hands in a defensive posture.

"What do you know?"

"People don't want to face the truth." Kennedy coughed a laugh. "Nobody believes a midget."

"I do, I do."

Kennedy forced a smile. "Falconer can plunge you into hell."

Chandler's armpits were sweating. He whistled below his breath and let his eyes search for the boss. "Pandora."

"What about her?" Kennedy asked.

"Could she be part of Falconer's malpractice schemes?"

"Part? She's the damn driving force," Kennedy said.

Chandler felt his lips quiver. "You're joking again. Let's leave."

"You're scared of the boss," Kennedy quipped.

Chandler dropped to his knees in Pandora's backyard by the edge of the pond. He stared at the gunshot wound at the back of her head. He looked at her Swiss Piguet watch, minute hand ticking. "She's dead! Oh my God!"

More thunder and lightning. "Mercy!" The head wound showed dry blood. He jerked his head around. Baraka picked up an open condom.

"Spit it out!"

The dog did, pranced away, and returned with something else. Chandler peered closer. He took the .22-caliber bullet from the dog. Four large human footprints imprinted on the soggy ground. The largest he had ever seen. Two sets of the same size. *Is this a random crime? A sex offence? A robbery gone wrong? Heroin?* His head throbbed and his heart thumped.

He sprang back a step, pulled out his cell phone, and dialed 911. His mind flashed to his orphan life. He had had a humble start in a faraway land. He came to America. He settled on Atlantic Isle. *Do I deserve this?* The carrion crows cawed and flew away. Baraka barked, and something dropped from a coconut tree.

He jerked around. Someone in a black mask and diving suit anchored on the ground. A blow to Chandler's head shocked him and numbed his skull. His world darkened. A voice rang in his head: *Everything happens for a reason.* The words annoyed him. He couldn't bring himself to consciousness to understand the dilemma.

CHAPTER 2

Chandler, unconscious, plunged into the Atlantic Ocean. The warm waves lapped on his skin. Baraka yapped and jumped in. Chandler came to, swam, and cleared his head from the shock. On land, in the hot sun, he drank bottles of American beer. They were giant bottles, the size of oxygen tanks. His deeper mind spat out faint words: *Part of Pandora's body floats on the water lily. Why?*

Somebody or something hustled away from him. Baraka barked, and Chandler's hands gripped the wet grass. His eyes blurred. His dog lay beside him. The dog nudged him, and Chandler felt his comfort. He rubbed his eyes. His vision cleared. "I'm on a paradise island." A sparrow twittered from a tree. The rain stopped. He passed his hand over his wet hair. His head still throbbed with pain. Shivering, he stripped off his wet shirt and brushed water off his hairy chest. He glanced around the grass. The scene changed. "Pandora?" He grew frenzied.

Three police officers stood over him. His stomach shriveled. The shepherd barked nonstop. The policemen grabbed Chandler by the arms.

"Don't touch me!" He jerked away, feeling a burning from their grip. "Listen to me."

He fought them, and they handcuffed him.

"Take the clamp off me!" His wet corduroy pants fell off his waist to his buttocks. He couldn't pull them up.

An officer held him up. The police dragged him.

He gritted his teeth. "I-I-I don't understand!" He shed a tear. "Pigs!"

"Not a word more!"

"Pigs!"

An officer grumbled, "You! You have five seconds to zip it."

"P-"

"We're taking you in."

Chandler blinked and looked around. The small green concrete police station bore the island's red, white, and black flag by the arched entrance. Inside, the air had an inky odor.

The cops fingerprinted him, took mug shots, and led him into the interrogation room. He dropped into a chair beside a rectangular table.

A plainclothes detective came in. He had a paunch and heavy gray eyebrows. He perched on the table and questioned him.

"The light's too bright!"

"Zip it, boy." The detective killed the lights. "We got recordings of Internet chats between you and Pandora."

He stared at the ceiling.

"Have you ever been angry with Pandora?"

"What?"

"Did you discuss cash transactions on the Internet?"

"Money?"

The man sucked his teeth. "Did you come here to get donations for your president's postelection campaign?"

"I-I don't know what you're talking about." Chandler's stomach knotted. He let out a strangled cry, "This is unjust."

"Would you can it?"

"Why, why do you question me, sir?" The veins in his temples throbbed, and blood surged to his fists. "I-I didn't kill my wife. I have no motive."

"You inherited a posh car and a big house. You married a rich woman." He switched on the high-power floodlight.

A tall, strapping bald man with gnawed fingers and a beefy African face marched in. He had a cup of coffee in his hand. The man sipped the beverage and turned off the light. Chandler feared another form of torture.

The officer studied him. His nasal twang instilled fear. "I'm Superintendent Bullard." Bullard turned to the officers. "He's a doctor working for a reputable hospital."

The sleuth's eyes smoldered. "He's the man who killed Gray's sister."

"We checked him out. He has a clean record here and in the States."

"He wasn't clean, sir, when we found him."

"He's a close friend of the US president."

"He was close to Pandora's body."

Bullard drank more coffee. "We have nothing to hold him on yet. Release him under *habeas corpus*."

Chandler raised himself from the chair. *The man is not a pig. He is a lamb.* "I appreciate this, sir!"

"Go kiss your boss's ass. We will follow you everywhere."

His heart bled. At home, dressed in a black Baja hoodie, Chandler phoned Kennedy at the hospital. "May I ask you a favor?"

"What can I do?"

"The pigs broke my arm. I need a few rolls of gypsum to make a plaster of Paris."

"Oh no, my man! Work is—"

"Can you slip out a minute?"

"Why?"

"It's urgent."

"I'll grab a break and keep my beeper on. I'm leaving now."

Kennedy arrived and rushed in. "Al, let me check the arm."

Chandler patted his shoulder. "My arm's fine."

"You dragged me out for nothing?"

"Do me a big favor."

"I'm working, Daddy-o."

"Here's a searchlight and a plastic bag. Hold on to the gypsum."

"Shit!"

Chandler shrugged and lowered his head. "I can't do it."

"Why?" Kennedy's beeper sounded.

"They're tailing me. Call your technician and let her do the X-rays. Check her when you return."

He called the assistant, and told him to work until he got back to the hospital. "Now, I'm giving you an hour of my time."

He explained the project.

Kennedy left, and Chandler paced the floor in his den. He waited. Half an hour went by. Another fifteen minutes.

"*Uh!*" Chandler shook his head. "The police picked up Kennedy."

Someone knocked. *The pigs are coming back for me after questioning Kennedy. They'll finish me.* He ran down and eased the door open a slither.

"Daddy-o, here's the molds and the condom."

He sighed. "God, you scared me."

"Going to your backyard was scary. Just to think of Pandora lying by the pond, dead. I managed to do two footprints. I had to run. The police came."

Chandler looked at the gypsum molds. "These are from big shoes. I have something here: OCMSFS14 ½. On the other: ACMSFS14 ½." He studied the codes. "Hmmm. The killers wore size 14½ shoes."

Kennedy's beeper emitted a twittering sound. He checked it. "Al, this is tough on you. I'm going back to work. We'll talk."

"You forgot something." Chandler held the plastic bag with the used condom. "Get the lab to analyze it."

"Al! Al!" Kennedy protested.

"Never mind."

Kennedy took the bag. "I know the female technician. I'll get the test done."

Chandler sat in the den. *What does my future hold? Only time will tell ...*

The ringing doorbell interrupted his thoughts. He killed the whistle of the kettle by yanking out the plug. His hackles rose. Thoughts of pigs rushed into his mind. He recalled the molds and quickly stashed them. He ran downstairs, pulled the curtains, and checked.

"Oh." He opened the door. Air from a mild cold front gushed in from the dark night.

"Mom!" He kissed her and looked at his father behind her.

"I'm sick," she panted. "I can't stay long. A taxi's outside. The meter's running."

"Meanin'?"

"I'm paying for this visit."

"I'll repay you, Mom. Please come in."

"Permit me to say my piece." She looked up at him with appealing eyes. "You'll regret it. I'm mad at you. You have become a monster."

"Pandora wasn't a devil. Now, do better than cry. Wipe those tears away. She was a demon."

She shuddered and cried.

Sam stepped ahead of Amelia. "This boy has suffered enough."

Chandler embraced Sam and clapped him on the back. "Come in." He turned to his mother. "Your eyes are red. Step in. I'll take you home later. I'll send away the taxi."

"No way, son."

"Mom, how about coffee?"

"It's bad for the heart."

Chandler's mind wandered to his wedding. Pandora flashed before his eyes.

"So?" Mrs. Chandler made a sour face.

"I didn't kill Pandora."

His mother inched closer to him. "Someone's framing you. You have stress lines on your face. I sense it ... enemies."

Chandler touched his cheek, and his voice waned to a guttural rasp. "Yes, and I hurt."

Sam paced the driveway with a walking stick. "Oh, my knee pains!" He sighed and grimaced. "You must clear your name."

"I will, Dad."

"The hospital is in a mess. We ministered to the sick; we know. The rumor is that Pandora slept with most of the foreign consultants. Maybe one of the doctors killed her." Sam limped back and forth. "Malpractice and insurance fraud is the big agenda in the hospital."

"Reminds me of a jungle of serpents, Dad."

Amelia burst out crying.

Chandler cuddled her. "I'll clear the obstacles."

"Those people will destroy you, son. You're not a chicken. Fight back with all your might."

The taxi horn sounded loudly.

"The fare's running up," Amelia cried. They all ran to the taxi. "Whip up a quick friggin' plan."

"Mom, you never cursed before."

Reverend Sam shouted from the cab. "She must be friggin' mad."

"Dad, I didn't know men of the cloth had foul mouths!"

Sam slammed the door shut. The vehicle sped off.

"I'll whip up a plan," Chandler vowed.

Chandler had to rush. By six the next morning, he was ready to go to work. Falconer would arrive by eight. Something by the mailbox on the door caught his attention. The manila envelope had a return address: The Office of the Prime Minister. He grabbed the envelope and ripped the flap open. It was a long letter with legal jargon. *"And Dr. Chandler, according to the attached will, you no longer can access any funds in Pandora's name. You don't own the Jaguar any more, as this was illegal. Leave the mansion. The only compromise is to put you in the servants' quarters. The two-story building is a small replica of Pandora's abode. It might serve as a posh prison cell for you."*

Loathing gripped his stomach. "I accept."

His sense of duty took him to Falconer's desk. His watch showed 6:30 a.m. Time was on his side. He crept into the office. He checked for clues to the medical misconduct Kennedy and Chandler's parents had told him about. He looked for Falconer's shoe size and ID. Falconer had several pairs in his office. He questioned intruding into Falconer's territory. He hesitated, but a second thought urged him to push for justice.

Falconer's mahogany desk looked more like furniture for a politician. It had flags on it and two miniature Falconer paperweight sculptures. His nameplate was in gold letters. An oversized initialed reading lamp towered above the table. Chandler pulled the chain for the light. Falconer's pet white rabbit frisked around the floor. Microsoft Word was open on his computer. Sweating under his bandanna, he searched the files. He found nothing to incriminate Falconer. Distraught, he shook his head. "No!"

The ringing phone made him jump. Maybe someone had spotted him and tipped off Falconer? He had to check Falconer's locker for his theater shoes. Time was on his side. It was 6:35 a.m. He had to run, but an open diary on the desk held his attention. He waited for the phone to stop ringing then waded through the notes. He walked away but returned to the book. Flipping the pages, his eye fell on his own name. He read the message: *Talk to the boys. Chandler—American, President King's man. Wants to get rid of the rich. Trying to boost the poor. Crazy!* Chandler gasped, and turned back the page. He scanned the desk for anything of interest. He pulled out the shallow middle drawer. Pandora's photo in a four-by-five frame! Scribbled below were the words: *To you, Obi, my love.*

Aghast, he stood and crept to the locker. He must have Falconer's shoe size and identity. He pulled on the knob, and pulled again. Locked. He tried to guess numbers on the combination lock. It didn't work.

OCMSFS14 ½. The thought permeated his brain. The last S might stand for size.

Footsteps thudded from the hallway. The digital desk clock showed 6:40 a.m. He still had time. The footsteps grew louder. In panic, he gazed at the door. Falconer barged in.

If Chandler could have dropped through a trapdoor, he would have felt safer. "Dude!"

Falconer grinned and gaped at him. He pulled out a doughnut from a paper bag, and bit into it. He spat it back into the bag. "So, you're snooping around?"

"I-I-I thought you had already reported for duty. Surgeons start working early. I-I-I wanted to tell you about—about Pandora."

"So, you're snooping around?" The voice sounded familiar. He had heard it by his wife's body. He wasn't sure.

Falconer's hairless, shiny face twitched from a tic. He still tried to keep his control. After biting his doughnut again, he pulled a disposable cup of orange juice out of the bag. His fox eyes seethed. "You're doting."

"Dude, I agree." He offered his hand in a handshake.

Falconer squeezed it hard.

"Be vigilant, or the country will flog you."

"It bothers me." During his lunch break, Chandler went to his parents. He had an hour to kill. They had left unhappy the last time he spoke to them. Their house was a one-story blue bungalow by the beach, a mile away. Coconut trees and white oleander filled the yard.

The door opened. "Al! Please come in and sit down." Amelia alerted her husband. "Sam, Al's here! Son, would you get us some milk sometime? You know our brand."

"I do and I will."

"Sam?"

"I heard you. Just got into the shower. Give me time."

Amelia shook her head and sobbed.

"I'm kidding." Sam came in right away and they sat.

His parents lived a simple life, with ordinary furniture and no ornaments. A large print of Jesus hung on the wall. Al's childhood photo lay on the living room coffee table. He smiled at himself. *Memories!*

"Son, I didn't know we were still speaking."

"Mom! Work can be heavy."

"You found the time for Pandora."

Chandler kept quiet.

"We sit on the patio and listen to the waves. We hear the wind rustling through the trees. You can enjoy it, too." Her eyes showed she was thinking hard.

"Atlantic Isle has some of the healthiest submerged coral rocks. It has the highest marine biodiversity. I support building reserves, protecting fish spawning. The islanders eat more fresh seafood," said Chandler.

"That's my son!" Sam eased himself up, and limped around the table with his walking cane. "A biologist and an environmentalist? Stick to medicine."

"Son, I blame you for stepping into Pandora's weird life."

"My cholesterol is still high." Sam raised his hands.

Chandler studied his father's reaction.

"The pills are useless. You stress us out, son," Sam added.

"The same here." Amelia patted the pleats on her black dress. "My arthritis and varicose veins hurt. I pop pills like crazy, but nothing works."

"Stop the medicine," Chandler suggested.

"This whole misfortune is killing me. You're our doctor, Al," Amelia said.

He sat next to her. "Consult the other medical brains."

"I had to pawn my jewelry several times to help you through medical school," she reminded him.

"It's ethics. Besides, I'm causing you stress. You've got to talk to one of the other doctors."

Tears filled Amelia's eyes, and her lips quivered.

"Pandora's gone."

Sam hit his stick against the floor. "You're a jackass! Like you were an idiot to keep a boa constrictor as a pet. In Illinois, I excused you. Youth! Now, we're stuck with the snake."

"It makes me feel as if I'm back home in Africa," Chandler said. "I sense my heritage."

"You gave the reptile a stupid name."

"Whistle-blower?" His beeper sounded. "What's wrong with the name?"

Amelia's eyes widened. "The snake is so darn big."

"The serpent's in his metal cage." The ER had called.

"Someday the monster might squeeze us to death."

"Mom! The island is trying to do the same to me."

Chandler had a long day at work. That evening, he went to the supermarket and bought a gallon of milk. He took it to his parents. Kennedy accompanied him; he had a newspaper folded under his arm. The sensor lights outside flashed and an owl hooted from a coconut tree.

"I don't like this." Kennedy peered about wild-eyed. "Owls spook me."

"You imagine that."

"Let's go back."

"Coward!" Chandler remembered something, and said peevishly, "Arnold?"

"Cut your tone of voice. What d'you want?"

"You never gave me the analysis on the condom."

Kennedy hit his forehead. "It tested negative for vaginal mucus or cells on the outside."

"It means no penetration."

"Guess what the rubber contained," said Kennedy.

"Sperm. We'll do a DNA and try to cross-match. We might find Pandora's killer or killers."

"You can't."

"Why?" Chandler asked.

"Inside the condom was glue."

"No! Pandora, dear! We aren't dealing with a sex crime." Anger tensed his muscles. "Don't know where to go from here." He unlocked the door and crept into the dark, Kennedy behind him. He stored the milk in the fridge and sensed his parents were already asleep. They took turns snoring in a laughable rhythm.

Kennedy jerked his head around. "I'm afraid of sooty places."

"Light's coming in from outside. D'you want floodlights?"

"You're not treating me right, I warn you."

Somewhere in the bushes, a dog howled.

His friend's eyes widened in fear. "Wolves!"

"Might be a wolf in sheep's clothing outside." Chandler faked the scary voice from Red Riding Hood. "Arnold, what big teeth!"

"Stop!"

Chandler tried to suppress a giggle.

"Something is not right, pal," Kennedy cautioned.

"Pal? The hippie word Daddy-o sounds much better."

Chandler flipped the light switch. He looked for the TV remote and pressed the ON button. The sixteen-inch TV played *The Addams Family.*

The midget shifted in his seat. "I'll stay put here. Snakes terrify me, Daddy-o!"

"The snake sleeps in a cage in the chamber. Whistle-blower is their pet now."

"You've got to be kidding. A serpent can kill your parents."

"No more teasing. Nothing more to fear. I'll go to the kitchen and check the cupboards."

Chandler checked the shelves. He pulled back. A cockroach startled him then slid into a crevice.

The radiologist opened the newspaper and ran through the first page. "I'll sit here and won't move until you're ready to leave." His fingers trembled. "I'm wearing a red shirt. Reptiles hate red."

"Cows do."

"Cattle, boa constrictors, cockroaches, whatever. I see one, I pee my pants. Worms scare me. Look, I see your worm." His face turned ashen. "I'll-I'll switch on the lights."

"Arnold! They're on."

"Oh!" Arnold perused the papers and creased his forehead. "Hey, Daddy-o, got something here." He pointed to the headline.

Chandler bent down and read the bold print aloud. "Shocking Medical

News." He waded through the subheading. "Pharmaceutical lobbyists use doctors and government officials to hype the sales of poisonous drugs."

"They make medicine from snakes, too, Daddy-o."

"Ye-e-s-s-s."

"You're getting on my nerves." Kennedy glanced halfway down the page. "Read below here."

Chandler perused in silence: *Falconer's Hospital. Medical Malpractice and Insurance Cover-up.*

"What d'you think, Daddy-o?"

"We'll stop Falconer."

"I'm with you, but Dr. Falconer is the chief surgeon. He's a desperado."

"We'll conquer him."

"Can we subdue Falconer?" Kennedy reared up and walked off a few steps. "T-the night's old. I'm off duty. I was forgetting. I'm doing a ten-minute stand-up late tonight at The Comedy Club."

"I'll call them tomorrow about the milk. They drink American 'Macarthur' only, and every morning."

"Power to America! Forward march, out!"

"Just a minute." Chandler stepped over to his parents' bedroom to check on them and on the snake.

"Al, the good boy. Mother's boy!"

"Arnold, shut up!"

"My knees are wobbling. Sheesh!"

The night-lights offered low light in the bedroom. He scolded himself for expecting trouble. He had to stop being paranoid. The sight froze in his brain. Blood siphoned from his face and made him dizzy. He rushed up to the bed and gripped the headboard. He touched his parents. The shock of discovery hit him full force. He was choking and freezing. He was losing consciousness. He screamed, "Oh my God! Mom? Dad? Dead?"

CHAPTER 3

Chandler put two fingers in his mouth and whistled. At The Comedy Club, they drank bottle after bottle of beer. Chandler grew tipsy and shed a tear. A dull ache gnawed at his soul. He welcomed the change from his grief, but every time he pictured the bedroom scene with his parents he wanted to cry. Liquor was numbing his brain.

Kennedy copied the whistle.

"You're open-minded," said Chandler. "It says humor's in your blood."

"You're my man, Daddy-o! How many nurses can you—?"

"Sheesh! I'm-I'm a one-chick man."

"I am, too. Everybody has a story to tell. Open up. Four minutes and I go."

"I-I-I enjoyed summer breaks from medical school. I traveled to Kenya and gave food, clothing, and bread to orphans. They had no television. I told them stories and even used a drum to-to-to entertain and inform."

"Kenya!"

"One summer, I flew to Indonesia, and showered the orphans with gifts. Did I say gifts? Right! I-I dressed like a hippie, talked kooky, and reasoned the same way as a beatnik."

"You're a smart guy."

"Once, a tsunami hit the island. Within an hour, I re-rescued twelve children from the raging sea."

"Now you're stretching the story, Daddy-o."

"It's true. I played party games with them and offered them food, drinks, and ice cream."

"Swell!"

Chandler hiccupped. "Some days I wore a wizard's hat and on other days a miner's hat, a pirate's hat, or a cowhand's hat. It depended on what stories I had to tell the orphans. Their drumbeat kept me dancing. I love children. I want a houseful of them. Two, maybe."

"One is your unlucky number." Kennedy rose to his feet. "Just one man may want your head on a silver platter." He walked down the aisle to the stage. The crowd applauded.

Chandler burst out crying. Midnight had passed. He was in his car, going back home.

Kennedy touched him. "They're in a safe place in heaven."

Chandler had to work at seven, and rushed to get at least four hours sleep. He revved up the speed. "You're brave," he said to Kennedy. "You were roasting Falconer, the prime minister, and the goddamned government."

"Many a truth shows up in jokes. Sam and Amelia—?"

"You want to roast them, too?" Chandler asked.

"Daddy-o, I never would roast the revered dead. The speed limit here is forty-five miles per hour. You're inebriated and doing sixty-five."

"I know, Arnold."

"I'd hate to die with you, Daddy-o."

"Mom and Dad emigrated from Florida. The stress of big cities was too much. My father worked as a chaplain at Falconer's institution. Mother helped him."

"We're talking years ago."

"They mixed with the residents, volunteered in the Kiwanis Club, the Rotary Club, and the Red Cross. They're Irish. Mom and Dad advised politicians, one of whom led the country to independence in 1973. The politician gave the Chandlers citizenship." He floored the pedal to seventy miles per hour.

"Ease it! My mama and papa died in a plane crash in the Everglades. They were white island people here from the English colonial days. Mama and Papa were in Florida on holiday." He sniffed.

"Oh?" A siren wailed. Chandler's words slurred. "Sounds like one of our ambulances." The siren grew louder. The police stopped him. He earned a traffic ticket. He looked up at the pig. "What?"

The stranger smirked.

Kennedy huffed, "That's Adolph."

A day later, Chandler walked in and ordered food as Kennedy was finishing off lunch at a bistro. Chandler's head bowed with sorrow. They drank beers.

Kennedy listened as Chandler recounted his parents' medical history.

Chandler's phone had rung one day while he was in ER. The caller ID showed O. Falconer.

Chandler answered it. "The renowned friend of the rich!"

"The nurse is telling me Reverend and Mrs. Chandler are here to consult me."

"They believe in you, Dr. Falconer."

"Chandler, you show promise in my institution. Oh, they're here. Talk later."

Amelia and Sam Chandler had walked into Falconer's office. He put down his phone, and patted his white rabbit.

Amelia sat on a side chair. "Doctor, my varicose veins are bothering me."

"I'll strip them."

Agony showed on her face. "I have a weak heart."

Falconer rose and headed for the door. "I'm rushing for surgery. Talk later. Just wanted you to know: Al's becoming a problem."

The following day, in the upstairs theater, Falconer stripped the veins. He felt culpable. He had treated the Chandler parents badly while they ministered the word of God at his hospital. He was doing a good deed to compensate for his years of wrongdoing. The cardiologist helped the anesthetist to monitor Amelia's heart. The varicose stripping went well.

"We must talk." Falconer rushed off to another operation room.

A day went by. Falconer walked up to her in the ward. Sam was there.

Amelia rubbed her knee joints. "Doctor, I've had arthritis for many years now."

"I'm sure Al can prescribe you something. He's now a citizen. Pandora helped to make him head of the Doctors and Allied Workers Union." He responded to a call. "I'm coming." He hung up the cell phone.

Sam spoke up. "About Al's writing a prescription—we're family. Leave him out. It's ethics. He's busy, and we only write prescriptions for the soul."

"Your proud son is a Working Class Party member."

A nurse approached him to sign a requisition.

"And so are we." Amelia showed a simple smile.

Falconer's voice keyed up. "Can you persuade him to leave the Party? I'll then tell him how Atlantic Isle works."

Sam hit his walking stick on the floor. "Let me think—"

"I do the thinking," declared Amelia.

Falconer took her chart. He signed Amelia's discharge and prescribed the arthritis drug Morgex for her.

"Reverend Sam, is there anything I can do for you?"

"D'you know any good drug to drop my cholesterol? I tried them all. They don't work."

Falconer took a pad from his white jacket pocket and wrote something.

Sam read it. "DED-statin. I'll try anything."

Falconer was ready for the kill. He puffed up. "You have a handsome son. An adopted white African boy! I like him. Advise him to slow down. Tell him he's not America's commander-in-chief. He has no one hundred-day plan to fulfill." He had lowered his voice to a whisper. "He's a good boy."

Chandler bit his lip. "That's my parents' story." He sobbed and covered his face with one hand.

Kennedy held Chandler's shoulders. "I understand."

"Heavenly Father knows what's in store for them. I know what's in store for my enemy."

The light in the police interrogation room was terribly bright. The police had been questioning Chandler and Kennedy for hours. They put them in separate rooms.

Superintendent Bullard said, "What did you do with the snake?"

"I took him to the vet and had him put to sleep."

"Is this a trend, Dr. Chandler?" He stomped around, and turned to face him. "We'll release you, research the Chandlers' death, and monitor you."

"How would you interpret this?" He swallowed hard and looked at his right palm. For the first time, Chandler was driving at twenty-five miles per hour and avoiding the main road.

"A trembling hand?" Kennedy answered.

"I see blood, pain, sacrifice, anger, and death," Chandler said.

"You're mixed up, Daddy-o."

"Pandora, and now Mom and Dad." He craved a channel to his soul. Barbs and thickets lined his way. He had to clear the way, solve the puzzle, and experience peace. "I would research their death."

"I'm with you," Kennedy agreed.

"Am I next?"

The car lurched forward as something hit its rear bumper.

Chandler pressed his gas. A car appeared in the rear view mirror. "Who's that?"

"Daddy-o! Hit the gas."

"What the hell—?"

"Someone's following us," Kennedy warned.

CHAPTER 4

Sirens blared and flashing lights reflected off the double glass doors of Falconer General emergency room. An ambulance took off. Another screeched to a stop.

Chandler slipped on a white coat. "Let's go, doctors."

Saturday night traffic accidents crammed the ER. Police officers gripped handcuffed criminals. Paramedics ran in. They nursed casualties in wheelchairs, stretchers, and gurneys. Patients moaned in the prep room. Nurses screened them, and Chandler worked nonstop. Human suffering touched him.

"Help me, Doctor!"

"A pain killer, please!"

"Let me die!"

With his team, he continued to assess them. "I'll get you well."

"I can't afford this," moaned a patient.

"I'll pay your bills," he responded.

He spoke to another patient. "I'm here to help you, sweetheart. Don't worry. Soon, you'll be pain free."

Life support wall monitors, hooked up to patients, filled the ER. It housed twelve beds and three procedural rooms. Two glass-encased operating theaters and an Intensive Care Unit treated casualties nonstop. The smell of blood and iodine floated in waves in the air-conditioned, fluorescent-lit room. The white tiles showed spots of bloody shoe prints.

A fair-skinned, bright-eyed boy with red hives and swollen face cried, "Mommy!"

Chandler held his hand to reassure him. One day he hoped to have a son—a son and a daughter. "Your name is—?"

"I'm Nicholas Andros. I'm Nick."

"I'm Doctor C. Or Duck C. 'Quack,' says the duck."

Nicholas forced a laugh. "I have a mango allergy."

"Gets it all the time," his mother commented. Nicholas hugged her.

"Mrs. Andros, how old is he?" Chandler asked the slender woman with the long auburn hair.

"He's three." Chandler detected a tinge of anger in her soft, smooth voice. "Children run around and pick up doo-doo. A week ago we consulted a genuine doctor."

"Who?"

"Obi Falconer."

"The doctor with the white hair on his lip," said Nicholas.

The mother blinked and looked away. "Sorry, this isn't the great doctor's field, but he's a friend."

"Mommy, I-I can't brea—"

"Epinephrine and hydrocortisone!"

The child settled with drugs.

Chandler took out a paper note from his pocket. "Ten dollars for being a good patient. No more mangoes."

Nick hugged him. "You're the bestest! I don't like the big old doctor."

His mother feigned an angelic smile. "Obi is the genuine doctor." She gripped Nick by the hand and marched out.

"She's Falconer's main squeeze," a nurse mumbled to Chandler. "At least, he thinks so."

The beep of an EKG monitor sounded in another room. Chandler dashed across. An eighty-eight-year-old man stretched out stiffly on the bed. He wasn't breathing. Dilated pupils. He had no pulse. No heartbeat. The EKG bleated a steady tone—flat line. Chandler started CPR.

The old man grabbed him by the arm and opened his eyes.

Chandler's skin crawled. "I thought you were—"

"Dead. Doc, this place is for the rich." The man motioned for Chandler to come closer. "The giant doctor's a sucker. He bills the insurance company, turns around, and demands cash from us." The man hacked until he started to laugh. "I have a little money in the bank but—" He coughed again. "I'm an artist. I make life-size mannequins. Free for you anytime. As for Falconer, we'll remember his ashes."

"Some doctors are knee-jerk villains from the time they became interns," Chandler continued. "A few achieve villainy. A small number have under-the-table knavery thrust on them. Falconer is all three."

A nurse ran up to the bed. "Doctor, someone's on the line for you."

"Take a message," Chandler responded curtly.

"They insist on speaking to you."

He provoked a screech from his black Florsheim shoes as he turned on the tile. He hustled to the station.

A purring, professional voice came on the line. "Doctor, I'm Michelle Lang, the hospital administrator. I have a pathology report here for you. It's the results of your parents' postmortem."

"Read it to me."

"Only in person."

He liked her tone of voice.

He knocked and went into Lang's office. A camera flashed in his head and gave him instant joy. "Beautiful," he mumbled.

She stood erect and adjusted her skirt. She was a chick of substance, purpose, and sex appeal, and had to be of Chinese and African descent. About twenty-eight, she was fit at five-foot-five. Chandler's heart flip-flopped. Her long, delicate hands gripped a sheet of paper. She looked down and to the side, a touch of humor on her lips. She handed the report to him. His fingers touched her seashell-pink polished nails.

Her beauty mesmerized him. For the first time since Pandora's death, life began to have meaning. He dismissed the emotion.

He opened the envelope and read the report.

> *The postmortem and toxicology report showed Amelia Chandler succumbed to cardiac failure. The potent drug, Morgex, caused it. Sam Chandler died of liver damage and a clot in the lungs. Blame the deadly anti-cholesterol drug, DED-statin. You can drop by pathology to get the full findings.*
>
> —*The Pathologist.*

Loathing welled up in his gut. *Life is cruel to me, giving me sour oranges.*

Michelle came over and touched his arm. Her big, almond-shaped cinnamon eyes showed sorrow and her high cheekbones paled. She patted his hands. "I'll call pathologist Dina Dower for you now."

"Later," he insisted.

She smiled, her full, ripe, sensuous lips saying hello. She dialed the number and put him on to Dower.

"Thank you for the report."

Dr. Dower spoke in a mature voice. "My deepest sympathy. Morgex, in its pure form, is a bittersweet chemical with an earthy-leafy smell. High doses of Morgex cause fainting, heart dysfunction, and death. The antidote is Nosiop and hydrocortisone."

The postmortem results tugged at his heart, but Michelle's presence warmed it. He stepped away from the desk. Life was beginning to have pleasant and unpleasant meaning. He stopped and looked beyond her shoulder. He noted the ginger speckles that graced her skin.

"I-I-I'd love to chat sometime," she stammered.

He smiled at her. He was a child again, playing with his boa constrictor. "I was thinking the same." He nodded his head and strutted back to ER.

Chandler, junior doctors, and nurses hurried to a man on a gurney. The patient's middle-aged, pale-white body gave off a sweaty, meaty odor. His legs jutted beyond the blanket.

"Was he in an explosion?" Chandler had years of ER experience, yet this sight made him cringe.

The man lay in a torn, bloodstained white T-shirt. His voice was feeble. "Where's the big chief, Dr. Falconer?"

"I'm your doctor now." He removed the paramedics' bloody bandages.

Blood smeared the man's giant face and his stocky neck.

"Pain! Do something, Doctor!"

The nurses cut off the casualty's shirt. His cracked thighbone stuck out from a ten-inch wound, and his thigh twisted. Blood drenched the blue jeans covering his other leg. The man had massive bruises. Chandler palpated the man's chest. It crackled. "He's got broken ribs."

"Where's the chief?" the patient demanded again.

Chandler's felt anger surge, but he suppressed it. He ran through the vital signs the paramedics had documented. They had plummeted. "Mercy!"

he cried out. "Hydrocortisone!" He pumped 500 milligrams of it into the man's veins to keep the pressure up. "Demerol!" He added the painkiller and withdrew blood for the lab. "We need a transfusion. Call the lab. X-rays. Alert Dr. Kennedy."

Even under sedation the man mumbled, "Falconer, please."

Kennedy rolled in a portable X-ray unit ahead of his undersized frame. He took quick X-rays, which confirmed Chandler's diagnosis.

"The stomach shows nil contents. He's safe to have anesthesia."

Chandler grew optimistic. He patted Kennedy on his back. "Thanks for coming on time. See you after work?"

"Not today. Vanessa and I are on a date. Romance says never to say no to Vanessa." Kennedy snorted a chuckle. "Remember a car hit us the other day?"

"Who was it?"

"The infamous Adolph."

"Who's he?"

"We'll talk later." Kennedy left with his machine.

A nurse rushed in. She carried bags of O-positive blood. Chandler and his staff wheeled the casualty into ER Theater Two.

The anesthetist, a short middle-aged Filipino man in green scrubs, inserted an intravenous needle. An intubation tube jutted from the patient's mouth.

Chandler performed a bloody surgery on the leg and the chest. He reduced the femur fracture. He put in a steel rod and screwed metal plates on the ribs. In four hours, exhausted and sweating, Chandler emerged with the patient.

"Doctor!" yelled a woman.

A stocky woman in her thirties appeared in the hallway.

"Ma'am, who allowed you to come in?"

Her hoarse voice had a Latin American accent. "I had to."

"Visitors are forbidden here."

The woman slipped behind them. The nurses tried to send her out.

Chandler raised a hand. "Give me a second."

A senior nurse stepped in. "We'll call security."

"Go easy with her."

The woman had a worried and sick face.

Chandler pushed ahead to ICU. "Give her a mask, a gown, and a cap."

In ICU, the nurses closed the blue curtain. Interns rechecked the blood pressure. Chandler evaluated the signs with the Filipino doctor.

Without warning, beeps erupted from the monitors.

A soft gasp escaped Chandler's lips. "What the hell—?"

The man heaved in paroxysms.

The woman's black eyebrows knitted. "Zis my *hombre*, my partner." Her voice box grew more hoarse. "Speed up, Doctor. Goddammit! *Muerto!* He's dying! Get the hospital chief!"

The anesthetist helped. Chandler connected the mouth tube to a respirator. He gave emergency drugs: Lidocaine, bretylium, and epinephrine. The man convulsed, and his skin turned a mottled blue.

"Jesus!" Chandler's heart throbbed.

The patient's eyes dilated and remained fixed.

"He's gone." Chandler's cheeks grew heavy. He spoke to the interns and the nurses. "He suffered chest contusions, a broken thigh bone, and massive hemorrhage. His heart stopped. We tried to help, but ..." He faced the woman. "You were with him to the end. You did your part."

She blustered and jerked her head away.

The anesthetist defended Chandler. "Ma'am, don't blame him or anyone."

"This American doctor! You ended my man's life! You refused to call the boss."

The staff remained tight-lipped. A junior doctor spoke out. "The ER chief followed the right protocol."

"You shut up!" snapped the wife.

The anesthetist put on a stern face. "I've watched him. He has saved many lives. Blame him for nothing. This is just a bad case."

"You didn't call the real surgeon in charge!" She coughed and cried. "I'm sick."

Chandler escorted her from the ICU into the ER lobby. "Ma'am, I get the picture."

"You don't! You're a stubborn doctor." She wept and tried to take her mask off. "Falconer woulda save him."

"Keep it on." He fished out his handkerchief and offered it to her. "I did all I could, but—"

"Stop!" She took the hanky and wiped her red eyes. "I was dying sick. The police called me to zee accident scene. I have zis terrible sore throat,

Doctor. Give me pills, and I go." She rubbed her neck. "Prescribe me something."

"We're in the ER. It's against the rules to do that. You go to Medical Outpatient."

"Doctor, no time. Treat me."

He called a nurse for a digital thermometer and checked for fever. "High."

"I'm looking for an actual doctor."

He slid the mask down. "Open your mouth, please. Ma'am, the hospital has documented hundreds of swine flu cases in the past week."

"*Dios*! God!"

He examined her throat. Red mucous coated it. He put back the mask over her mouth and nose and listened to her chest. The lungs appeared clear, but mucous rattled in the bronchial passage. "Your name?"

"It's Matilda Aguilar."

He scribbled a prescription. "You may just have a viral infection. You got sick a day now?"

"Two."

"I'm giving you Paracetamol for the pain, and loratadine to dry the mucus. Antibiotics don't work on viruses. On the fourth day, we give antibiotics if necessary." He slung the stethoscope around his neck. "If you're still running a high fever, go to Outpatient."

She jerked her head away. "Some doctor you are! *Dios*! You butchered my husband and killed him dead! I'll sell myself to any man who slaps you."

A siren blared outside the automatic sliding door. Paramedics loped inside with a moaning man on a stretcher.

Matilda sniffled, giving Chandler the once-over.

"Mrs. Aguilar, my sympathy, too, on your husband's death. I have duties."

She harrumphed, and a female intern led her away.

A nurse approached the ER chief. "She'll roast you."

"She could be Falconer's mistress, and I'd care less. Rules are—"

"Doctor, most island people are part of a big family. When Falconer's your nemesis, expect trouble. He's got a crueler brother named Adolph. He's worse than the pirate Blackbeard." She closed her eyes. "Just be careful."

Falconer walked in. "Chandler!"

"Dude, you're connected to the drug industry. I challenge them to admit they sell prescription drugs that can kill patients."

Falconer eyed him. "You think well."

"Did you test my father for hepatic malfunction before giving him DED-statin? No! The statins cause liver problems."

"He showed no signs or symptoms of them."

"You didn't do the test."

"We would have done it in three months."

"You gave him enough time to die."

"Not wise thinking. With your mother, the side effects from Mordex are uncertain and unpredictable. Other similar anti-inflammatories can cause the same heart problem."

"If you weren't sure of Mordex, why prescribe the poison to human beings?"

"I didn't write the prescription."

"Strange. Who wrote it?"

"Dr. Ivanov did."

"I understand the government accepts medical lobbyists' bribes to bring in illegal formula medicines. You prescribed my mother and my father banned drugs."

"Prohibited in America only."

"Dude, you poisoned my parents."

"No!"

He eyed him. "I hold doctors accountable. It's my reality, man. I'll sue you."

"This isn't the United States. No law here says I cannot prescribe a drug banned in your country. Besides, I did not write any prescription."

"You're aware of the side effects."

"You can't predict that."

"Read the literature."

"We have our own laws."

"I know."

"This is not America. You could lose your position for squealing on—"

"I do no harm, dude! Ban the poisons. People will continue to get sick and die." He found himself rubbing his Adam's apple. "Patients recount funny stories about this hospital. Mom and Dad, too."

Falconer's white whiskers bristled. His leathery cheeks furrowed. Falconer had caused his parents to die. Chandler would move on, but he wouldn't forget. He lived in an unjust society and would have to work with it.

Michelle Lang entered the room. Chandler noted how her short casual dress showed off her long legs and her dainty frame. She held a package. "Our office staff had a cookout. I brought you barbecued chicken and coleslaw."

"That's kind of you." He took the food. "Dr. Falconer and I are having a little talk."

Falconer inched closer to Michelle. "He's whistle-blowing."

"I'll come back." Michelle walked out.

"Just remember, sir, the wheel will spin, but the hamster will always die," Chandler warned.

"Me, a what?" Falconer stepped aside. "I'll never, ever die. I'm going off to Switzerland for a few days' vacation. When I return, I expect a new you."

"May I ask you something?" Chandler asked.

"Go ahead," Falconer replied.

"Where were you the day and hour Pandora died?"

"Are you suggesting ...? Adolph and I had a massage at the Seaside Parlor. Take your mind off me." Falconer smiled, turned around, and left.

An intern ran up. "Another big traffic accident, chief!"

"Coming up!" *Will Falconer destroy the people's dream of freedom?*

Michelle came back in. She lowered her head. "About Pandora?"

CHAPTER 5

The wheezing nine-year-old was pale and sweating. In the ER Chandler examined her, concerned about her severe shortness of breath.

He connected a nebulizer to her face. The nurses helped. He treated her for an asthmatic attack. He loved helping children.

A short, stocky black nurse ran up to him with a cordless phone. "For you, Doctor."

A female voice came on. "I spoke to the chief executive of the hospital. I'll take you to court for a million dollars."

He gulped air. "Who might this be?" His patient began to gasp again. "Hold the line a minute," he ordered. He handed the phone back to the nurse and listened to the girl's chest. She needed emergency drugs. He eased in the intravenous medicine. Her breathing regulated.

The nurse handed the phone back to him.

"Who's speaking?" he demanded.

"Zis ees Aguilar," said the voice.

"Mrs. Matilda Aguilar!" Tension built in his head.

The voice on the phone changed to panting. "I can hardly-hardly breathe," Aguilar stammered.

"Got an emerg—" Static stopped him. "Come to us now."

"Doctor, but it's j-just zee f-flu."

"What did you say?" He shifted the phone to his left ear. "I'll send an ambulance."

"If I come to you," Matilda wheezed, "I faint. Will remind me of … zee state my husband was in." Her voice dropped to a whisper. "Prescribe me anti … antibiotic over zee phone to zee pharmacy. Many pharmacies on island. A friend will collect. *Por favor,* please."

He was feeling the pressure from her.

"Doctor!" she insisted.

"I'll-I'll phone it in," Chandler replied.

"Doctor, burn my house and me. Not coming back to the hospital."

He phoned in a prescription for amoxicillin and turned his attention back to the child.

Her chart showed the name *Noelle*. The passport section told him that he was treating resident oil tycoon Abdul Ali's daughter. He turned to a junior registrar. "Falconer referred this beautiful girl to us."

"He's money-crazy."

"I'm learning a lot about him. The ritzy clients still go to see him first. He meets them at social gatherings. They are the Falconerites. He likes to advise clients with silver spoons in their mouths." Chandler sighed. "Falconer collects fees from the rich and double bills National Insurance. He then throws the opulent patients over to us for further treatment. I have to think of ways to outsmart him. Six months max."

"I'm getting wiser," the registrar said.

"So am I." Chandler suddenly remembered Matilda's call. Sweat seeped into his bandanna.

"Sir." The nurse inched closer to him. "Someone's gone into your office."

Noelle started to wheeze again, and her face grew pale. Beads of sweat poured from her forehead.

"Let's repeat the intravenous." Chandler eased Noelle of her burden. "Who went into my office?"

"Looked like a woman."

"Watch Noelle for me." He hustled to his room. The judicial hearing on the death of Sam and Amelia Chandler loomed on his mind. The judge had said, "The charge is baseless with no tangible evidence. The case is dismissed."

Michelle sat by his desk, her face sour.

How do I get her closer to me? Chandler's heart skipped a beat.

"Dr. Chandler—"

"Call me Al."

"Al, something bothers me."

He went around the desk and dropped into his chair. "Go on, I'm listening." A buzz sounded. "Excuse me a sec." He put his cell phone to his ear. "Should we continue Noelle's oxygen?" he heard.

"Sure," he answered, and put the phone down.

"Let's talk about Pandora," Michelle said.

The thought froze in his soul.

"We had a close friendship," she said.

"I'm listening," replied Chandler.

"She was getting too wild for me. I had to slow down."

"I agree, Michelle."

She rose to her feet. "Pandora had a reputation."

"Are you sure—?"

"Let me finish. Pandora loved control over men and she used them."

He stifled his conscience. He looked away and then back at her. "I slobbered over her."

"She was screwing Obi Falconer. She loved the power. She had her fingers on his money. Al, I'm telling you the truth." She walked out.

Her words puzzled him. He passed his hand over his face and cringed at his own touch. He had lost Pandora. He was losing Michelle. She sounded genuine. *I'm falling in love with her.*

He returned to the ER bay. "Darn!"

An intern walked up to him.

Chandler scratched his head. "Matilda's prescription?"

He checked the time. "It's too late to stop it."

The intern stepped back. "Too much in your head, Doctor."

"Blame my self-esteem." He took Noelle's file, and feigned studying the notes. He slid the chart back to the desk and studied his hands.

"T-t-thank you, D-d-doctor," said Noelle with a smile. She perspired, convulsed, and left for the angels above.

That afternoon, Chandler lazed on the sofa in his living room. He was casually dressed in white corduroy pants and a blue batik shirt. He was thinking back on his life. He had to clear his mind. Munching on KFC spicy drumsticks, he focused on a football game. He pictured Noelle and vomited. She had chronic bronchial asthma.

The ring of the telephone interrupted his thoughts. He snapped up the receiver.

"I'm Alfred Smith," the husky voice on the line said. "I'm an attorney at Bootle Law Firm."

Chandler's neck muscles stiffened. "Peace from the cosmos," he said, and lowered the volume on the TV.

The lawyer hesitated. "She's dead."

A hardball hit him. "What are you—?"

"During his student days in Jamaica, Dr. Falconer had a Latina woman. She bore a daughter who married a Cuban man, a resident here. The daughter's name was Matilda Aguilar." The phone tinkled off.

Fear paralyzed him. He had to fight for justice. He dropped the receiver to its cradle. Amid his emotional turmoil, a sweet and loving Michelle called for his love. He was willing to suspend the worry of the world. He took the phone off the hook and glued his eyes on the TV game. He felt fidgety. Every turn of the ball gave a different perspective to the people he met on the island. Noelle's voice played in his head: *T-t-thank you, D-d-doctor.*

The phone pealed. "Smith here, again. Dr. Falconer is observing you from a distance. He'll behave like this until he's ready for you."

The click off jarred Chandler's senses. *Should I leave the island?*

CHAPTER 6

It's already morning! I'm late! Chandler slid into his Chevy Blazer. *This day won't turn out right. I just know it.*

He sped to work through the downtown traffic. Huge hotels, motels, nightclubs, big-name stores, and duty-free shops flew by the car windows. Some of the buildings had *CLOSED* signs. He pondered the impact the US economy had on Atlantic Isle. He counted his blessings for being on an island rather than living in America's turmoil. Good or bad, the natives survived. He studied them. They lived even if it was on coconut alone, or on a neighbor's loaf of bread. The islanders ate plantain or sweet potatoes from each other's kitchen farm. He called Noelle to mind, and a stabbing pain needled his skull.

The red traffic light flashed.

He slammed his brakes. The car screeched to a stop at the intersection. He panted and jerked his head around. His heart raced. Jitney bus horns blared. A police officer directed traffic. Chandler saw the officer stomping up to him. The officer's white, black, and red uniform and white cork hat with red tassel fascinated him.

"I'm late. I'm stuck. I get a ticket."

"You're a good doctor. Slow down, please."

The traffic light turned green and he sped off. "I'm cutting and running from this island."

He drove past the American embassy. The flag made him glow. He passed the McDonald's building and the multistoried British Colonial

Hotel. His mood improved. He began to whistle. He loved colors. Tourists shopped and bargained at the straw market. Sellers hailed customers. Still, Noelle's death emerged to haunt him and made him sweat. Chandler saw himself crawling back to America with only the shirt on his back.

He accelerated up a hill, heading for the Falconer General Hospital. He drove the Blazer along the cut-stone driveway up to the three-story peach structure. He prayed to one day own the hospital and change the color. *If Ali spares me or if Falconer doesn't punish me in excess ... am I dreaming?*

He begged the gods to let Michelle fall in love with him. Michelle and he might return to America someday when the economy improved. He glimpsed into the rear view mirror. *A wonderful, but sad, tale to tell our friends and children!*

The morning sun glowed on the horizon.

"I enjoy nature," he declared to no one in particular.

He gazed at the green-roofed cathedral and the glass tower at the foot of the hill. Next to them was the high-rise Atlantic Isle Hotel. The deep toll from the church belfry suddenly reminded him of his Sunday school days. Again, however, Noelle surfaced. The screech of blue and gray herons echoed as they flew into the cloudless sky, over the evergreens bursting with clusters of felt-blue flowers that lined the entrance. Chandler stepped past frangipani that grew along the curb, their fragrance greeting him. *Even the hospital is a paradise,* he thought. *Except for the devils milling inside the institution.*

He spotted Falconer, sporting a white coat. The fat man was looking through his office window and patting his rabbit. *Speak of the devil!* thought Chandler. *Why can't the doctors inside behave as peacefully as the trees outside?* He parked his car.

He checked his watch. "Mercy!" Matilda's death had made him absentminded. He stumbled on the curb but regained his balance. Complaining wasn't a habit of his. He could make a silk purse out of Falconer's sow ears. Cosmic aliens would have to descend from heaven and help. He didn't want Falconer to spot him coming in late. "Well, not today. I wiped Falconer's daughter off the face of this world!" he muttered to himself.

He went down to the cafeteria for a quick breakfast. The scrambled eggs, pancakes, orange juice, and coffee from the buffet were appealing. He sat in a corner. Looking up, he saw someone rushing in. His temple veins throbbed against his skull. *I'm hot.*

The dainty hospital administrator, Michelle Lang, strolled in. She held an envelope. Her blue suit covered her one hundred-twenty-pound body. Her caramel-colored hair was tied back in a tight roll. It twisted into a circle near the nape of her neck. She moved with grace, showing off her svelte figure.

"Hi!" she greeted him.

He found himself smooching Michelle. A hint of her Chanel No. 5 perfume soothed him.

"I saw you come in." She handed him the manila envelope. "I'll grab a tray."

He tore the envelope open. *Dear Dr. Chandler: I grieve, and I shed tears. I'm not myself since Noelle left us for Allah. My wives are depressed. The Mighty Allah spoke to me. I praise you for doing your best for Noelle. She's in heaven and wants to say thanks.*

Michelle came back with a tray of corned beef, grits, and coffee.

He gave her the letter to read.

"Great!" She kissed him on his cheek.

Stammering, he told her about the Aguilar case.

"She's Falconer's descendant. He can twist your neck for her untimely death."

"Must I pack up?"

"Al, good doctors are like tree trunks. Dogs will pee on you." She touched his arm. "Millions of Americans are losing their jobs." She sipped her coffee and bit a buttered toast. "Pandora used to have long, late-night parties and end up sleeping with Falconer."

He dreaded what more she had to say.

"Dr. Ivanov, Falconer's confidant, knows everything. He keeps quiet to guarantee his position at the hospital. Oh, and he carries a .22-caliber automatic. It's to protect Falconer." She spooned grits into her mouth. "The consultants belong to the rifle club."

"What a mess I got myself into."

He saw Falconer and Ivanov in the wall-to-wall mirror. Ivanov, although only five feet tall and bald, had a fit body for his thirty-eight years. He walked behind his superior.

Michelle commented, "He dresses like Falconer and promotes Falconer's wicked ways."

Chandler gagged on his breakfast. *I ended Falconer's bastard child's life!*

Falconer's furrowed brow creased, and his doughy face turned fiercer. He fiddled with a hair sprouting from a mole on his left cheek.

Kennedy entered the cafeteria. He hailed Chandler and then rushed to the food counter. He waddled to the table on his bowlegs with six assorted doughnuts and coffee on a tray balanced on his overflowing beltline. "Hey, Daddy-o!" His sorrel-brown eyes were as sincere as his friendship.

"Al, the elephant is the largest, most intelligent, and most faithful animal. I'm the elephant, just smaller."

Michelle's swan-like neck inclined as she leaned to the side and arched her delicate shoulders. Her sensuous lips unfurled in a broad smile.

"Falconer will fall with his own weight." Chandler turned his head away, still anxious about Falconer's presence in the room.

"Al, you were walking Baraka yesterday morning." She was veering off the subject. "Baraka has a medallion-winning stance. He's fit for dog shows. Meditate on it."

"He's a good dog." Chandler glanced at the doughnuts. "Arnold, you're thirty-seven, with a solid body. You're my trump card. Cut down on the doughnuts." Chandler peered into the mirror. Falconer headed toward him. "I'm quitting."

"Where are you going, Al?"

He rose and moved off the table. "Far from evil."

Michelle half-stood. "Al, don't leave."

"I'm-I'm going … to the washroom."

Kennedy got him back to his seat.

Chandler murmured, "Falconer and his specialists!"

Falconer strode up, his knock-knees giving him a crooked profile. His barrel chest rose, his swinging belly protruding. "Chandler!"

"Dude, I'm eating."

Michelle held her head down and murmured, "Entertain the boss."

Chandler let his cutlery drop to the table.

Ivanov's brown cross-eyes shifted. "The talk is, Dr. Chandler, you've come here to cause trouble."

"Far from it."

Ivanov sucked his corn-kernel teeth.

Falconer assumed an air. "Chandler, I served as an insurance claims officer before I studied medicine. I know the operation."

"You did well. You do everything for a good reason."

"I appreciate the way you think."

Chandler looked at Michelle. Her lips tensed, and his mind slipped from hate to love, and to hatred again.

She touched his arm. "Take it easy."

Ivanov's face grew tight. "Michelle, you're wrong to show this orphan American doctor compassion. Falconer's brother, what's his name?" He scratched his head. "Adolph. He thinks you shouldn't either."

Her forehead wrinkled.

Chandler sipped his coffee. Ivanov pushed a wood chair and let it scrape across the rough-tiled floor. The sound made Chandler's skin crawl. The atmosphere was tense. Ivanov had no eyebrows, but his forehead spoke of anger and he tensed his jaw.

Saliva collected at the corners of Falconer's mouth. "You missed the morning conference, Chandler."

"I know. No one should miss the conference. You're the boss, and respect is due."

Falconer affected a caring smile.

"It was hectic in ER last night."

Falconer whispered into Chandler's ear and clapped him on the shoulder. "You're still in my den."

"I honor your position and plans to consolidate finances."

"Do you recall treating a woman with a throat infection?"

Mercy! A chord of fear sounded in his head.

"She came in with her husband. He was in a traffic accident and died under your care. It was Matilda Aguilar. You killed—

"Dude!" Chandler sprang up. "I did not!"

"Did you think about doing a throat culture on Aguilar?"

"Thank you, you're the learned one."

"She died because of you. Why didn't you prescribe a potent and expensive antibiotic? Our pharmacy needs the money."

"So bread's the focus here." He glanced down at Falconer's feet. "You're a genius to deal so well with National Insurance. I savor your rich taste in shoes."

"I respect doctors who stick to the rules."

Chandler shook his head and snickered.

Ivanov's ruddy cheeks grew redder. He teased Chandler. "We rang the pharmacist. We spoke to an intern of yours." He rubbed his nose and turned to Falconer, grinning slyly.

Chandler boiled inside.

Ivanov raised his chin and played with it. "My goal is to get to America."

Chandler affirmed, "Do America a favor."

"You're not America, okay? I adore Dr. Falconer. I care for his country. I enjoy working in his hospital." He faced Falconer. "Ease off the case before the media reports the scandal."

Falconer mumbled, "You slipped up, Chandler."

"Newspapers, radio, and television," warned Ivanov. "It's wiser to leave the matter alone. Slander is bad for your hospital."

Falconer's lips twisted into a wicked smile. "I spoke to lawyer Bootle, about the Aguilar case. Bootle says you're liable for breach of duty of care."

Chandler raised his voice. "Are you serious?"

"I can't be. I'm fond of you. I'll fire you."

Chandler felt a numbness settle over him. He drank more coffee and gulped juice. He dropped his jaw in astonishment. "The order is unconstitutional, *ultra vires*: outside your jurisdiction."

"Come again?"

"The director and the board can fire. Only they can."

"I'm the chief of staff. I'm in charge."

"You're just one of the members. In Section 777 of the advisory rules, the director ends an employee's contract."

"Would you listen to him?" Falconer ramped up. "I'm walking out of here."

Ivanov pulled him down. "Please sit, sir."

Chandler continued. "The hospital high command recommends—"

"I'm a chief of staff of few words." Falconer's age spots darkened. "I prefer to act."

"I suggest you quash your order and forbid any action to enforce it." Tension still gripped Chandler. His words emerged tight and strained. "You violate the express wording of the constitution. You broke the consultative body's rule."

"What an intelligent man you are! I'll boot you out."

Chandler glared at him. "You mustn't do that."

"You're saying I can't?"

"The council decides."

"I—I-I-" Falconer stammered.

"You're playing politics," Chandler charged.

"I'm the hospital head. I may end my employees' jobs at my discretion to run this hospital well."

"You're wrong, Dr. Falconer."

The skin on Falconer's bald head creased. "Doctors come under my brass hat."

"In your skull."

"You fall under me," Falconer insisted.

Ivanov stepped in. His Russian accent had intensified. "Dr. Falconer is a veteran doctor and surgeon with over thirty years of experience. He acts in the best interest of the department. Dr. Falconer has terminated the services of ten other employees this year. He's ending yours for good reasons."

Chandler grew defiant. "Dr. Falconer fired ten people—opposition party members."

"I object to that." Falconer made a sour face. "You're—you're twisting the facts."

Chandler studied Falconer's features. "I refer to Section 101 of the commission rules. The staff chief could recommend that the administrator end the jobs of nonmedical staff."

Falconer snarled and pointed a finger at Chandler. "Explain yourself more."

"The right to dismiss medical staff rests with the director of the panel, Larry Lang. Father of the administrator Michelle Lang. Owner of the pharmacies on the island."

"You've been listening to gossip?"

Michelle's eyes opened wide. "This is overwhelming."

Chandler vaulted and shuffled off. "I'm abandoning this wreck of a hospital."

Michelle went after him. "You can't do this."

"Why not?"

Her voice was stern. "You get a very good tax-free salary. Cool off."

"Michelle, I'll fight."

"Hey, you people!" Falconer called with his hand. "Come back here, Chandler. I hold you in great esteem."

Chandler and Michelle returned to them. Chandler noted Falconer's now high-and-mighty posture.

"I run to the board every time a gripe or a grievance pops up, right?" Falconer said. "Then, we're questioning the integrity and judgment of the doctor-in-charge." He blinked, trying to make up stories. "Patients say you're rude."

"You're perjuring yourself," Chandler retorted.

"Refusing to sign sick leave slips for patients."

"Fib!"

"And a host of other complaints."

Chandler stiffened, not knowing what to say. An instinct told him to leave.

Kennedy came to his rescue. "To err is human and—"

"Arnold, let me answer." Ardor crept into Chandler's voice. "I read the hospital's standing orders and terms of contract. Section 120 of the board's rules says the employer must bring complaints to the employee's attention." His stomach clenched. "The rumor is you gamble too much, and I wish you'd change."

"Chandler!" Falconer's emphysema made him wheeze. He tried to lift his stooping shoulders. He was showing courage. "Oh, Mighty Jah!"

Ivanov shot up. "Let's get away from here."

They stomped to the door.

Chandler followed them. "Dr. Falconer, I value you, but you just don't walk out on people."

Falconer and his man marched out of the cafeteria without saying another word.

Kennedy said to Chandler, "You know Michelle's father owns a string of pharmacies."

Chandler whistled under his breath.

"Rise to the challenge, Daddy-o!"

"Al! Al?" Michelle's head fell into her plate, and she groaned.

"Michelle!" Chandler grabbed her. He wondered if it was stress or the beginning of some illness.

She didn't recover.

CHAPTER 7

"I'm not sitting here alone, goddammit! It's Saturday night. The cafeteria ordeal. No!"

Chandler invited Michelle, Kennedy, and Kennedy's girlfriend, Vanessa, for dinner. He cooked barbeque New York steak with sliced potatoes, carrots, and corn on the grill. They gathered in Chandler's quarters and sat in the back patio behind the kitchen, among the white, pink, and purple orchids that grew in hanging pots. Chandler served red wine.

"Fifteen years ago I came with Papa," said Michelle. "We got resident status. Father invested in the country."

"Cool," said Kennedy.

"About the cafeteria. I never fainted before. Tonight, I'll retire early." She leafed through a 2009 edition handbook. "Royal anthem: *God Save the Queen*."

Chandler closed his eyes. "Queen! You still sing that? It's colonial."

Vanessa's hundred and twenty pounds and flashy eyelashes made her sexy. "We follow British law. Falconer calls me his queen."

Michelle narrowed her eyes at her. "Why?"

Kennedy downed his wine. "If he doesn't stop, I'll name him something he's not."

"Queen!" Chandler squared his shoulders. "Time to remove royalty's influence and confuse Falconer's rights."

Michelle meted out the statistics. "'We're 85 percent Black, 12 percent European, and 3 percent other. A parliamentary democracy and a constitutional monarchy. The monarch: Queen Elizabeth the Second."

"Monarch? I am one." Kennedy hit his chest. "King of karate."

Chandler raised his chin and wagged his index finger. "The Honorable Obi Falconer will kill you."

They reeled with laughter.

"We're independent." Vanessa's creamy-white skin blushed, emphasizing the bleached blonde feathered hair that framed her face.

Michelle held the handbook closer. "A governor general represents the Queen."

Chandler lowered the book with his little finger. "Is our chief of staff the monarch?"

The crowd laughed, and Vanessa had to hit Kennedy to stop. Chandler knew they would never be a match.

"Falconer is a buddy friend of the Queen's man." Michelle read, "'Currency: dollar. Calling code: 242. Traffic: drives on the left.' We know that. 'This country has a Gross Domestic Product of nine billion dollars.' Wow!" She put away the book.

"Don't remind Falconer." Chandler narrowed his lips. "He'll get his hands glued to the money, gamble it, and bankrupt the country."

They rolled with joy, drank, and ate.

"Al, I have an idea," Kennedy said.

"A concept from you? Please!"

"Don't be so naïve. I'll hot-wire the engine."

"What engine?" Chandler pushed back. "Yes, you can."

Vanessa shot her arms up. "Yeah!"

Michelle stretched and yawned. "I'll go to my bed and rest."

Chandler held her hand. "No, you join us."

"So, you're leading me to an early grave?"

Chandler had no idea he was heading for trouble. Kennedy did his hot-wire trick. Chandler and his friends sped along the airport highway in Pandora's Jaguar. Few cars traversed the road so late in the night. Chandler built up a speed of ninety miles per hour and sang Beyonce's *Single Ladies*. They chanted and hummed.

A drink in his hand, Chandler toasted. "To my first newsletter publication!" He drank his wine, reached for the glove compartment, and gave out his newsletters. "You are the inner circle of this production." He switched on the inside light and focused on the asphalt. After overtaking an airport bus and nearly hitting it, he glanced at the caption. *Good Doctor–Patient Relationships.*

Michelle shot her hands up. "Al, watch out!"

Baraka raised himself from the back seat and grazed against Chandler's neck. He whined and barked at the steak on the dashboard.

Chandler bit the meat. "You don't need this. Lang Pet Pharmacy supplies you the best dog food."

Michelle leaned back in the front seat. "You make me proud. My papa owns the company."

"Information is power!" They raised their glasses to Chandler and continued eating and drinking in the car.

Kennedy gargled with his brew. "Wow! A picnic ride in a Jaguar." He swallowed the liquor. "Let's start the revolution!"

"Arnold," said Vanessa, "cool off."

Kennedy's plum mouth pouted. In the back seat, he put his other hand around Vanessa's shoulder.

Chandler glanced at the rear view mirror. Vanessa eyed Kennedy.

At high speed, they swung by a school.

"Al, Al!" exclaimed Michelle. "Slow down!"

Kennedy swigged lustily. "The building we passed is a private college. Falconer's the owner. One of his investments. The teachers are on his payroll. So you know where to send your little ones." Kennedy touched Michelle and Chandler.

Chandler raised his glass again. "Let's toast to the precious pearls!" He was giddy with drink. "This baby's a real car!"

"Years ago," continued Kennedy, "Falconer organized pre-prom beach parties for the graduates. He enjoyed frolicking with the girls."

Michelle coughed and choked. "Guys, we should go back. We're tipsy. The police catch us, and we're in trouble. We can crash."

They stared at each other. "No."

Chandler swerved to the corner, and glanced at Michelle. "What's wrong, babe?"

Her eyes rolled to the side, and her head bobbed. She recovered in a flash and nodded sleepily. "Watch where you're going."

Kennedy delved into his back pocket and took out a booklet. "Comic books are good literature."

Vanessa snatched it from him and hit him on his forehead. "Bad manners in company."

"Super to read Superman in a car like this. Want to follow me home?" He hiccupped. "We could watch *The Three Stooges,* you know, and monkey around."

She punched him on the head.

Chandler gripped the wheel and pressed his back to the seat. "Too much laughter leads to gloom. How many pharmacies does Mr. Lang own, Michelle?"

She drank, her speech slurring. "T-ten." She showed ten with her fingers and counted them like a child.

Chandler sipped his wine and overtook a trailer. "Let's fill our glasses to ten!"

Kennedy teased Michelle; "Your father has friends in the government."

"Arnold, stop it." Chandler's head was a bag of bricks from the drinks. He held on tight to the wheel and kept his foot on the pedal. The meter read ninety-eight miles per hour.

"He bribed his way into big business and citizenship. He's a crony of Falconer. I'm not trying to hurt you. Oops! I'm wallowing in this, Michelle. Could you unwind the windows?"

"Arnold!" Chandler unwound the back window. He smacked his lips. "Lang works hard."

"Open them all. The breeze is island cool." Kennedy's voice slurred. "Daddy-o! Can you fight the clan?"

Chandler dropped the windows. "Let's reduce the speed. We're going 105 mph."

Kennedy giggled and hummed the national anthem. "Let's experience the Jaguar beauty."

"Right!" Vanessa bunched a fist. "You-you-you can fight the Falconer clan. Y-you've got to slug harder together."

Kennedy tapped Vanessa on the thigh. "I spent seven years in university. Three extra for radiology. I work like a coalminer."

"Got ya, honey."

"Dispensing drugs at the hospital pharmacy only puts money into Falconer's pocket, Vanessa." Kennedy gulped his wine. "You get no perks as a pharmacist. Dispense me love for life, and let me plant seeds for more midgets." He giggled. "I'm a karate black belt—an upright man."

"Got ya, honey." Vanessa whacked him on his head. "Bear children yourself."

"Jaguar! Wow!" Kennedy rubbed his scalp. "Last Friday I performed at a comedy club. Five of us competed for the stand-up comic of the year. I won by roasting Falconer. I'm shooting for the national one, and I'll win."

They chuckled and clapped. "Got ya, honey."

Chandler drank his wine. He rested his glass in the holder and slurred his words. "This breeze is good. I always thought the island was a paradise." He turned at seventy miles per hour. The tires screeched and rubbed against the curb. "Seventh heaven is in a Jaguar!"

"You speak the truth." Michelle held on to her seat belt. "Ease up on the gas. Set an example. We're sixty minutes away by air from Florida." She hiccupped. "Listen to me, people. This country prides itself on an economy based on tourism, banking, and shipping. A unique combination for a small island."

Chandler increased his speed, overtaking a dump truck. "Fewer cruise ships are coming in, and banks are closing. Six cruises used to come in the harbor every day. Now, there are only three or four. The domino effect will empty Falconer's purse. Recession messes up the economy." He was racing at one hundred miles per hour.

"Whoops!" Kennedy and Vanessa sang, "*Jag-Jag-Jaguar!*"

Michelle touched Chandler's hand. "Enough of this joy ride."

"Slack off the throttle, Daddy-o." Kennedy looked up outside. "Now, veer to the right. See Falconer's nest?"

The house stood on a hill. A road surrounded the mount. Floodlights bathed the mansion, a white two-story building. Towers on both sides protected it. Chandler circled the hillock.

Kennedy stretched over to the wheel. "Blow a Jaguar horn and entertain Falconer."

Chandler pushed him away. "In a quiet zone?"

"Al, you're a lame chicken."

Chandler pressed the horn. "It's a wake-up call, Falconer!"

Chandler blasted it again. The speedometer showed ninety-seven miles per hour. They cupped their hands to their mouths. "Falconer, Falconer, down with Falconer!"

Michelle tightened her seatbelt. "Al, let's go back. Now!"

Baraka scratched the seat and barked. They got into a fit of giggles and sped off to the main highway. Just then, a Mack truck raced from the left. Chandler slued to the right. The screech of tires was drowned by the blast of the truck horn. Chandler hugged the wheel and twisted it to the right. The car plunged into a pond. The passengers yelled and swore.

Water gushed into the Jaguar. The passengers screamed and scrambled from their seats. They arrowed through the windows and swam to the surface. Chandler grabbed Michelle and waded through the mud to shore. Vanessa swam to land. Kennedy was on her back. Smeared in mud, Baraka followed. The pond reeked of rotten fish, salt, and mangrove.

Chandler sniffed and spat. "I'm in hot water. Nuclear radiation!"

Sirens blared, and the police came.

"You've wrecked the Jaguar." The officer planted his fists on his waist. "You smell of alcohol." He surveyed the scene and spoke to Chandler. "My job is to take you in for questioning."

"For a simple accident?" Kennedy clasped his hands in prayer.

The police officer relaxed his fists. "Doctor, I'll call vehicle rescue, get the Jaguar fixed, and take you off the hook."

"Why are you doing this?" said Chandler. "Isn't this an offense?"

"Dr. Chandler, you mightn't remember. I was in a police car accident. I was with my cop friend. You treated me for a spinal injury, sciatica, and whiplash. My colleague went to Dr. Falconer. He had similar injuries. He died. I'm pain-free, thanks to you. Now, do what you must."

Michelle walked off. "I'll pay for the damages."

Bubbles floated on the pond and the Jaguar disappeared.

The officer shot his hands up. "This is a good car! It's salvageable. I'll escort you home."

Chandler touched her arm. "Please, Michelle, you're coming with me."

Another Jaguar raced toward them and screeched to a stop. Falconer stepped out.

The cathedral belfry rang. Chandler and Michelle arrived at his home and showered. They sat in the den and sipped wine. The aches went away. "Let's switch on the television. After the news, I'll usher you home."

Community News announced the mail boat schedule to the outlying islands.

Michelle took in the information and nodded. The station spotlighted the annual dog show. "Falconer owns it. He's spreading his tentacles like an octopus in varied financial ventures. Money is his only objective."

"He gambles it out. Let's sit and drink. I'm still achy."

"No more drinking, Al."

He gripped his glass, downed the wine, and laughed. "Falconer fell for the late-night swim in the pool and our hunting for crabs. Glad Pandora's Jaguar went under."

"I'll salvage the car and get it back to normal."

"Thanks." They watched TV in silence.

"Midnight is long gone. I'll go."

"Michelle, I'm the happiest man with you. Please don't leave me alone." He gave her a blend of merlot, cabernet, and sauvignon. "Keep me company."

She nodded, winked, and kissed him. She drank the wine. "Al, where do I start?" She gazed at the glass and took a bigger sip. "Despite the economy, this is an affluent island. The sick visit the hospital and buy drugs from Lang Pharmacies. We give them a wealthy man's price. Well-off pet owners rush to the pet pharmacy to buy pet paraphernalia. We offer the right quote for their pockets. The government controls the value to suit the opulent man's pocket."

Chandler gave her a smug look.

Michelle cut her eye at him. "Despite the economic crisis—and the dry Public Treasury—the hospital is making money. The super-rich American residents here still support us. Falconer loves the business. The rich get richer!" Michelle regarded her empty glass. "We run an efficient enterprise."

Chandler poured her more wine and helped himself.

"Where was I? Foxy and rich people here own shares in Falconer's hospital. They own stocks in the pharmaceutical and food companies. The prosperous even infiltrate the veterinary pharmacy." Her face grew taut.

"I'm listening."

She hiccupped and slurred her words. "Falconer bought the dog track with profits from insurance fraud, drug, and food company bribes."

"That's white-collar crime!" Chandler licked his lips.

"Falconer has to launder the money." She touched one side of her high cheekbones. She was thinking.

"I was keeping a special bottle of Kenyan wine just for me and you."

Michelle's words slurred "T-tell me your life story."

Chandler told her. His wineglass slipped off his hand and fell, shattering.

She helped him pick up the broken pieces. "Your pinkie's bleeding."

"Oops. Nothing much to worry about. As I was saying, what did you ask?"

She sucked the finger. The bleeding stopped. "I-I-I wanted to know you."

"I nurture a profound secret."

"Keep it to yourself. All's well, and I like it this way."

They found themselves kissing passionately. Chandler was experiencing the joys of life. His hand bled again.

Breaking news flashed on the TV. The anchor announced, "Pandora Gray's death is still a mystery."

Chandler's heart beat against his chest. "For mercy's sake!"

The screen zoomed in on a corpse fished from the ocean. "The police suspect the body to be Pandora's."

He focused on the TV. The Jaguar came to mind. He wiped off the blood from his hand. "The good-for-nothing pigs!" Chandler lost his sense of equilibrium. "Michelle?"

"I-I-I'm right here with you."

"Fill up my glass. Double."

"No more for me."

The earth opened to swallow him. A dinosaur emerged and chewed on his sinews. His mind went back to his happy campaign days with President King. *I'm going to jail.*

CHAPTER 8

"Hey, you! It's early in the morning, but you look stressed. Like you can't cope." Chandler faced the bedroom mirror. "Now give me a smile." He showed his teeth. "You're hippie material, dude." He slipped on the diamond-studded bandanna. "Such is life." He had sixty minutes to spare. He headed for the union building to attend a quick union meeting. Five representatives from the different departments of allied medical personnel graced him with their presence.

A female representative spoke. "The hospital owes us an increment."

"Falconer won't part with the cash. What money are you taking about?"

"Overdue pay raise. A hundred dollars more a person and we're five hundred plus allied."

"Any documents to support your pretext?"

The woman handed Chandler the papers.

He scanned the contract and shook his head in disbelief. "The claim is valid."

He still had thirty-five minutes to spare before another meeting. He went to the radiology department on the ground floor to kill the time. He shifted on a stool. In the subdued light, he listened to one of Kennedy's ballads on a CD player, *Wind Beneath My Wings*. He hummed along, trying to make himself happy. The pigs had not called him in. Pressure built in his head. The media worried him more than anything else did. They loved to put you on trial before the law kicked in.

The karate doctor put on shockproof gloves and adjusted a light bulb in his aquarium. An electric eel squirmed in it. "I'll be careful. He's my pet, but he can paralyze you."

Chandler grabbed a nail file from the desk. "What do eels do to the reefs? If global warming continues, the ice up north will continue to melt. It will swell the ocean and this island will disappear." He filed his nails. "The eels will take over. They'll shock us and we'll go to Arnold Kennedy's locker." He laughed aloud and handed him a copy of his free monthly newsletter, *Do No Harm*. It was for the following month. "The readership is close to ten thousand. Like, that's my reality, man."

"Daddy-o! Are you using your girlfriend to do the typing again?"

"She's a darling."

"Readers' response is mythical."

"Michelle does the typing and printing on her computer in the evening, when Falconer is off." He blew the dust off his nails. "We're the peacemakers." He stood, and paced the floor as he read from the newsletter. "'Worldwide, two hundred thousand patients die of heart failure from Morgex arthritis pills.'"

"That's homicide."

"One hundred and nineteen died in the country."

"Murder!"

He searched the desk. "I need a nail buffer."

Kennedy pulled open a drawer. "Here you go."

"Doctors' prescriptions on the Isle amounted to nine and a half million dollars and worldwide, ten billion."

"Shocking! Pissing rich, these people!"

"Healthcare reform is the answer. President King is following the right path." He buffed his nails. "The greedy CEOs will go downhill!"

"The islanders will say, 'Out with you.'" The radiologist sat and reviewed an MRI scan. He dictated a diagnostic report based on the images into his mini-recorder.

"The senior consultants, who are shareholders, are upset. They're supposed to share the profit. The prime minister is angry with Falconer and alluded to the rip-off in a TV broadcast."

"He'll crucify him."

Chandler blew on his nails again and continued buffing. "Falconer's got connections."

"Most greedy people do."

Chandler fanned his fingers and took out a package of his natural daily vitamins. "I'll be in top shape for Michelle's love."

Kennedy sat and read the newsletter. "Al, the statistics for every country are fine. Falconer and his big shots will pin you for exposing him."

"He can poke holes in me. So far, he hasn't made any direct attack on the publication. I'm hungry."

The phone dinged and Kennedy grabbed it.

"Michelle, ah … Al?" He pressed the speakerphone on.

"Let him know Falconer will talk to him. He must stop circulating the newsletter." She breathed heavily. *"He plans to tell the American embassy of Al's wayward behavior. According to Falconer, Al has citizenship here. He's still American. I'm beginning to hate the publication, too."* She cut him off.

Chandler cracked his knuckles. He feared losing her. The tension was overpowering him. "I'll leave you for a short while. I'm attending a meeting with the hospital board upstairs." He puffed on his fingers.

He went up and sat in the conference room with the board. "Our allied personnel are over half a thousand strong."

"What are we here for?" sniffed Lang.

"The board promised an increment but my people aren't getting the money."

Falconer hit a pencil on the desk. "Everything takes time."

They argued among themselves.

A board member jumped up. "This American doctor is a pig."

Chandler had little to say.

Another was piqued. "More of a snake."

He kept quiet. His head ached. He thought about getting up and leaving.

Falconer slapped his hands on the desk. "Lang's got the final word."

Lang glared at him. "I'm thinking."

Chandler threw the personnel agreement before them. "We'll call a strike." Closing his hands, he admired his polished nails. He whistled a tune, took back the document, and sprang up to leave. "You're a great asset to my people. We'll catch up."

"Did you say strike?" Falconer drummed his fingers on the desk. "Hold on."

"Sure." He pushed his chin up.

The Board debated. He wasn't listening anymore.

"No!" Lang raised a pointed finger. "We will pay."

He went down back to Kennedy and told him about his union victory.

"That's a tough sell with them, but you're the victor. Wait for the reaction." Kennedy sprang up, unleashed a karate chop, and muttered something indecipherable in Japanese. His shirtsleeve tore at the shoulder. "Oops! I'm black belt since I attended the University of Miami."

The CD player stopped.

"Dead batteries." Kennedy mimicked the knuckle punch and blurted something in a foreign language. "I move like a kangaroo, and if you step into my pouch, consider yourself pouched."

Chandler checked his wristwatch. "Time to get to ER."

"You're in deeper shit, Daddy-o." He sighed, and shook his head. "Join our club." Kennedy performed a finger jab and made a swishing sound. "Karate stresses self-discipline, positive attitude, and moral purpose. We'll pummel Falconer together. Hang out with a combatant like me."

The phone dinged once, and Kennedy picked it up. "X-ray department."

"Falconer speaking." His voice was loud over the speakerphone.

Chandler mimed, "I'm not here. I'm leaving."

"Hold on a sec." Kennedy pointed a finger at Chandler, and spoke into the mouthpiece.

"The whistle-blower is in your office. Put me on to him. Okay, tell him to call me."

The phone died off then became alive again. The little doctor grabbed it.

"Arnold, it's Michelle. Put Al on. Falconer's on the line."

"No."

"The chief wants to talk to him in his office."

"I'll tell him. Refrain from paging him now. He's coming." He dropped the phone. "The devil needs you."

Chandler folded his fingers and admired his nails.

"Your boss is clamoring for you."

"I'll let him wait," Chandler said.

A nurse came in. "A patient for a Doppler scan, Dr. Kennedy."

"I sent that." Chandler glanced at the form. "I'm going to my office. Keep me informed."

"Daddy-o, don't piss your pants if you bump into Falconer."

The phone pealed off its hook. Kennedy waited.

"X-ray Depart—"

Michelle spoke low. *"Arnold, put Al on now!"*

He heard her voice on the mini-speakerphone.

"I can't."

Michelle spoke quickly. *"Find him and tell him to vamoose from there while Falconer's cross. He's on his way. The newsletters are driving him mad. Falconer's making up a new story to pin on Al."*

Kennedy dropped the phone. "Al, run. Falconer's coming down."

Chandler pushed the door shut and folded his arms.

"Al!"

"I'm going nowhere."

"Holy shit! I'm with you, Al." Kennedy turned to Roberts. He read the requisition. "Varicose veins?"

"Chandler suspects DVT."

"Deep vein thrombosis. I'll scan the leg right away."

He decided to wait.

Kennedy checked the notes. He applied gel to the patient's leg and ran the probe along the leg. He studied the monitor as the distorted images changed from red to blue to black.

"Mr. Allen has three clots in the right leg. I see one high in the thigh, one behind the knee, and another in the calf," Kennedy reported, "but the ER chief did an urgent angiogram a week ago."

Chandler nodded.

Allen assumed a sour face. "Doctors make mistakes like crazy in the hospital."

Roberts wheeled the patient out.

Kennedy went into his side office. In the mild light from the desk lamp, he wrote his findings. Chandler scratched his chin. Roberts came back in. He handed the report to her.

Someone knocked on the door. The telephone rang again.

"Don't answer it," Chandler ordered.

Kennedy cried out, "The ring or the door?"

The phone continued ringing.

"The bloody telecom crap!"

"Why?"

"Might be Falconer again."

Falconer crashed in. "Chandler!"

Chandler sat and held his head down. Not wanting to face Falconer, he raised his left wrist to eye level. "My watch says ... got another minute to kill."

Falconer squalled, "A woman complained about your behavior toward her daughter. You surprise me."

Chandler crossed his legs. "Did you make up the complaint?"

"Roberts and I had a short chat," said Falconer. "You're a fine doctor."

Chandler folded his arms. "DVT is a possible complication from any angiogram. The newsletter had that."

"I asked my consultants and my political friends not to read the newsletters." Falconer stretched his legs. "Our specialists do such procedures. You're embarrassing me."

"I wanted to make sure the coronary arteries were clear. He's a pensioner. He can't afford to—"

"Still, Chandler . . ."

"I accept that." Chandler turned to Kennedy. "Picture this: Falconer or any of his specialists do the operation. Big money in the kitty for the good chief. *Ching-ching*! Cool, Dr. Falconer."

The giant chief of staff chuckled. "You're a friend of the human race. Friends and fortune make a healthy handshake."

"No pussyfooting, please." Chandler shot his arms up. "My time is up. Got to work."

"Hold it." Falconer turned and spoke to Kennedy. "Recommend additional routine scans to the doctors." His lips burst into a cocky grin. "My hospital runs on a budget."

"Chandler ordered a scan of the right leg."

"Must I repeat? Do the other leg. Always! Forget what the doctors say. Disregard Chandler's orders. You're the radiologist." His tone softened. "Ten or more scans a day and we're in the money groove."

Chandler teased, "Call in crabs and centipedes. They have legs to make you an Arab sheik. Good fodder for my newsletter."

Falconer stood stone stiff, his breath quickening.

Kennedy kept his mouth shut.

"Arnold Kennedy!" Falconer swung around and pointed a finger at him. "My orders are two legs: sick leg and healthy leg."

"It borders on insanity," affirmed Chandler.

"The cost doubles."

"Just listen to your words!"

"I won't pretend to be subtle, Chandler. The economy is dropping. Blame the bloody Americans."

"Man shall not live by bread alone."

"Don't ask me." Kennedy dropped his eyes. "Tell the staff about the leg scanning."

Falconer stiffed his arms. "You take orders from me."

"I'm a radiologist. I follow the doctors' orders."

"I adhere to rules," Chandler said, "and stick to ethics."

Falconer stomped to the door. "You're a first-rate doctor. Clean up the newsletter."

"You're ripping off the insurance to juice your pocket. About my news roundup, thousands of union members, relatives, and well-wishers desire to read the facts."

"I'll speak to Gray."

"Gray spoke against your financial dealings."

"Chandler! Gray announces one story. In closed chambers, he tells me another."

"Dr. Falconer, be careful of under-the-table deals. I'm in the way. I'll fight back. Filthy doctor dabs in dirty politics."

"You'll live on the Isle for a long time. America is in a recession. You're on contract."

"I'm unable to get away from your drug-pushing doctors. You're working with the giant food boys. You're collaborating with major pill pushers, lobbyists, and corrupt political wheel horses. It's a mafia!"

Falconer affected a sinister smile and hustled out.

"I empathize with him," Chandler commented.

"I give you a plus, Daddy-o. I'm getting to like you more."

Chandler walked about, not mindful of ER. His pager vibrated. "No!" He ignored it. His resolve grew firmer.

"He's testing you, Daddy-o. The minority hates you. The majority of the people adore you."

He slapped Kennedy a high five. "I'll go for democracy." He had a bright idea and discussed it with Kennedy.

The following day, he called the administration office. "Connect me to the person who handles sick leave for the staff, please."

"Sure, sir," sang the receptionist.

"Personnel here."

"I'm Dr. Chandler. Dr. Ivanov and I were talking. Check your system. When was he on sick leave this year?"

"Our computers are down."

"You've been employed in the office for a while, right?"

"Years, but this has never—"

"I'll call back."

"Wait a minute; is this Michelle Lang's admirer?"

"If you need a favor, phone me anytime."

"I remember Ivanov had a sick day. It's the first time ever. It was exactly two weeks before your parents died."

"Good memory. How come you're so sure?"

"He asked me for a date, and we went picnicking all day."

"He's the best."

CHAPTER 9

Today I'm done. Chandler had chosen a green T-shirt and a yellow bandanna for the occasion. He sat at the far end of the conference table in a red-carpeted room. The fluorescent ceiling lights competed with the sunlight coming in through the wide-paneled windows.

By 8:00 a.m., union members massed at the hospital to rally for their president.

Chandler glanced around the rectangular room. The connections were crystal-clear. A huge gold-framed portrait of Gray, lit with an ornamental picture light, dominated the front. The Atlantic Isle Chemicals president, National Insurance director, and private health insurance presidents shared smaller spaces.

The curtains were a macabre red. The wall clock showed 8:25. The back wall displayed an oversized color photo of Falconer, also in a gold frame. On both sides of Falconer's portrait hung the consultants' black-and-white pictures. He saw an empty slot. It was his.

The wall clock said 8:27. He sipped cold water from a plastic glass with the Lang Pharmacy snake, mortar, and, pestle logo etched around the rim. He wasn't going to interfere with the private insurance companies. He waited until 8:30. The clock showed 8:35. Believing in time, he shifted in his seat and got up to leave. His watch indicated 8:36.

Falconer entered, wearing a white coat over his black suit. He joined the dark-suited members, who settled down around the table.

Larry Lang rose. He was Michelle's father, the board chair, and owner of the pharmacy chain. He stroked his gray Kung Fu mustache and addressed Chandler. "Dr. Chandler, our report says you're insubordinate to staff members. You ignore Dr. Falconer's orders. You show gross disrespect to Falconer. He's our venerable high command, whom Gray and his cabinet respect. In the ER, you do only emergencies. You do work you shouldn't do. You refuse to refer patients to the relevant consultants. They know how to follow the rules." His hairless eyelids, showing habitual spasm, opened wide, exposing his big black eyes. "You spend precious time with the union." He pushed back a strand of his salt-and-pepper hair. "Then, this strange newsletter. The doctors here think the news roundup is defamatory. We can't tolerate a staff doctor making controversial statements." He paused and took a deep breath.

Chandler studied the directors. Conniving politicians appointed the cronies with rich backgrounds. They had no medical education. "I'm no psychologist, but here we see people of average ignorance."

Lang made a fist, the age spots on his hands lightening. His voice rose. "I'll hold you in contempt!"

"If you tell the truth, you're a whistle-blower. If you lie and you're jobless, you're still a bad person. If you do unnecessary procedures or prescribe too many drugs, you're an idol."

"You're out of your element." Lang lowered his fingers to the belt on his narrow waist.

"What's the final word?" Chandler listened to his spirit within for words of hope. "You've painted a target at the center of my forehead." He steeled himself against the pain inside. "For love and peace, I'm guilty as charged."

Lang's tic increased. "You're not fighting us?" He turned to Falconer. "Sir, your comments, please."

Falconer coughed up a laugh. "Free love and sex is what these people worship."

"We reviewed the report you filed."

Sweat beaded on Falconer brow. He took off his coat. "I thought this adopted doctor was a gentleman."

Chandler knees grew weak but his faith strengthened. He reflected on his parents. He searched his mind for a flicker of advice. He got none. "I stand for helping the poor."

"Lang, this man is behaving badly."

"I treat and cure people," Chandler continued. "I never push poisons to our patients."

"Are you referring to me?" Falconer made a sour face. "I object to the insult."

"I work for an honest day's pay." The agony of the trial was easing. He was in the presence of vipers. "Falconer rips off National Insurance and private insurances. He pushes for doctors to follow him."

Falconer knitted his brows and smiled in defiance.

Lang gripped the desk. "Chandler, the attitude you show to work is not changing. Dr. Falconer is the master of the ship."

Chandler's voice grew firm and final. "I promise to do what's right. I'll defend medical workers. I uphold the new-age spirit of America and the world. Free at last!"

A director covered his mouth and snickered. "Leave us alone."

Someone tapped on the door and opened it. "Excuse me, gentlemen. Just a note for Dr. Chandler."

He read it. *Remember, in support of you, a crowd's gathering outside. It's getting bigger. Keep up your self-esteem.* He became wide-awake. God had sent his angels. Dread was becoming as familiar to him as the air he breathed. He gained sudden strength.

Falconer stared at Chandler and affected a smile. Lang grew red in the face. Falconer jumped up.

"Sit down, Dr. Falconer." Lang rubbed his chin and turned to Chandler. "You're defiant; you disobey rules and whistle-blow. The board has decided to suspend you for a month without pay. We hope you'll reconsider your behavior."

"He can't." Falconer dropped to his seat and sniggered. "He's suffering from orphan identity crisis."

Chandler swallowed hard. The words hurt him. He forced grandeur into his voice. "You can beat a horse as much as you can. You cut off a cockroach's head and he lives ten days more. You decapitate me. I live to fight the chief and his cronies for a lifetime."

Falconer wrote a note and slid the index card across the table to Chandler. "Read the message in your spare time."

Chandler took it, face down, and folded it. He would wait. He had enough to deal with.

"*Woof.*"

The dog's bark sounded from the corridor. He had a friend outside. He had hundreds of friends waiting for him. Falconer permitted himself a withering stare.

Chandler shoved the note into his shirt pocket. "Baraka's looking for his master who's in trouble."

"We suspend the bitch from the institution," said Falconer.

Chandler pressed his hands on the table and pushed himself up. His fingers ached.

"Both you and the dog are out."

"Baraka brings love to patients." He forced a smile. "The waiting room is public domain."

"He's your shadow."

"Watch out, Dr. Falconer. Baraka's bark is worse than his bite. I'm the reverse." He jumped up and surveyed the glum faces focusing on him. He took a long breath and walked out, brooding, enraged.

The people applauded, and gave him an adrenaline rush. "Mercy! Mind-blowing! This is like Woodstock." He spoke up. "Well-wishers, allied medical personnel, and union members! Peace!"

They clamored, "Peace!"

He showed his peace sign to them. "You've come not to stifle me, but to rejoice." He managed a small, tentative smile and explained the board's decision.

The crowd bawled out "Down with Falconer!"

He read Falconer's note. His temper soared. "Here's a love letter from Falconer. 'I, Obi Falconer, will silence you, Al Chandler, and all your blind followers.'"

His patrons raised their fists. "No!"

"Health for all is our objective. Without you, my people, no healthcare exists. Victimization we'll never tolerate. Slavery days are over. The affluent doctors are still getting richer. You continue to die of the rich doctors' poison. We must run before we walk. The day will come when we'll reflect and rejoice. No one can stifle our hopes!"

The fans shouted, "No!"

"The fight goes on for our rights! We won't pretend or shake plastic hands! The mighty will perish before the battle is over!"

"Yes!" they screamed.

"You're not like me," he roared. "You didn't fall from the sky. Doctors bleed the veins of the sick to fill the whims of their egos. You'll enjoy the prerogative to choose your treatment. Pushing deadly drugs must stop."

"Yes!"

"Remember the children and parents of our land." He passed his hands across the crowd. "Your lives and health are worth battling for."

The supporters lost their tempers. "Shame on Falconer!"

"Falconer insulted my orphan background. Ponder the millions of orphans throughout the world, victims of poverty, family tragedy, and war. You defend justice, and the doctors think you're deranged."

"Shame, Falconer!"

He opened the newspapers. "Point of interest: Here's today's newspaper headline. *Falconer Sold Old Yacht. Buys Another One. Twelve Million Dollars.*" He looked up. "It is your bread!"

Pandemonium erupted among the people. Police sirens blared. Chandler raised his arms. "Go in peace, my people." He made a fist. He hammered it in the air. "If the devils harm us, remember: We are like cockroaches." He slapped his wrist on his chest. "We will continue to occupy the earth for countless years."

The crowd blew white balloons and released them. They filled the sky with a cloud of shining moons. He wasn't fighting alone.

He walked to the parking lot for his car. Baraka jumped into the back seat. He slipped in and rubbed Baraka on the back. A human sound echoed behind them. The dog's hackles rose. Baraka broke wind. "Boy!" He called Michelle.

She sounded distant. "Papa's establishing PR with the doctors. He and Falconer are coming any moment to see me about the business. I have much to do."

"And less to do with me."

"Falconer ordered Vanessa to make ten million this year in the pharmacy or else."

"Not at the people's expense."

"He warned Vanessa to order the substandard generic drugs from underdeveloped countries. She had to dispense them 'to the poor bastards without insurance.' Falconer's words."

"We need healthcare reform."

"They'll start rationing pills."

"Everyone will benefit."

"Al, zip it. He offered Vanessa a mountain bike and a two-week Mediterranean cruise for two. Papa's paying for the gifts."

"Your Papa didn't even give me the right to take out the trash."

"But he's my papa. He has a heart problem."

He ducked his head. "Now the sympathy factor."

"He told me I'm his only beneficiary in his estate. I'll care for him."

"You're obliged to."

"Many pharmacies to worry about."

"You'll become a drug pusher, too."

"Al, stop this revenge. Worthless for me, pathetic for you. Go on a holiday. Falconer's going on another vacation. Switzerland. For a few days."

He glanced at Baraka through the rear view mirror.

"I'll drop off Papa. I'm having lunch with a group of hearing- and speech-impaired persons at one thirty."

"You are busy. I—"

"I'm planning a fund-raiser for my pet project. A school for the hearing and speech impaired."

His temple vein throbbed from her excuses. He craved jazz music. He yearned to look out at the yachts in the ocean. "I had much to handle today." He ran his hand over his shaved face, taking comfort from the touch.

"I hear footsteps. Someone's knocking downstairs. Have to go. Sorry, the postal worker is here."

"I'll go and clean up the beaches. The tar comes from North Atlantic. Tar kills marine life and healthy reefs. Sorry for the poor turtles! I'll organize cleanup campaigns and keep busy."

"You're putting me under stress."

His voice grew husky. "With nothing else to do, the devil in me might evolve. I'll be busy on my computer."

"I'll be looking over your shoulder."

"Kind of you," he retorted.

"The prime minister is calling Falconer to a private meeting. The health minister and the finance minister will be there. Tomorrow. Guess we'll never know what they have to say. Oh, they're here. I didn't hear a knock."

"Will they discuss Greed Identity Crisis?" He chuckled. "You have to go. I'll feed my dog, every day, for the rest of my spare time. Your papa imposed it on me."

"You're unfair to say. Papa, Dr. Falconer, please come in. Sit down, P-P-Papa, Dr. F-Falconer," Michelle said.

"Your father stinks!"

"My-my Papa—? I'll-I'll be with you in a minute."

Chandler clicked off. Baraka farted again and stank up the car. "*Ugh!*" He rolled down the window and drove off. The barbs of gluttony worried him. "The world stinks. It's a colossal task!" *Somebody has to clean the shit. Someone will, this year. Starting at dawn.*

CHAPTER 10

"I have a great idea." He made a fake ID with a piracy program.

Dressed in a black suit, he put on wrap-around shades and went down to the rifle club. He stepped inside the one-story red-roof building.

A short man smiled at him. "Yes?"

"I'm with the FBI. I'm helping the local authorities investigate a murder case involving club members."

"Sir, I can't give any information."

Chandler studied him. He slipped two hundred dollars in the man's hand.

"No, no, no, I can't. What do you want to know?"

"About a Dr. Ivanov?"

"From the hospital?"

"Correct."

"Not much to tell." He pulled Chandler closer to him and whispered into his ears.

"Most grateful, sir," Chandler said.

Chandler picked up the phone at home. He dialed Michelle but then put the phone down.

"I'll wait."

He hunted down emails of corporate heads, presidents, business managers, and food-store supervisors. He found emails of politicians, doctors, nurses, civic and religious leaders, and island big shots. Phoning secretaries of hard-to-reach people, he retrieved company listings for executives.

He called Michelle on his cell. "I need a favor."

"Al, it depends what."

He told her.

She murmured something he didn't understand. He was about to put the phone down when she spoke.

"Yes!"

"You live alone, Al. Be alert for Adolph. He's been around the hospital asking the nurses where you were. Adolph is a known hit man for his brother."

He used a hippie expression. "I dig you. I'll cool off."

From an underworld agency, he got an extensive email list. "Yes! Everything is going well."

After returning to work on his desktop computer, he emailed everybody on the list. He told a story. An unknown, wicked doctor had a secret plan to keep people sick until they died. He elaborated on some of his favorite themes: side effects of prescription drugs, supermarket rip-offs, and hospital bacteria.

Chandler copied his last email ten times in a large, red, italic font. He sent the copies to Falconer. The chief was certain to know of the conversion in healthcare for the better of all.

He bit into a pie. Baraka licked his snout. Chandler fed him half of the pie. "You're no Clyde! That's hippie for moron."

Through the window, he saw rain drizzle then pour from gray clouds. He restarted his computer. It didn't come on, and his spirits sank. He drifted across the room and glanced outside. The transformer on the electric pole still had a beacon light and streetlights worked. Something funny was going on. His cell phone rang: *"I'm Adolph. Just saying hello."*

"What?" Chandler felt he had heard that voice before—in the backyard when Pandora died.

Someone knocked downstairs. He spilled his Campari. His nerves throbbed. Baraka barked. Chandler ran down. Baraka followed, ran ahead, and jumped on the door. Forks of lightning heralded a blast of thunder. He tiptoed to the window and split open the curtain an inch. He saw nothing. He cracked the door, ready to slam it shut in case Adolph swooped on him.

"Hi!"

Chandler felt like peeing. He checked again and breathed a sigh of relief. Baraka pushed through the door crack and rubbed against the familiar person outside.

"Michelle!" He pulled the portal open wider. Rain splashed inside.

The taxi revved up and took off.

She rushed in. "Just wanted to drop in."

"Oh!"

"I was checking your emails." She took off her raincoat.

She had a basket in her hand; a plastic sheet covered it from the rain. He smooched her on both cheeks. Baraka yapped again.

A car pulled up outside.

She shaded her eyes from the lights. "That's not the taxi."

Baraka bared his fangs. "*WOOF*!"

Something stirred in the shrubs. Chandler's brain froze. A giant male Afro-Islander popped into view.

"Who the hell's that?" Chandler demanded.

The man grinned, showing his teeth. He huffed and slid behind the bushes. Thunder clapped one after another. Baraka snarled and dribbled. "Adolph!" Chandler panicked. "You bloody Clyde!" He gulped air furiously, gripped Michelle by the waist, and jerked her to him.

"Adolph?"

"I noted his rotten teeth. Falconer has bleached dentures." Chandler peeped through the slit in the door.

"High school dropout."

"Dumb!"

"On heavy drugs."

"Dope dude!"

"Alcoholic. Done a few killings for the island mafia."

Chandler kicked the door open wider. "What the hell d'you want?"

Michelle affirmed, "Adolph! Falconer pays you a thousand dollars a month to keep you alive. Get out!"

Chandler pulled the door in, still leaving a crack.

"Out!"

Michelle pushed her head out. "Adolph! Dr. Falconer gives you a place to sleep on his new yacht. He orders you to do mischief. You dream of winning the lottery. You're thinking of growing marijuana for you and your brother to sell to innocent people. Now, go away!"

Behind the bushes, Adolph blurted in his raspy voice, "Michelle?" Adolph guffawed and fired a gun into the air.

Chandler slammed the door. His nerves recoiled into a tight rubber-band ball. He peeped from the corner of the curtain. Adolph hopped into a black car and sped off. Chandler's temples throbbed. He squeezed Michelle's waist. "I'll keep him on my radar and follow his shadow." He walked up the stairs.

"Falconer's getting away with murder, Al. He's ripping off National Insurance. That means he's robbing the country of its assets. I've seen the reports. He and Gray call up each other every day and talk like friends."

Chandler was beginning to wonder if Adolph was not the one who killed Pandora. He suspected Adolph had knocked him unconscious when he'd discovered Pandora's dead body. "I'll put the Clyde on my target list." By June of 2009 he wanted to end the absurd happenings. "My parents' death has taught me self-sufficiency." He kissed her lightly on the lips. "I live for a cause in a land I've come to call my home."

"America is still your homeland." She hugged him, and shot him a romantic glance. "I'll go now. I checked Falconer's records. He's made seven million dollars illegally at the hospital. The amount far exceeds his salary and individual patient consultations. The specialists speak of his sociopathic behavior—all for Falconer, none for the consultants. Falconer has a hook on the foreign doctors. He amasses wealth."

"To gamble big time at the baccarat table." Chandler touched Michelle's trembling lips with one finger. "Thanks." His sex hormones surged to his brain. It put him in an easy mood. "Let's—"

"No! You had too much for the day."

"Then I'll get on the Internet, on Facebook, Twitter, and MySpace. I'll get anti-Falconer messages to every user."

Congratulations! His computer signaled incoming mail. *We read your emails. You are a freedom fighter. We love you.*

-Union Members.

The computer beeped. Chandler read the mail:

My dog show and dog race are coming up soon. You and your supporters keep out. You're getting nowhere with the propaganda. People are working to rebut your smear campaign. Oh, Chandler, I had hopes for you. I hope you change.

The next email came from Dr. Sam Pierre, pediatrician. It reflected Falconer's sentiments.

He read another one. *I'm safer putting you down. Oliver Jarvis, psychiatrist.*

"I'm getting ideas."

CHAPTER 11

The wall clock struck one. That Saturday was Valentine's Day. He slipped on a cloth apron over his khaki pants and hibiscus-print red T-shirt. He sported a red bandanna.

He and Michelle busied themselves at the downtown fair, which they had founded. The hospital administrator donned a red polka-dot skimmer dress.

They made a big dish of curried oyster pâté. All the funds went to charity for the disabled and the orphanage.

They stepped into the Atlantic Isle Hotel ballroom, onto a maroon carpet. A string of dimly lit chandeliers hung from the white-domed ceiling, illuminating a stretch of tables covered with red cloths and displaying international dishes. Sunlight filtered through the pink tieback draperies. In the spirit of love, Java doves cooed in a huge bronze cage. The red-carpeted platform had fresh roses in crystal vases.

A piano version of *The Wind Beneath My Wings* played from ceiling speakers.

"It's exotic here." Michelle touched Chandler's arm. "It's the perfect place for the fair."

He pecked her on the cheek. "The atmosphere is right."

She returned the kiss.

He spoke with an air of authority. "Respect for Falconer is light-years from me."

"He and his boys might—"

"People dehumanize politics here and brutalize medicine. We'll correct the problem. Family is the only humanizing force left in the country."

She tasted the pâté. "Early in the morning I went in to work and snuck into the chief of staff's office."

"You're braver than I thought."

"Credit me for something. I tried to tap deeper into his computer to know the score on him. *NO ACCESS* flashed on the screen."

"You're in for trouble."

"He installed a surveillance camera. I panicked." She panned the crowd and changed the subject. "You made this fair a five-star occasion."

"Let's hope no one turns the day into a one-star disaster. You never know."

She looked down. "Al, you're the man I was searching for my entire life."

He whistled, and his heart thumped. "Today is our day."

Vanessa, sporting a red floral dress, strolled up to join them. "Our Falconer is messing up the pharmacy bills. I'm missing five hundred thousand from the account. Falconer went into the funds and removed the money."

Kennedy appeared behind his girlfriend, his white pants and black shirt far less exotic than her dress. He sneezed and ogled her. "Hmmm. Your cologne's sexy. Short men like me can eat an elephant and carry their weight around."

She stooped to his eye level. "Cut the stupid jokes."

He gazed at her. "But my lips are red and sweeter than wine."

"Silly talk!" Vanessa disappeared into the crowd.

"Something to think about." He patted his clothes. "I'm wearing black because we might grieve if Falconer comes. He won't come." His hands made a karate move.

Michelle wiped a food spot from the tablecloth. "The funds go toward the abused children's group. Some to the old folks' home and the Humane Society. A part of it is to rehabilitate dogs abandoned from dog races."

The good doctor spotted Falconer entering. His spirits sank. "So, he is coming."

The hospital specialists followed him. Larry Lang walked in. Chandler was dismayed. They were all dressed alike: in hibiscus-red long-sleeved shirts and ankle-length off-white pants. A soft gasp escaped Chandler's lips. "The circus is in town."

Adolph milled around with his cronies. He took off his studded cowhand hat, revealing a shiny, bald head. He smoothed out his white whiskers, as he glanced sideways at Chandler. He whispered something to his brother.

"The hell-hags are in." Chandler sniffed, and bunched his fists. "The Medical Mafia—the M&Ms. You bet they're about to commit the perfect crime."

Adolph pushed up his tinted gray executive glasses and scratched his boxer's nose.

"Papa took his heart pills and went to bed last night. He shouldn't be here today. I sense trouble."

Adolph came close to their stall. Chandler noted the difference between the two brothers. Adolph: rotten incisors, right cheek facial mole.

"I had a plan." The ER chief winked at his fiancée. "I brought a thousand fliers."

Her forehead creased.

"The message focuses on Falconer and his medical specialists."

"Al! The bad guys are here."

"Give me a minute; I'll be back." Fliers in hand, he went out and returned.

Music was closing the two-hour fair with *Endless Love*. Couples danced and hummed along, eyes closed.

Chandler showed the fliers to Michelle and said to Kennedy, "Help me give these out. Quick!"

"W-what's this about?" He read a pamphlet. "I'll pass them out."

"Not now." Michelle scanned the crowd.

Chandler followed Kennedy.

"The guests are still dancing." She shook her head. "*Uh!*"

Chandler tapped on people's shoulders and handed them the fliers. Falconer chatted with his M&Ms. They smiled, clearly thinking the leaflets contained a message of love and peace.

Chandler climbed on a chair. "Attention, ladies and gentlemen! I'd love to run through the brochures I gave you."

The crowd gathered closer, and he read aloud.

Avoid psychiatrists who push mind-altering drugs. They may hook you for life or cause you to kill yourself. Last year, the island psychiatrist saw 151 patients. Fifteen of them committed suicide after taking the antidepressant drug Mordare.

Eat well, and make friends. Reach out to relatives, and go on a holiday. Love people, believe in someone, and fear God. Listen to music you love. Enjoy comedy shows. Laugh to your heart's content. Remove Falconer's chance to milk National Insurance.

Avoid using the artificial sweetener aspartame. Do a candida cleanse. Eat wild salmon. Take omega-3 fish oil. Eat foods rich in vitamin B. Use St. John's Wort and holy basil. Attend an experienced doctor outside the hospital. Consult a counselor or search the Internet before you start any medication or regimen. Avoid the culprits who push dangerous drugs. Let's act now. Think healthcare for all.

The room grew quiet—for a minute. Falconer's jaw dropped.

Chandler forced a smile, sensing his lips twitching. "Happy Valentine's Day, everyone!"

Michelle was speechless. Then she spoke. "Ladies and gentlemen, our fifteen-member committee was hard at work tallying the proceeds. We made $25,998."

Chandler applauded three times, paused, and repeated the clapping. The guests did not.

"Three years now we've been collecting funds. We have $100,907."

The visitors raised the roof for a full minute.

"Money!" Falconer emphasized, "I can put it to better use."

Chandler seethed and stiffened. "Over my dead body, Mr. Gambler."

Falconer stomped up to him and gave him a folded note. "Here's a Valentine message for you and Michelle. Read it when you're free." He pointed a finger at him. "I still hope you reform. You've got talent."

Chandler put the paper in his pocket. Falconer left with his team. That relieved Chandler.

Lang shuffled up to his daughter. "I had to come out to warn you."

Her face grew pensive.

"Falconer told me you're sneaking around and messing with his computer. He identified you on his spy camera."

"Papa, Papa, I'll explain, Papa."

"Let me talk. I had to beg Falconer not to harm you. Stop being a fool. Leave the orphan man. Now! A day to think it over. Or forget I exist." He rushed out.

Chandler came up to Michelle.

She told him what Papa said. "Come outside for a minute. Papa gave me an ultimatum."

They scuttled from the lobby, and Michelle wrung her fingers. "Health tips, propaganda, whatever you're promoting!"

"I had to do what I had to do."

"You sure did!"

She gasped for breath. Fatigue settled in pockets under her eyes. He put an arm around her shoulder.

She mumbled, "I'm tired."

"You had a long day."

The power went off. He suspected Falconer's cat's paw, his rotten-tooth brother, was still doing his dirty tricks.

Michelle laid her head on his left shoulder. "This is a funny tired." He sensed her muscles going weak. "Al, let's go home."

Without warning, her eyes rolled and she fainted.

He grabbed her and held her tight. "Michelle, I've done you wrong. Forgive me, will you?"

CHAPTER 12

You left America and came here. You are restless. Stop probing the ants' nest. Accept what you can't change. Happy Valentine's Day, both of you. I'm stopping the fight with you. Everything is now in your hands. Sorry about the power cut. I'm not mad anymore—if you aren't!

In the driver's seat, Chandler sneered at Falconer's note. The sociopathic chief surgeon! He was precocious.

Michelle moaned and muttered something he couldn't understand. He thought of several diagnoses, but nothing made sense.

Michelle recovered in the back seat of Chandler's Blazer.

"You're in the hands of one who cares. Out of harm's way."

Chandler peered into the rearview mirror. "Move in with me." He gassed the engine for no reason. The speedometer read seventy-five miles per hour. He negotiated a curve and had to apply the brakes. "You can decide now. Good place to muse … before I drop you home."

"Al?"

"You think I'm nuts."

"Slow down, please."

He dropped the speed to fifty-five.

"Papa will kill me."

"He's an understanding man."

"He's San Francisco Chinese. They can be rough."

He depressed the throttle again. "My soul says I'll care for you."

She remained silent.

"I'm slowing down, the better for you to think." He squinted into the mirror. "I have ears." A car swerved ahead of him. "What the hell—?"

"I-I-I'll hang my hat in your house."

"I didn't catch you." The car had a bunch of drunken teenagers with beer bottles in their hands. "Where are the pigs when you need them? I'm still waiting, Michelle. We're getting closer to your house. What d'you say?"

She peeped through the window. "You're giving me a headache."

He gripped the wheel. "I'll do the cooking."

She coughed up a dry chuckle.

"Answer me," he demanded.

"I already did."

"You did?" He pressed the gas again.

The teenagers eased up speed, and drove parallel to Chandler. They giggled. One of them opened the back window and showed his middle finger. "Fuck her!" The pranksters guffawed and sped away.

The shock stifled Chandler's voice.

"Al?"

"I'm driving. No talking." He swerved into her street. "Your sweet home."

"I'll take up residence with you."

A passionate fluttering hit the back of his neck. "Did you say … fan-fantastic!"

"I'll live with you, but only if you behave like a good boy."

He took the next U-turn and sped home. His mind reeled. Chandler was born in Kenya. He hit America. He touched down on the island. He swept the most beautiful chick off her feet.

"Decelerate." She paused and said, "I saw Falconer's surveillance camera."

"I have an idea. Crashing into the boss's computer."

Michelle leaned forward. "I know the hospital computer technician."

"I achieved much. I'm happy." Chandler returned to work after the suspension. As long as his faculties were clear, he would succeed. He settled in his small office behind the ER bay. Medical books packed the marble shelf. He turned the switch on a mini water cascade. He ran his fingers on the rosewood wall chart. The room was his pad. It had to be snug and tranquil. At low volume, a portable radio played a Frank Sinatra song. Chandler expected Falconer to show up anytime. His blue T-shirt was comfortable: He was losing weight.

Chandler went to work with the spyware. An hour passed. After probing the giant man's computer, he printed out data. He erased Falconer's hard-disk memory and read the transactions. Falconer had drained millions from National Insurance. "Holy smoke! And you blow the money at baccarat." That was exactly what he needed to know. He spoke to an imaginary Falconer. "We'll talk, dude."

The next morning, Falconer squatted in his office before his computer. His crony consultants came in to have coffee with him. A helper served cookies and left.

"Dead!" Falconer peered into the computer. "Some jackass deleted my documents. This consigns my life to oblivion!"

Ivanov knitted his eyebrows. "You are saying—?"

"An ignoramus hacked into my computer and wiped out the files."

"I checked mine. I read an email from Chandler. He sent mail to us and to other people. About the hacking, do you suspect anyone?"

"Who would do that?"

"Think hard."

The day after, Kennedy popped into Chandler's office. He had a newspaper folded under his arm.

Chandler leaned backward. "I'm working out the monthly ER doctors' schedules this morning." He shot Kennedy a flat grin.

"The doctors are ranting from the last email. Falconer and his lobbyists are after you." Kennedy paced around the office. "Been doing scans for Ivanov. That man hates you."

"He hides behind Falconer for a living."

"You're hiding something."

"Arnold!"

"Falconer and his consultants are all wired up. Someone's exposing them. Falconer runs a full-page media smear on you captioned, *American Doctor, American Computer Hacker.*"

Chandler crawled up and gripped the edge of the desk.

"The talk is you have a big following in the union. Ivanov told Falconer not to touch you. Gray advised the same. Votes count to politicians."

Kennedy walked to the door. "It means, Daddy-o, you've got a longer rope with which to hang yourself. Three months, max. Just a hunch."

Chandler saw him leave. The phone struck a sudden tone.

"Dr. Falconer here."

Chandler's brain became a crazy mixture of hope and fear. He whispered. "So, it's Dr. Falconer?"

"You lost your voice?"

"Go right ahead."

"I walked into your office this morning."

Chandler stiffened.

"I came in early. Just observing. A walkabout."

"You talk like a politician."

"I'm your boss."

"Your point is?"

"Surveillance cameras never lie."

Chandler weighed Michelle's snooping.

"The room favors some lawyer's chamber," Falconer noted.

Chandler overheard Ivanov's voice.

Falconer continued. "From one colleague to another, create a better patient-friendly atmosphere. We differ in our reasoning, American man." He snorted. "I'd like to help you redecorate your office."

Chandler dropped the phone and slipped into his chair. A splitting headache hit him hard. He pulled on his bandanna.

The air vents in Chandler's office pumped a surge of cold air. He had to exit and go for a run on the beach. A nurse wheeled in an eighty-eight-year-old male patient in a wheelchair.

"Hello." Chandler opened his arms in welcome.

A urine odor preceded the elderly man. He had Parkinson's disease and trembled. He wheezed and coughed until he started to choke. He spat thick, slimy mucus on his clothes.

Chandler checked the notes: Jimmy Ford. American winter resident. Retired US governor. Chandler reexamined him and ordered more chest X-rays.

Someone knocked on the door. A light-skinned woman in a two-piece pink dress stepped in. She was a replica of Michelle Lang. Chestnut skin, almond-shaped eyes, broad nose, high forehead, and swan-like neck.

The nurse fidgeted and looked troubled. She took the file, scribbled on it, and returned it to Chandler. Her clipped English accent sounded deeper than normal. "I forgot to write down Mr. Ford's temperature, Doctor."

He opened the chart. The message read: *I recognize this young woman. She's trouble. Get her out.* He narrowed his eyes at her.

The nurse spoke in an upbeat tone, wheeled out Mr. Ford, and closed the door.

"I'm his wife." She smiled, her eyes fixed on Chandler.

He assessed her. She was a foxy woman with a rich elderly man. "Please, sit."

She was about thirty. Her fingers, covered in diamond and gemstone rings, played on her stock-tie sheath top.

Chandler extended his hand to greet her. Hers was warm and velvety.

She sat and crossed her legs. One of her red high-heel shoes dangled from her heel as she rolled her hips. She wriggled up, cat-walked around the room, and raised her sexy tone of voice. "Classy office, man. Looks like a lawyer's cabinet."

Falconer had alluded to that. Chandler shifted uncomfortably in his seat. Pride kept him from asking her questions.

She fanned herself with her fingers. "It's hot in here."

She loosened a tight French roll, and caramel hair cascaded down her shoulders. Diamond-studded gold bracelets jingled on her right wrist. Her vocal cords emitted a rough tone. She gazed into his eyes, half-closed hers, and winked at him.

"About your husband, he has a mild chest wall contusion from the steering wheel hitting him."

"I told the bitch to stop. He insisted on driving. I said, 'Your money, your morgue.'"

"He suffered minor injuries." Chandler's professional pride hid his reaction, but he glanced at her breasts.

"Tone down your voice, Dr. Chandler. He's past eighty and will die soon." She blinked, and her fake eyelashes sparkled. "I was observin' you. You're fighting Falconer. You are a hero."

"Could you wrap up, because—?"

She gritted her teeth, slid toward him, and roared. He guarded himself, catching a whiff of her perfume.

"You can jump me," she whispered. "You make me melt inside." She breathed in spasms.

Chandler held to his decorum and tried to keep his control. She wore a diamond-studded Rolex watch. "Mrs.—"

"Call me Bridgette." She inched up to him again.

"M-Mrs. Bridgette F-Ford."

"Cut the crap, man. The name's just Bridgette." She ran to the wall, switched off the tube lights, and crept up to him. "I know of Michelle Lang. I can show you I'm a better kisser than—"

"Y-y-your husband's in X-ray."

"Let the radiologist zap him," she huffed. "Jimmy's got dough to feed a thousand horses a day. You should've sent him to the morgue." She moaned, chuckled, and Eskimo-kissed him. She pinned his cheeks between her elbows.

She was strong. Chandler fought her off, stepped back, and put on the light. "Out!"

"You leave me like this?" She looked at him, breathless. "All you friggin' doctors are the same!"

"You're insane."

"You tried to rape me."

"Leave, please!"

"All I wanted was Demerol!"

"That's a narcotic pain reliever. It can kill you."

Her voice softened as she ran her fingers across her cleavage. "I crave somethin' strong for this frail, horny body."

"Demerol can take over your life," he said. He assumed a distant, professional tone. "Demerol's a controlled item."

"I had a neck fracture a year ago. I have pain. Nothing else helped."

"You either get out or I summon security."

"Or I'll speak to Dr. Falconer." She sprang up to him and seized his crotch. "Ooh! Steel magnolia!"

Someone barged in. Chandler's nursing assistant held the X-ray films. A flash of wild shock gripped him. He pulled himself free.

The nurse turned red. "I'll take the elevator down to the convent. Uh, sorry, to the cafeteria with Mr. Ford. I'll get him some brains. I mean, bran flakes."

Chandler's head spun. He wiped his face to clear his mind. The nurse pulled back and made the sign of the cross. She turned the wheelchair around, slid out, and slammed the door.

Bridgette gripped her husband's medical file and slapped it into Chandler's hands. "Think fast before your nurse checks on you again."

"You're giving me angina pain."

"Let me consult Dr. Falconer." She grinned. "He paid me well for this visit."

"Give me more breaking news!"

"The clock is ticking. He can organize the police to bring you in for the murder of Pandora."

Chandler shook his head vehemently. "I did not kill my wife!"

"Michelle, Michelle! Poor Michelle." She winked. She affected a wry smile and left.

"Mercy!" Bridgette was wasting her time. A clock was ticking—in his head.

CHAPTER 13

The clock struck seven. Chandler worked in the emergency room. He rubbed the small of his aching back, and called his fiancée. "Go ahead and have your supper. I'm running late."

"No, Al, I get a better appetite when you're around. I baked Chicago shepherd's pie. I'll shower and wait for you."

"You got it."

By five minutes to the hour, Chandler was driving home. "Hot home-cooked shepherd's pie!" Being a secretary of health or even a US president didn't appeal to him. He drove into his driveway at 8:30 p.m. The same black car parked by the curb. "Damn!" His hackles rose. No one sat in the car, and no one walked around. He took out his cell phone to call the pigs, but he hesitated. Adolph was a Falconer.

Michelle stood by the door outside. She had a brown paper bag with a flowerpot in her hand.

A gun fired, and Michelle fell.

"Oh, my friggin' God!" Chandler's heart hammered against his breastbone. He jumped out and sidled close up to her. Adolph's car sped off with a screech. He dropped on his knees. "Michelle! Michelle! N-o-o!" His mind froze. "Mich ... " His voice stuck in his throat. A hand closed around his throat—an invisible hand.

Someone opened a glass window by the steps upstairs.

Chandler jumped back.

"Hello? Al? Is that you? I just heard a gunshot. I'm coming down." Michelle bolted out.

He held his throbbing head. "What shit is this going on?"

She rushed up to him and gripped his shoulder.

Dumbfounded, Chandler anchored his feet on the ground next to the female corpse. She had a pistol in her morbid hand.

"Oh my God!" Michelle's brows creased.

"Who's she?" His pulse roared in his ears. "It's y-your look-alike."

The pigs interrogated him at the police station. A heavy mist loomed over Chandler. He was going to hell before he could carry out his mission. He was saying goodbye to his high self-esteem. "I never kill!"

The pigs withdrew from him. The waiting made him sweat. Soon they approached him.

"We accept your word. We have other leads."

Falconer was willing to stop fighting. "Damn!"

The pigs released him. He drove home.

Michelle embraced him and dished out shepherd's pie for him. He emptied the plate. He loved shepherd's pie, but he sensed something. The pie was bittersweet. He spat on the back of his hand. The saliva emitted an earthy odor.

"Oh my God! Morgex."

Michelle ran up to him.

"Bittersweet, earthy, and leafy. Heart failure. Death. This is a lethal dose!"

"Al!" She trembled and gripped his arm.

Vertigo hit Chandler. His pulse pumped in his head. His thoughts were dull and disquieting, and he stirred uneasily. "G-g-get me Kennedy." He coughed and choked. "T-tell him to get me—write it down—an injection of Nosiop and hydrocortisone. Fast! Hurry up, p-plea-se. I'm going to die!"

In fifteen minutes, Kennedy rushed in.

Chandler lay unconscious. His face was pale. Michelle embraced him and cried.

Kennedy checked Chandler's radial pulse. He found none. He looked for the carotid artery. It was there. "He's alive!" He eased the antidote into Chandler's bloodstream. "I'm not sure this will work."

"He had shepherd's pie." Her voice quivered. "I made it for him."

"You baked it." Kennedy gave her a long, searching look.

Her eyes misted, and she dissolved into tears.

Kennedy's voice was passionless. "Somebody's sick in the head here."

"Please!"

"Our Al Chandler might die."

She screamed, "No! No!" She stood as though shot and waiting to fall.

Kennedy eased the hydrocortisone into his friend's vein. His face twisted in anguish. He was losing his only real friend on the planet. "I can't take this." He sprang to his feet and lumbered off. He covered his face and sobbed. "Al, why, why, why?" He hugged Michelle. She shuddered.

Chandler opened his eyes a slither. His eyelids trembled, and his mouth quivered. "I'm-I'm-I'm in top shape."

They twisted around.

Michelle threw her hands on Chandler's shoulders. "I quite like you, Al."

"You're a jerk!" Kennedy laughed and clapped.

Chandler tried to get up. "Shit, I'm dizzy."

Kennedy put him back to lie down. "Take it easy, Daddy-o. Someone poisoned you."

Early the next morning, as the sun peeped above the horizon, Chandler sat up in bed. His muscles ached. Kennedy slept and snored on the couch.

Chandler sipped coffee and spoke in a sickly tone. "Arnold, I've been wondering all night. This might be the result of my own actions. Every action has a reaction." He avoided Michelle's gaze. "I'm beginning to detest my emotions."

"Love, for example, Daddy-o?"

He inclined his head.

Michelle cringed, her eyes watering. She bit her lips and sobbed.

"The hate and anger of terrorists pierce me like needles. The anxiety of a child and the grief of mourners do the same to me. I'm a mess. Orphan complex can go to hell. I realize who I am. Pandora is gone. Why doesn't anyone lock me up? They accuse me of her death. Yesterday, I was dying. What's going on?" He looked up.

"I swear I didn't poison you!" She sobbed and dropped her head into his lap. "No idea how it happened."

"Then who did it?"

"I don't know!" Tears filled her eyes and she trembled.

"Whoever it was, the world has taught me good counsel."

"What lesson, Al?"

"I'm changing my life."

A soft gasp escaped Arnold's lips. "Holy Mary! Daddy-o, for the first time, I sense justice, mercy, and holiness in you. I see transformation in you. Al, believe me."

"I'll speak to the god in me. I'll listen to what he says. This earthly way of living, of fighting and getting nowhere is not good for me."

"Nothing is wrong with change, Al. You mean well." Michelle touched his cheek. "I'll never hurt you. I didn't."

The epileptic patient in ER convulsed. He bit his tongue. Chandler settled him. "You have to eat well."

"I have no money. No shoes."

Chandler wrote off the hospital charges.

He rushed to another bed. The monitor showed heart attack and fibrillation. He worked on her.

"I'm a widow and pensioner."

He touched her forehead. "I'll charge the medical bills to my personal account."

Chandler drank orange juice. A message filtered from the ceiling speakers. "Dr. Chandler to ICU. Dr. Chandler to ICU."

He went up the concrete corridor to ICU. A long wall mirror reflected a flushed face. Chandler was already looking like his father. He was aging. The people who surrounded him were causing it. He changed his mind. He was getting more mature, day by day.

Falconer barged out from ICU. Dr. Amoono and Dr. Jarvis tailed him. Falconer masterminded the poisoning. Flashes of Adolph's car injected his brain and gave him a throbbing headache.

Chandler sniffed. "Hello, gentlemen, good black coffee is somewhere around."

"Well!" Falconer's rancor sharpened his voice. "Dr. Death in person."

Chandler suppressed his rage. He riveted his eyes on Falconer. "Back to you, dude."

"I'm rushing for theater in ten minutes. I admire you for being a clever doctor." His forehead wrinkled.

Consultant Jarvis stroked his peach fuzz. His apple cheeks blushed and his swan-like neck crooked to the side. He showed his yellow teeth and his clipped accent grew deeper. "I have a procedure to do," he said, as he walked off.

"Hold a minute." Falconer ran up to him and held his shoulder.

Jarvis' cold eyes sniped at Chandler.

"I'm skedaddling from this." Amoono's vexation chiseled his features. "It's clinic time." He shuffled away.

"My African friend!" Chandler called him with a beckoning hand.

The doctor's jutting lips curled back and showed his gap-toothed mouth. His oily Afro glistened beneath the fluorescent ceiling light. "Gentlemen," he murmured in a hoarse voice, "let's discuss this in private, not in the corridor."

"We'll talk about this *now*." Falconer shuffled. "We had a shooting accident last night."

"I'd love to investigate that. Bridgett—"

"I'm referring to an incident at the hospital. We had to send the victim to the morgue to chill out."

Chandler seethed and looked away.

"I'm alluding to the woman. Mrs. Bridgette—"

"What more about her?" Chandler sensed danger.

Falconer jumped on the question. "The autopsy showed she succumbed to an overdose."

"Have mercy, she *what?*" Chandler fought hard to keep his composure. "The man you share your DNA with murdered her!"

Falconer's voice grew hoarse. "You killed her! It was the Demerol."

"Someone shot her. I witnessed the scene!" Chandler insisted.

"You're smart."

Chandler dreaded the hint. "I-I-I didn't kill her!"

"So, you deny killing her. I close the case." Falconer teased Chandler. "You prescribed the pills for an addicted junkie."

Heat rushed to Chandler's face. "I never did!"

"You gave her sixty tablets! The rule here says ten for a prescription. Come on, my good doctor. You just slipped up."

"She asked me to give her Demerol. I refused to."

The doctors stared at Chandler and made him uneasy.

"Then the nurse is lying." Falconer feigned a smile and stepped closer to Chandler. "My advisers say you're to take the blame for a breach of ethics. You know better."

His veins pumped hard against his temples.

"I'm saving your ass, son," Falconer continued. "According to our lawyer, you breach the Law of Causation. Who's to say what is wrong and right. No shooting done."

"Get Adolph in for questioning." Chandler's knees quaked. He had someone to consult in ICU. "Got to go."

"Your medical negligence caused the woman to die. It's simply so," Falconer said. "I'm going to keep this quiet."

"You're doing me a favor?" Chandler walked off. "I didn't do anything wrong."

"I do it to preserve the name of the hospital."

Chandler retorted, "For your deep pocket."

"I've consulted the board. I'm sure you haven't done anything wrong, son. From today, you're on probation for another three months. The board chairman said it's to adjust your behavior."

"You're sick." Chandler turned and stomped away down the corridor.

The ceiling speakers buzzed with static, and a female voice announced, "*Dr. Chandler. ER. Code Blue. Dr. Chandler. ER. Code Blue.*"

He returned home to a table that Michelle had set for dinner. He had lost his appetite. The walls were closing in on him. His appointment book was already full. He began to perceive himself for who he was inside. He had courage. He was on a pink sand beach, and stripped naked. The Atlantic breeze played with his body. He inhaled the cool salty air, and plunged into the warm water for a long swim. Michelle and Baraka were there.

He thanked God Michelle was alive and not shot. "Michelle?"

"You have to eat."

"Michelle?"

Michelle came up close to him and passed her fingers through his hair. "A penny for your thoughts," she murmured.

"To give thanks, I want to adopt an orphan."

"Make that two."

He smiled at her.

"Be careful," Michelle said. "Falconer still hates you, Al."

Holy mercy! Someone had to pay for that very soon.

CHAPTER 14

"Damn you people!" Chandler had a lot on his chest. He sat in a room in his house he had made into a study. A breeze blew through the open French window and refreshed his spirit. Sparrows chirped on trees. Contemplating his probation, he sipped hot coffee from a white mug. It had the hospital logo stamped in bold blue. He gazed at the label and then pitched the mug against the wall.

Michelle rushed up to him. "Al, slacken up. Time heals everything."

The orphans pounced on the bed Chandler had bought for them. Seven-year-old twins whom he named Abraham and Abigail. He made the first floor into their bedroom. He intended to teach them about life as they grew and became ideal citizens.

The kids jumped around and roamed the quarters. Baraka loved the company. People carried trinkets and key chains for luck, but Chandler's little darlings were his lucky charms. He cooked and meditated with them. He lectured to them on his philosophy. If he was busy, he ordered in food. They had to wash hands six to eight times a day, as he did. Cleaning the house twice a day was a joint task. He bought them laptop computers with webcams. He intended to set up a trust fund for his orphan sweethearts. The children changed his life. His self-esteem soared. He was more playful, and laughed more. He felt less stressed and more motivated. Life was more than the tip of the iceberg.

Abraham looked across at Pandora's mansion. "I admire the big house, Dad."

Abigail smiled like an angel. "Why don't you live there?"

"It's a long story. I cherish the modesty of this little place."

A thoughtful smile curved Abraham's lips. "One day we'll live in the mansion?"

"Dream big, son."

Chandler patted Baraka on the head. *If Michelle's father dies, who inherits the pharmacies? R Power-drunk Falconer? No! Michelle gets it.* His thoughts twirled from the deluge of complications.

A dog whined outside. Baraka ran down and bolted through the dog door. Chandler switched on the bamboo floor lamp. He read the *Atlantic Isle Daily News*, the *Family Tribune*, and the *Sip-Sip Weekly*.

Michelle helped him with the cooking. If her father sustained a heart attack or became disabled, Chandler planned to welcome him home. He was going to live with someone who pushed doctors to prescribe deadly drugs.

In a blue executive suit, Michelle was ready to go to work. She had fifteen minutes to spare. She donned a white apron, and helped Chandler serve breakfast. It was an egg white and mushroom omelet, diced tomatoes, orange slices, and whole-wheat toast.

She fetched the sugar and the cream. "Al, I was thinking about us."

Chandler sipped coffee. "I'm in the dumps. I'm jumpy."

"I've got the same bug." She sighed. "Enjoy your breakfast. Got to leave for work now." She took off the apron and pecked him and the children on the cheeks. "Al, I appreciate you, no matter what."

Abigail chuckled, and Abraham stifled a laugh.

Chandler passed his hand over his chin.

"I've seen you working. You treat patients well. You play with the family. You're their father."

"I am, Michelle."

"Stop fighting the people on the island." She glanced at her wristwatch.

He foresaw her new position as executive head of the pharmacies if her father died. He opened his mouth to talk. He changed his mind.

"Rich, evil forces are bent on crushing you. Surrender before—"

"The devils are already brainwashing you. I'm not a martyr, but my courage of conviction stands."

"You're still American."

"The sky keeps its stars."

Michelle looked at the time again. "Let's elope to America, and carry Abraham and Abigail with us."

Chandler raised his chin and looked up to the ceiling. "We can take the children. Sure. Fulfill their dreams in America." His suave smile put her at ease.

"I'll forget the administrator job."

"Hallelujah!"

"And the pharmacies. Well, Papa is here. Let's get away."

"Michelle, fleeing is adopting a defeatist attitude."

"If you say so."

"I'll write letters to all the newspaper editors and expose Falconer's medical trickery."

"Call me."

"Enjoy your day." He winked at her.

She left.

He reviewed the woman who might one day be on the other side of the fence. Looking out, he made sure Adolph's black car was nowhere in sight. He sent the children to the basement. They had to tidy their beds and prepare for home school.

Chandler focused on his philosophy. He jumped on his Apple desktop computer. He started writing chapters of his bible for the good of everyone.

> *Some surgeons perform operations at the flick of a thumb. On this island, one in every two hundred patients dies of a nonemergency surgical procedure. That person could be a near relative.*

He recounted a story of a woman who went to a hospital to remove an ingrown toenail. The doctors could have taken the nail out without general anesthesia. She succumbed from anesthetic shock. Fifteen such atrocities happened in one year.

He wrote about a man who checked into the hospital with a tiny, uncomplicated belly button hernia. The surgeon operated and the patient expired. Two incidences occurred within the same week.

He documented a mother who brought in a boy for a routine circumcision. The boy died from shock. Three boys perished in similar incidents.

He sent the letter to the *Sip-Sip Weekly.*

Baraka barked in the yard. Another dog yapped. Chandler raised his head and listened. A dog moaned. Someone was having a sporty time. The children were laughing downstairs. Chandler enjoyed their laughter, but he ordered them not to look outside.

He wrote a letter to the daily *Family Tribune*:

> *In Falconer General Hospital, over a five-year period, 349 women had uncomplicated, no-bleeding, pain-free fibroids. Two hundred and ninety-nine had hysterectomies. They had money. The rest are alive, and opted not to have surgery. All the biopsies turned out benign. The greed for bread motivated our surgeons to butcher our women. The procedure costs $5,000, but Falconer billed for $20,000. A commandment against atrocity has to exist somewhere.*
>
> *Think healthcare for all.*

Chandler quoted mothers protesting fibroid hysterectomies. Unwanted surgery was the backbone of surgeons' bank accounts.

He addressed the *Atlantic Isle Daily News*:

> *In five years, a hundred patients on the Isle perished in surgical wards. The hospital tells you the clients die of the conditions under which the doctors admitted you. They died of resistant strains of bacteria in the hospital. No antibiotics are available to fight those parasites. The patients end up dead. National Insurance pays.*

He missed treating casualties, but he had to remain sober. With Abraham and Abigail around, he was compelled to. He ate more Big Apple steak and hamburgers than a pubescent boy would. Time was still crawling for him.

One night, before he shut down his computer, he went to Facebook. He saw a picture of Pandora. Her fake dainty body leaned back. Her Irish face had a superior grin. Her hazel eyes beamed. She looked full of life. She was dead.

His off-time expired sooner than he thought. On the first morning of his return to work, a young nurse brought him coffee. She held an envelope. "A letter here from Dr. Falconer for you."

She left with a nod. He tore the flap open and read the note:

> *You have maligned us. We granted you provisional freedom on the promise of good behavior. We had you return to this hospital. The good citizens of this land took pity on you. Gray patronized them to avoid national chaos. Thanks to the thousands of union members and their families. Your intellect shifts. We warn you to stop smearing the good works of our doctors here and that of myself. We'll ignore the people's threat and have our board try you. What I can control, I will. I consulted the committee and advised the Medical Association to suspend you. Enclosed is the president's response.*

Chandler drank his coffee and read the letter aloud. "*This body has rules. Dr. Falconer gave his testimonial. Members recommended we suspend you for six months. Correct your unethical behavior toward doctors and pharmaceutical agencies on the Isle.*"

His heart leaped. They've captured him and ostracized him. He sucked in a mouthful of coffee and choked. The Enemy of Mankind punished him for revealing the truth and the light. He consulted the God in him. He worked in the ER bay, but his mind was far away. He returned to his office and Googled Falconer. He was even able to Skype some of Falconer's old friends abroad.

Later that day, Chandler was busy documenting patients' info on the computer. Falconer and Ivanov showed up.

"I'm passing through on my way to a meeting," said Falconer. "I never give up, Chandler."

"I can see."

"My Jamaican experience taught me strength of character."

"I researched you."

"Who gave you the authority?"

"Often, in Jamaica, you went into drug withdrawal and attempted suicide."

"Those were difficult days, but you had no right—"

"Even then, you befriended glib politicians who cleared you from trouble."

"Who asked you to?"

"The road you trod is popular."

"What?"

"Your experience shows."

Falconer twisted his face. "Ivanov, can you explain this?"

"Ivanov, from Russia, knows nothing about your life in the Caribbean. Your Jamaica ganja affect speaks for itself."

Falconer checked his watch. "I'm late for my meeting."

Chandler assumed a sarcastic tone. "I envy you."

"I am the modern Caesar." Falconer shot Chandler a patronizing smile. "I'm not prone to murder."

Chandler hated the leer on Falconer's face. Ivanov again whispered into Falconer's ear.

Falconer gave him a hostile glare. "The union population and hundreds of other nitwits support you. Please don't play Jesus. Why not let me reign as Caesar over you?" He laughed. "God, I'm late." He verified the time. "Wasting time with a hippie." He stomped out. Ivanov followed.

Chandler picked himself up and stepped to the window. Lightning flashed and thunder rumbled in the distance. Falconer disappointed him.

Kennedy strolled in. "Daddy-o. Waiting on the nurses to prep a casualty for X-ray. Falconer just emerged from your office. What's up?"

"I wouldn't allow Falconer to put pressure on me."

"No torque, no."

A nurse came up from the bay, "The patient is ready, Dr. Kennedy."

"Coming."

Chandler forced dignity into his voice. "I won't let Falconer manipulate me."

"No manipulation, no. Got to go, Daddy-o."

"I'm no prophet. Jesus, and many prophets in history, didn't fall for wire pulling either."

"You're dead right."

The nurse called again. "Dr. Kennedy?"

Kennedy sang out his answer, "I'm on my way."

"I'll leave with Michelle and the children for America."

"You can't. I'll tag along, too."

"Hello, Dr. Kennedy?" shouted the nurse.

"Bringing up the rear."

Chandler watched him leave. *A friend indeed.* His phone rang once. "Hello, Michelle."

"What's going on?"

"I don't know. Tell me."

CHAPTER 15

The children ran up to Michelle when she came home. Chandler pecked his fiancée on the cheek. The kiss was awkward. He thought about the first time he had met her. Her exquisite beauty excited him. It still did, but life was becoming a fitful sleep. Engaging in no small talk, they ate a meal of ribs, mixed vegetables, and boiled potatoes. The children had chicken nuggets and Coke.

After dinner, Abraham pounced on him. Abigail ruffled his hair. The boy rolled on the floor and played with him until bedtime. Abigail led them in prayer.

"Amen." The father kissed them goodnight.

The mother squinted and shook her head. "Al, the children are rough."

"Why d'you think you're my companion?"

They slunk into each other's arms. His world was on the island.

Hundreds of lively members met that weekend at union headquarters. They discussed the union's regular affairs and special events scheduled before the union year ended. Union president Chandler prized the islanders' support. He had to do something big to gain maximum backing to keep his position. The deadline was today.

He committed himself to correcting his union members' problems. Their children's future concerned him. He found fifty-five higher education scholarships to Canada, England, Russia, China, and Cuba for them.

Dr. Edita Pratt, medical council chairperson and adviser to the union, stood and sang. *We shall overcome …*

Abraham and Abigail ran behind butterflies in the yard. Abigail capered up to him. "The daily papers for you, Dad."

"It's a new day." Abraham caught a butterfly. "Have fun, Dad."

The red sun eased above the orange horizon. It painted the clouded sky a dark crimson. Chandler said thanks for the glory of nature. He stood by his front door. Shock overtook him. He opened the newspapers and saw a paid advertisement. A cartoon depicted him as a long-horned Satan. At the bottom the ad read: *Ad sponsored by Falconer. Chief,* he thought, *if you think that's what I am, I'm thirsty for your blood.*

The ring of the wall phone sent him rushing to the study. The ringing stopped. He walked away. The LED screen signaled a message. He grabbed the receiver.

"Morning!" came a soft singsong voice.

"Yes, it is." Chandler dropped on the sofa and turned on the floor lamp.

"This is Janice from administration. I had to come in early to prepare some papers about you. The hospital's board asked me to tell you, sir—"she held back long enough to make him gulp— "you're called to an urgent meeting this morning at ten."

"I take note of that."

She mumbled, "You're fighting an uphill battle. The big chief plays a dangerous game." Her breathing sounded labored. "My daughter is getting one of the union scholarships. Thanks."

He eased the phone down to its cradle. He tensed up. Troubling thoughts needled his brain. He rose and looked outside. The sun floated behind fluffy clouds, which turned to a dark cherry-red. He didn't like nature's art anymore. Abraham and Abigail rushed into the dining room. That pleased him.

Michelle fetched breakfast for her and the children. "I'm late again for work." She breathed in.

He goggled outside through the open French window.

"Got a call." He told her about it. "I'll ignore the board." He glanced at the time. "You're running late."

Her voice sounded grave. "I'm under attack." She shook her head and bit her lip. "Don't know." She adjusted the collar of her light blue suit. Her purring voice became grave. "Like something worse than the plague will happen." Her eyes rolled back, and her face turned pale. "Al, I'm—" Her neck grew limp and she fainted.

"Michelle!" He jumped for her. He eased her to the floor and raised her legs. He turned her head to the side. He rubbed a point between her upper lip and her nostrils.

The children panicked. "Dad!"

She opened her eyes. "Al, thank you. Be so careful." She spoke to the children. "Take your breakfast and go down to your room."

They went away.

He caressed the nape of her neck. "Your safety against the vultures at work means more to me."

"It was my first time," she purred, tears running down her cheeks. "I enjoyed having carnal knowledge of you last night."

His self-esteem ballooned.

Larry Lang stroked his gray Fu Manchu mustache and switched on the lectern light. Chandler was giving them half an hour; he sat on one side of the hospital conference table and stared straight ahead without looking at the board members. His sanity meant more to him than their meeting.

The tinted fluorescent bulb jaundiced Lang's face, and his salt-and-pepper hair looked yellow. "Dr. Chandler, we had no other recourse but to ostracize you, to avoid friction in the hospital."

Chandler tensed his neck but kept his mouth shut. His eyes scoured the room.

"During that time, you smeared the medical profession and the pharmaceutical trade." Lang's eyelids went into their habitual spasms again.

The members mumbled, and Falconer clawed his tensed fingers. "Let me make this clear."

Chandler was clocking them.

Obi Falconer rubbed his hands together. "Chandler's a mighty good therapist, but he's disloyal to our profession."

Chandler's anger rose. "I sense double standards."

Lang drummed his fingers on the lectern. "Our chief has the floor."

Falconer continued. "The police have no concrete evidence, and they respect this hospital and me. You're lucky."

"That's some luck," Chandler replied sardonically.

"It just ran out. You killed Bridgette Ford!"

"I did not!"

"Thanks to Michelle and her father and our good prime minister, I've been protecting you. America would have put you in the slammer." Falconer raised his chin in self-importance. "A bullet in Bridgette's head. One by Pandora's."

"What're you talking about?"

"The detectives found a torn condom package at the scene of your wife's death. Another one by Bridgette's."

The half hour was getting close. He rose to leave.

Lang gestured with his hand. "Sit down, please."

He sat, a heavy weight in his chest.

"The police are debating arresting you."

"Let them do their job."

"We're protecting you for reasons you might not understand."

"So suddenly I'm your friend?"

"It's business politics."

"Trying to frame me? I'll always be loyal to my patients, but you prostituted your duty." Chandler slammed his right fist on the desk. "National Insurance is becoming sick and comatose. Your white-collar crimes are causing the disease."

Lang raised a hand. "Let's stop the arguing."

Chandler reared up and pointed his index finger at Falconer. "I can't sit and fold my arms. Your bread grubbing drives you to do harm to the sick. The mighty dollar rules your waves." He kept his chin up high, an eye on his watch. "Stop living for you. Exist for others. Subsist to please your hopeless and innocent patients. I'm so disappointed in you." He stared at his enemies and dropped to his seat.

Silence reigned in the room.

The giant doctor's eyes clawed Chandler like talons. "Gentlemen, you've heard him."

Lang stood and scratched his chin. His narrow chest expanded as he inhaled. He coughed, and his tic increased. "Dr. Al Chandler, we hate to do this. We relieve you of duties at the hospital."

Chandler grew frenzied. "Did you say—?"

Falconer affected a smile. "What a pity. The directors just relieved you of your duties! You're fired!"

Bones weighed down on his chest as he shook his head in defeat. He rose and headed for the door.

Michelle barged in.

Falconer gave her the once-over.

"Something here for Al. It says *Urgent*." She handed the letter to Chandler.

He read the address on the legal envelope: *Atlantic Isle Medical Council.* The board was waiting for him to carry on. He walked back to his seat but remained standing. "Michelle, your father fired me."

"Papa!"

Sweat formed on Lang's forehead. He fidgeted with his fingers. His eyelids drooped, and his head fell forward. Members cried for help.

"Mr. Lang!" The chief looked confused.

Chandler supported Lang as he grew heavy, his body turning limp. His pupils dilated, and he stopped breathing. No pulse, no heartbeat.

Michelle gaped in stunned silence.

Chandler eased him down to the floor and started CPR. "Someone call ER! It's Code Blue! Tell them to bring the Life Pack!"

The ceiling speakers livened up: "*Code Blue, boardroom. I repeat, Code Blue, boardroom. Code Blue, boardroom.*"

"Help him, please," Michelle cried.

The team charged in. They had oxygen, an EKG monitor, an emergency kit, and a defibrillation machine. Chandler continued with CPR. He defibrillated Lang twice, pumped in intravenous drugs, and set up a lifeline.

Falconer stomped away to the window. "I don't want to witness this."

Lang eased into the eternal night. The members moaned and seethed. They glowered at Chandler. "Who are you playing? God?"

Michelle fell on her father. Her face was a snarl of agony. "Papa!"

Chandler put his hands on her shoulders, lifted her up, and hugged her by the waist. "He has done his last job. What matters is how well he lived and loved." He meditated on his parents' death and glared at Falconer. "At least certain prescription drugs didn't poison Lang."

The chief of staff seethed, his eyes narrowing like a snake. "You're killing us."

"What I've caused?" Chandler's mind whirled with tension. "You'll pay."

"Who sent you to us?" Falconer pulled back his lips.

"No one sent me."

"Rubbish!" Falconer held his stomach.

"From now on, don't look back. Someone might be gaining on you." Chandler sizzled inside. "America is a democracy with equality and justice. Your agenda is to amass wealth and let the poor suffer. Our new America stands for the opposite—benefits for all."

Falconer folded his arms, slapping his fingers on his forearms.

"I have an agenda for you."

CHAPTER 16

"Al, it's not even dark yet. I'm not in the mood."

Chandler and Michelle showered. He soaped her with Dove soap.

She sobbed and bit her lip. "I think of all the good things my father did for me as a child. He made me who I am." She cried and wiped her eyes.

The doorbell chimed.

"Oops!"

He smooched her on her neck.

"Go."

He kissed her, his hands caressing the small of her back.

Once more, the bell signaled someone at the door. It tinkled and resounded.

He wrapped a towel around his waist and ran downstairs. A boy stood on the asphalt driveway with a bouquet in his hands.

"Oh?"

The boy sang out, "Flowers for Michelle Lang."

"Oh!" He tipped the boy, and ran back upstairs.

She took the arrangement, the shower massage still trifling with her hair. In a sorrowful tone she whispered, "H-how sweet of y-you."

He leaped into the full soapy tub. "They're not from me. Read the card."

"Please accept these flowers. My deepest sympathy on your beloved father's passing. Obi Falconer. He's sweet."

"See if you can decipher the fine print."

She tilted more closely: *I bear what you're going through. I'll pay for Mr. Lang's coffin and funeral expenses. It's a gesture of goodwill to your wonderful father and to you. I've chosen the Promethean casket. It's custom-made solid bronze with a 14-carat gold finish. I paid $25,000 for it. He deserves the box. My condolences to you.* She fiddled with her fingers and stroked her chin. "I-I accept." She kissed him but her lips trembled. She pulled back. "Al, my father loved me."

He said sarcastically, "Good gesture of Falconer to send flowers." He grabbed her and made rough love to her.

"No, no, no, Al ... Yes, yes, love you, Al."

Like a beast, he squeezed her, as she did him, in climax. He would punish Falconer.

Chandler still tossed in bed, although it was three in the morning. The conflict was spiraling. He had to protect himself and pummel for justice. He opened his eyes. His anguish grew more acute. An owl hooted outside. He was hurt.

At 4:00 a.m. he eased himself up. He tiptoed out of the bedroom and picked his way to his computer. He clicked on his Miami bank account and compared the statement with his island deposit. It was the same financial chain. He electronically transferred $100,000, withdrawing from both accounts, to a safe institution in Zurich, Switzerland. It was his total savings. He didn't trust Falconer.

He vowed to avoid going to Lang's burial for security reasons. At 4:15, he treaded back to bed. Michelle's eyes opened. He threw an arm around her.

She yawned and covered her mouth. "The bed was cold and empty. I was dreaming. It was a nightmare."

"I was right here by you."

"A bird howled." She sat up. "Mama and Papa appeared in the dream and scared me. The old folks had a bitter divorce. It soon led to my mother's death from breast cancer."

He turned on his side, his hand supporting his head. "I can't sleep. Tell me more about your parents."

She lay on her back, her hands behind her head. Her voice had a slur. "Mama and Papa lived with dark spots."

"Oh, mine, too."

"My parents quarreled. Many of their relatives and friends separated. Mine stuck together for 'our teddy bear's sake.' The marriage ended. Don't know why." Her mouth quivered as she stifled a sob. "Maybe I caused the problem."

"Never blame yourself for their divorce." He gripped her, empathizing with her. "I adore you." He sensed her nipples firming.

She moaned and grabbed him. Exploring the rosy peaks of her breasts, he sensed her trembling. He slid his body over hers, and she gasped. He possessed her, flesh against flesh, big bear face-to-face with teddy bear. He succumbed to the hysteria of delight gripping him. It sent them soaring to a shuddering ecstasy. They slept until the sun rose and touched their faces.

He kissed her on her neck. "Morning, teddy bear."

"Hi, tabby bear." She hugged him and sobbed. "I have no father."

"You have me. I was thinking. The printout from Falconer's computer—should I publish the info in the daily papers?"

She raised herself up, leaned on the headboard, and shook her head.

He rubbed his nose against hers, went to his computer, and checked his Zurich account. He blinked at the screen. His heart thumped. The hundred thousand had disappeared. "Not for all the ganja in America!"

She strutted to him in her duster and stroked his hair. "Enlighten me."

"Michelle, no way!"

"Spit it out, Al."

"Falconer."

"Falconer? Yes, the note did say the flowers were from him. What—?"

"I know."

She dropped into his lap. "Feels as if I'm a little girl and I'm on Papa's lap." She switched off the computer and cuddled him. "Screw the computer—and me, too."

Chandler drove to the Seaside Massage Parlor by the beach. He left Michelle sleeping. She was on compassionate leave. It was 7:00 a.m. He'd be back by eight, before she awakened.

The sun was just beginning to warm the ocean and the sand, and travelers milled around. Seagulls cried and pounced on morsels of fish guts. Tourists in bikinis entered the parlor, the scent of coconut suntan lotion in the air. Chandler went into the parlor and rushed past tourists. He spoke to the young, blond receptionist.

"I'm Dr. Chandler. I'm checking on two patients. Doctors. Friends of mine. Obi Falconer said he forgot his watch when he last came here."

"He has a brother named Adolph." She searched the lost and found records. "Nothing."

"Didn't they come for a massage?"

She ran through the appointment record on her computer. "I'll search under F." She pressed a few keys and dissented. "The Falconers were never here."

"I'm sorry. Maybe the brothers visited another parlor."

"We're the only one, sir."

He bent over the counter and dropped a hundred dollars into the receptionist's hand.

She talked with gusto. He returned home. Michelle was still sleeping. What the parlor woman told him stunned him.

A pianist played *Abide with Me* on a portable keyboard. Abraham and Abigail sang along like professionals. Chandler was proud of his darlings.

Lang's funeral occurred on a clouded Sunday morning. The mourners assembled at the tree-laden manicured cemetery near the sea. A three-foot-high white concrete seawall separated the graveyard from the beach. Cemeteries reminded Chandler of death. He decided to attend and not leave his fiancée alone.

Everyone sweated in the humidity. The prime minister, the director of Atlantic Isle Chemicals, doctors, pharmacists, and uniformed nurses attended. The dignitaries sat in mahogany chairs under a yellow tent.

Michelle grabbed his arm. "Al, Papa requested *Abide With Me*." She trembled and cried.

He caressed her and stroked her hair.

Without citing the Bible, a justice of the peace presided over the funeral. The closed golden casket hovered at ground level above the burial site.

Flowers and wreaths lay on top. Chandler disliked the weird perfume sprayed on them.

An old island woman sang *When Peace Flows like a River*. She dragged the hymn off tune.

"Al, she cooked for Papa."

"Want her to come and cook for us?"

"I'll prepare meals. I'm fatigued and feverish, Al, for some time now. Many times a week. Oh, my br-breathing i-is getting l-la-labored."

The idea of her falling sick made him feel a tingling all over.

"I saw the internist."

"You never told me."

"I hate to bother you. We're too close. The doctors say you cause me to be sick."

He steeled himself against the pain her words caused. "I know who would criticize me. I didn't grant my Mom and Dad the favor, and guilt is eating me inside. Will make up. I'm the one to put an extra pillow under your head. You're sick." He squeezed her hand and patted it with his other. "We'll study the problems and put you on something safe."

The old woman ended with the hymn's chorus, "*It is well … with my soul … it is well with my soul.*"

Gray delivered a trite political speech. "This isle has lost a giant of a man. He was gentle but firm, an executive of high caliber. The pharmaceutical business revered him. He supported doctors, backed me and my nation, and made us happy." Closing with a regular promise of heaven for God-fearing citizens, he gave Chandler a sidelong look. "Mr. Lang died because of defiant tendencies in the medical field."

Chandler was an outsider. He pushed back his chair and stood. Rain clouds hovered to the east and crawled toward the cemetery. Chandler's voice grew wooden. "On Michelle Lang's behalf, I thank you for the condolences, sympathy letters, and flowers. Despite religious and philosophical beliefs, cry we must at a loved one's death. Parting makes the spirit obtuse. I've had my own experience with sorrow." A vision of his mother knitting away on her rocking chair flashed before his eyes. Pandora lay on the water lily. "God had a master plan for Larry Lang, and He fulfilled his life's program. The abuse of others, whose aims were monetary, marred his blueprint." He swallowed air. "Mr. Lang was hardworking and earnest and proved to be a heaven-sent father. Some had designs. They wanted to promote medicine amid poisons under the guise of prescription marvels. The influential above him used him. The underdogs feasted on his moral intents to fatten bank accounts. He doesn't breathe any more to serve man's whims." A wave of discontent filled the air. "Again, I apologize if I'm making your heart heavier. Bless his spirit. Mine is far from blessed. May his soul rest in peace."

Michelle sobbed, her face lined with grief. Her little fingers twitched. Her skin blanched over her cheeks and forehead.

Chandler squeezed her hands. "Relax." He spoke to a funeral organizer. "Get us some water." He stroked Michelle's face and arms. Then he called after the attendant. "Rush, if you can."

The woman took forever.

Chandler ran to a dwarf palm tree, climbed it, and ripped off a young coconut. He banged it on the concrete wall until it burst, and raced back to her. "Open your mouth. Drink this."

He sniffed the nutty scent. "It rehydrates and provides electrolytes."

"Y-y-you're right."

The pianist raised the keyboard volume higher with *The Old Rugged Cross*.

Gray, Falconer, and their cronies walked out before the ceremony ended.

The attendant slouched up to him with a note. "The chief asked me to give you this."

Chandler read the paper. *Allow me a month or two. I'll screw you!*

Chandler, Michelle, and the children drove home. They chanted sad folk songs. He played a father's role. Dark stepped in as he approached the house. Something aroused him. Lights shone inside.

He drove closer. Flashing police cars blocked the driveway. He sped up and screeched to a stop. "What's happening here?"

The pigs gave him a note. "A warrant to search the premises."

"Could you explain?"

"It's concerning Pandora's death."

"My soul's a hammer, not a nail." Chandler spent hours putting the house back to order. Michelle, Abraham, and Abigail helped him.

The following morning, he rubbed the sleep from his eyes. He wanted to defy the board's order.

"I'm going to work."

Michelle jumped up. "They'll hammer you and nail you."

He went to the kitchen. He pulled down the white Rasta hoodie and switched on the gas stove. For the children, he prepared a breakfast of grits and tuna. For him and Michelle, he fried eggs and sausages. The radio was on. A hell-and-damnation preacher heaved and screamed warnings of Hades. "I'm getting goose pimples. What do you plan to do with the pharmacies?"

Concern showed on her face. Her fingers fiddled with a fork. "I'll keep the business."

"As hospital administrator, you'll suffer too much undue stress."

"Who says?"

"Please yourself, darling."

"Wrong attitude toward me, Al."

"Whatever pleases you puts me at ease."

She pushed away her plate, slid off the stool, and paced the floor. "I'll quit the hospital."

He opened his mouth to speak. He kept quiet.

"Talk," she ordered.

"It's going to be a complicated job. You, Gray, and Falconer working together in the pharmacy business," he said.

"I'll handle them."

"Michelle, I'm sleeping with the enemy."

"You're giving me a headache."

The radio announcer heralded the *Wake-Up Call Show*. Listeners called in. A male caller requested *Lady in Red*.

Twelve white roses in a crystal vase added class to the air. He watered the flowers. "I ordered them for you, dearest."

She pecked his cheek and leaned back. "Al?"

"Your tone of voice is scaring me."

"I want to say something," she said.

"I'm the sounding board, go ahead."

"Al, I experience this …"

"What?" he asked.

"As if I'll pass away."

He gripped her arm.

"Al …"

He ran to the first aid cabinet in the kitchen and took out ibuprofen. He poured water in a glass. "Here, drink these two pills."

She showed him rashes on her arms. "And now this."

"Goodness, dear, we have to do blood chemistry."

He again went to the medicine cabinet. He gave her an antihistamine. "Your fatigue worries me."

"I'll succumb to something."

"You'll have to trust me," he said.

He returned to the cabinet, found natural multivitamins with antioxidants, enzymes, and amino acids. He made her swallow three of the green tablets. "I pop them, too, to keep fit."

"Doctors!" An enigmatic smile curled at the edge of her lips.

"I'll take you to a small private clinic downtown. Trust me to examine you."

"I'll be fine." Her eyes clung to his.

His heart raced.

They finished breakfast and sat at the front patio, taking in the warm, fresh air. He inspected Michelle's rash. His medical mind computed the prognosis.

"Grief's many heads." Michelle grimaced and clamped her teeth. "My chest is tight."

Pain deepened her wrinkles. A mild lip tremor accentuated them. From the fridge, he took out mango-tangerine juice and gave it to her. He opted for his regular American beer.

"A father's loss drains you." She sipped from her glass.

"The grief will pass. He's safe in heaven."

"You're trying to make me happy."

"I am, yes."

"He was a phenomenal father."

"Michelle, I agree." he said. "You're telling me. I trust you."

"You don't!"

"Chill out, Michelle. You're not well."

"Blame everything on my health. Tell the world I'm a sick woman." She shook her head and bit her lip. "He left the estate to me."

He embraced her, almost squeezing her.

"You're already celebrating," she accused.

He stepped back. "I'm taking you to the lab."

"I'm not going anywhere. I consulted a few specialists. They say nothing to fuss about. Falconer confirmed that, too." Her eyelids closed and trembled.

He reached for her hand and gave it a reassuring grip.

"In your eyes, I'll be in perfect health."

His voice rose as he fought the fear of the unknown. "I'm pushing, but dress, and let's put our best foot forward. Look as smart as you can. Life is still a gift."

He was ready to fight for Michelle's well being—and the good of his children. They stepped out. The hot morning sun blazed on Chandler's cheeks. He jumped into his Ford Blazer. She hesitated then slid in. His brain shifted from her sickness to his jobless status.

She tweaked his arm and shook her head. He backed the car off the driveway.

Someone bolted into the bushes. Chandler felt his skin grow clammy. The man slammed on his car door, sucked himself in, and sped off. "Goddammit! It's Adolph again!"

Michelle turned around and saw the car. "Let's go home."

His nerves tensed but he forced himself not to show the tension. "Every dog has its day."

"You can do nothing about him and his contacts." She leaned toward the dashboard.

"I'm preparing his snare."

In twenty-four hours, after Chandler had Michelle take the test, the phone summoned them to a call.

"This is the technician from the Atlantic Isle Lab. Dr. Chandler, please?"

"Speaking."

"Dr. Chandler, I finished the blood work. I can send the report—"

"Read it out, please."

"It says *High titers of anti-double-stranded DNA antibodies*. I'll post you the result."

He drew in a quick breath and suppressed the pull in his jaw. "Michelle, you're positive for—"

She cried out and grabbed at his shirt.

"You have SLE. Systemic lupus erythematosus." His world grew dark, as dark as when Pandora died by the pond. As dim as the day his parents passed away. He freed himself from the agony. If disaster was the fate of all his loved ones, it was his destiny. Someday Satan would strike him. Who was Satan? He was next. Someone, or something, was stressing Michelle. Stress was weakening her body and killing her. "I feel with you, Michelle. As long as I can breathe, you won't die."

Michelle swallowed hard, and managed to say, "Never?"

Once more, the phone buzzed. "I'm the technician. I called a minute or so ago from the lab."

Chandler turned the speakerphone on. "The test was wrong? Negative?"

"No, no, no. One Adolph just called to ask if you're still here. He said you're buddies."

He forced a smile. "We're great friends." He eased the phone down.

"He's damaging my mind," Michelle said.

"He's not worth worrying over."

"Al, the man's evil."

"Worry about other matters. Your health, for example," Chandler declared.

"Damn!" She cowered into his arms and cried.

Nauseating spurts of adrenaline coursed through his veins as he thought of Adolph. His problems were squeezing him like a shark's bite. He dared not let his emotions show. Michelle's life was more important.

"We're both tense," he said. "Let's go for a drive. Anywhere. We'll leave the children."

His cell phone vibrated. He was about to negotiate a curve by a forested area of town.

"Patsy here, Dr. Chandler. I'm sorry to call you," the voice said.

"Who?" He took the turn and slowed down. "What's the matter?" A car clipped him on the bumper and sped away. "Damn!"

"Just got back from the grocery," said Patsy. "Abraham and Abigail were reading and giggling over child pornographic fliers. Vivid pictures, too."

He swerved to the curb and pressed the brakes.

"A few brochures were on the open windowsill."

His heart jostled.

"What's the problem?" Michelle asked, hearing the tutor. "Al, talk to me. The funny events around here are making me sicker."

"Take the fliers away!"

Michelle raised her voice.

"I'll explain later." The line clicked off.

"Adolph will turn you from a two-legged mammal to a four-legged baboon."

"Give me two full moons."

"To do what, Al?"

"The long rope around his neck will shorten."

He could barely speak. It was the morning after. Chandler noted an unsightly rash on Michelle's chest and elbows. "Typical malar butterfly erythema." He put on the bedside lamp and studied the scalp. Her hair fell out in clumps. "It's focal alopecia." He played with a few strands and fought to keep his composure.

"That was happening a good while, in small bits." A sotto lisp dulled her voice. "I dismissed the condition as just work anxiety. Falconer can stress out anybody. Only now I'm beginning to feel it."

His mind turned heavy. "I'll refer you to a specialist in Miami."

She spoke in a hoarse whisper. "You'll come with me."

He passed his fingers over his chin and pondered the dire complications of the disease. "I have another idea." He hugged her. "We'll get you well." He picked up the bedside phone and dialed Kennedy.

"D'you know what's the time, Daddy-o?" His cackling voice grew heavy. "In karate we believe in self-discipline, positive attitude, and high morals. Shoot!"

"Michelle has lupus."

"People die of it! My God! What d'you need to get her well?"

Chandler told him.

Chandler heard him sigh. "You're asking for a lot, Daddy-o. Vanessa is here for that. Besides, I get to kiss her early in the morning."

He listed other medication.

"Wow! Vanessa will kill me."

In no time, Kennedy arrived with a package. He joked, "Federal Express delivery!" He embraced Michelle, who was sitting on a bar stool by the stove. He punched Chandler on the shoulder playfully. "I'm working. But keep me informed, Daddy-o." He slapped Chandler on the thigh. "Hey, Daddy-o, midgets have equal rights."

Chandler administered the shots to Michelle for several days. "I'll continue with prednisone." Treating someone so close was heavy on the heart. Falconer was using island voodoo to punish him.

She pulled back. "The oral steroid—I'll develop a moon face, and my immune system will drop."

"You're thinking too hard."

"I'll get a broken hip from steroids."

"If you take the drug for long periods."

"I'll still die." A wounded expression veiled her eyes.

"I'll include the antimalarial drug chloroquin and taper the steroids."

Her features fell.

"You need the drugs now," he said.

Her eyes turned pale. "You're experimenting."

"I'll add DHEA. It's a more natural androgenic drug."

She patted his cheek. "I admire you. Let me die in peace."

The phone rang, startling Michelle. "Chandler's residence."

A female voice came on. "It's Pandora, your best friend." The phone went dead.

"The voice seems to be your deceased wife's," she told Chandler.

"Michelle, you're hallucinating."

"I'm not!" she insisted.

"Take it easy; I understand."

"I know myself. I'm not imagining things."

"Try to get some sleep." He came into the bedroom and checked the LED screen. "The country code is 41?" The telephone directory was in the kitchen. He went for the book and looked up the area code. "Switzerland."

"Something funny?" Early the next morning, before the tutor arrived, Chandler ambled into the children's room. They laughed at their computers. He moved closer.

"This is child pornography! The origin is untraceable. Switch it off!"

He breathed slowly to calm down and spoke to Abraham and Abigail.

"The computer is good and bad. It entertains, educates, and informs. It can also be dangerous. Bad people with bad designs produce those Internet shows. We call them pedophiles, child abusers."

Innocence shone in their eyes. They cocked their ears, eyes fixed on him. Together they sang out, "Yes, Dad."

Abraham pointed a finger. "They won't feed on me."

"I'll pray for their evil souls." Abigail clasped her hands, closed her eyes, and flipped them open. "They'll never prey on Abigail. Not in my whole life."

He put child locks on the laptop computers. He slammed his fist into his open hand. "Someone will pay."

The children sang uplifting songs to Michelle. Chandler took her hands; they gave out special warmth, calming his soul. He mothered her. He cooked, cleaned, and did the laundry. He tended to her bedside needs. The children pitched in and did their part. He played soft jazz for her all day. Abigail knelt by the bed and prayed for her.

The phone rang. Chandler grabbed the receiver.

Falconer's voice was demanding.

"I gave her sick leave. I'm still a doctor, and she's my fiancée."

"She has work to do here at the hospital. I've been struggling for the past two days with work she ought to be doing."

"So, a woman in poor health has to come to work?"

"She must get back here soon."

"Really?" Chandler was flabbergasted. The LED screen indicated a local call. Falconer was not in Switzerland.

The children continued bedtime chants. Chandler gave Michelle potassium-rich foods daily, like bananas, dates, and broccoli. He spoon-fed her aloe vera and green tea. He stopped giving her red meats, refined sugars, and starches. He let her take herbal supplements and started her on sound therapy. He ensured she had nine hours of sleep each night. When slumber evaded her, he led her in breathing exercises, relaxation techniques, and meditation.

"Michelle," he told her daily, "repeat after me: *ohm* ..."

Michelle was twenty-eight. In two weeks, she looked twenty-one. Her chestnut skin and ginger speckles assumed a brighter hue. Her high cheekbones were gaining more flesh. Her lips gained fullness, and her hair was starting to grow. Her eyes brightened. "Al, I'm a good patient."

"Ideal patients heal well. You can blow a flute?"

"I did in secondary school, but I've forgotten much."

He arranged for a flutist to give her lessons. A tall, dark, and handsome man with a pleasant smile came to the house. After ten sessions, Michelle was playing like a pro. She practiced daily. The children surprised her with a flute rendition.

Michelle raised an eyebrow. "Marvelous!"

Abigail shrugged her shoulders and giggled. "We learned at the orphanage."

Chandler joined Michelle on a thirty-minute walk each day. The children followed her, played, joked, and laughed.

From a distance, Adolph tagged along.

Chandler included thirty minutes of weight lifting in her day. He increased the weights. Soon, she was walking an hour and a half a day with him, morning and afternoon, with dumbbells. The children urged her on.

So did Falconer from afar.

She frisked around. "I had another hobby. I did archery in school. Shake my hand."

They gripped hands, and she squeezed his very hard.

"Ouch!" He thought he was holding a vise.

Early the following morning, Chandler went out and bought high-tech archery gear. "I'll get you a tutor."

"Save the teacher. I can still shoot arrows." Every day in the back yard, she practiced with the bow and arrow. Birds chirped on bougainvillea flowers. She tried to train Chandler. He never hit the bull's-eye. The children learned the game and killed themselves laughing at Chandler's errors.

So did Adolph and Falconer. From a distance.

Michelle regained her health. One day, as they practiced archery, something strange happened.

"Al!" She said, "I heard a rustle in the bushes, behind the hedge. I saw Adolph."

Chandler didn't see anything.

"I'm not imagining things, Al! Stop thinking I'm crazy."

He put his arm over her shoulders. "You're the picture of health."

"Bravo!"

"Avoid doctors at all cost: every one, except me. You'll live longer."

One day, Kennedy came, dressed as a clown. He surprised Michelle with a roast of Al Chandler and Falconer in conflict.

Michelle, Chandler, and the children bubbled with laughter. Every evening Kennedy delivered a different comic routine on life, love, women, doctors, and politicians. Another day, he arrived in a karate outfit.

"Oooh!" exclaimed Abraham.

"Enough, Arnold," Chandler cracked up. "Keep the costume for the judo fool, I mean *school*."

"Daddy-o, happiness lies in controlling the present. Forget the past and the future. Do you hear me, Michelle? At work, Falconer's peppering your name and Al's. Do what's best for you."

That night, the children ran up to their stepfather. They glanced at each other and were shy and reluctant to speak.

Abraham looked down, eyes up. "Sir, remember you warned us about bad shows from bad people?"

He inclined his head to him, and interlaced his fingers.

"Well, our computers are full of stuff again."

He sighed. "I'll see to that." It could never be Adolph. He pondered Falconer, or one of the consultants. The web of intrigue was getting thicker and nastier. He discussed the matter with Michelle.

"For money, the hospital computer guy will do anything, and he's trustworthy. All he wants is a few dollars to buy liquor."

The computer technician came. He added a recording gadget to the laptops, connecting it to the webcams.

"Why are you doing this?" asked Michelle. "Sounds like one of your weird plans."

"That's good security. I'll record pictures coming in and going out around the clock. It has a two-way recording. I'll rectify the problem. I'll deal with evil people who try to shatter my world."

CHAPTER 17

That Saturday, Abraham and Abigail played hide-and-seek outside. Chandler stood by his front window. The sun flared from a cloudless sky and shone on Pandora's castle. A breeze caressed the lilies in the pond and gave the atmosphere a sweet aroma. Doves glided in the sky and cooed. Chandler ran downstairs and played with them.

He organized a barbecue. Someone shouted from the road. He saw the mail carrier. The little darlings ran for the post.

Michelle walked up to Al.

He opened the letter. "It's from chairperson Dr. Enida Pratt of the National Medical Council. Oh, heavens! I forgot to go to the council meeting."

Michelle shook her head. "Al, Al—"

"I'll read it to you."

> *The Hospital Board put you on probation, but you refused to reform your conduct. The Medical Association suspended you, but you are still flouting the profession. Falconer loathes you. Gray thinks you incite the nation to fight his government, Atlantic Isle Chemicals, and the pharmaceutical business. The Food and Drug Commission abhors you. Prominent specialists like Ivanov, Amoono, Demos, Parco, Jarvis, and Pierre hate you. They're not interested in any socialized medicine.*

> *Your conduct in the medical profession is shameful. We can revoke your right to practice medicine.*
>
> *I'm with the union, and so I have a dual role here. We, the council, the supreme national body, have decided to give you a last chance to adjust your behavior. You may keep the license to practice medicine. We'll review your status.*
>
> *—Enida Pratt, MD*

The phone sounded inside.

Abigail sauntered in for it. "For you, ma'am."

Michelle forged in. Chandler could discern her through the rear glass window. Her mood changed from ecstatic to dismay. She continued to listen to Falconer's voice. *"Leave Chandler for your own good."*

"I'll do that." She slammed down the phone. She didn't go outside.

Chandler rushed in.

She was faking a smile. "Just someone from work. Problems follow me."

From home, the following day, Chandler called up the hospital pharmacy. "This is Dr. Chandler. I wonder if you would check your computer for a little information."

The soft female voice sounded reassuring. "I'm a new technician. One sec, please ... go ahead now."

"I'm calling about a prescription for Mordex for Amelia Chandler and DED-statin for Sam Chandler. I believe Dr. Ivanov wrote them."

"One second, Doctor."

Chandler waited. The computer beeped.

"Doctor?"

"Did you find anything?" What Chandler heard made him recoil. "I'll buck out from this crab hole."

CHAPTER 18

Pigeons cooed and fluttered, plucking morsels of food.

Michelle said, "Al, you bring me here because you know I'll kick the bucket soon."

That was the following night. Chandler, Michelle, and Baraka stepped up the marble steps of the downtown Atlantic Isle Hotel.

"That's not true." Chandler adjusted his navy-blue corduroy jacket, his light-blue T-shirt, and purple bandanna.

The children preferred to lounge and play with their laptops. It exposed them to the world.

"I leave the world and you'll woo another woman."

"Darling!" he objected.

The full moon added luster to the two kissing marble marlins on the rooftop. Glittering red-and-blue neon lights flickered. A gust of wind swished between the tree leaves from the hotel garden. Night jasmine essence sweetened the air.

"We're celebrating life."

"Rubbish! I'm dropping you, dirty boy."

His heart leaped. He stopped, gripped her hands, and locked her gaze. "W-what did you—?"

"Let's forget the night."

"I won't let this evening be for anyone else but you, dear."

Her eyebrows narrowed. "I'm not up to dinner."

"We're on a date."

She exploded. "Smell the rose."

That puzzled him. He forced a smile, clasped and unclasped his hands. "We're giving thanks for your health, my work, and our two great children."

"You're a troublemaker."

"Trouble?"

"The world is against you. Stupid communist healthcare! Society thinks I'm a fool to be in your company."

"You're unfair to say so, Michelle."

"Unjust to you."

Her purple chiffon wrap slid off her shoulder.

He recovered the shawl and put it back on. "You dress like a star."

"I have a hearing problem and I lisp."

"It means nothing to me."

"Look for an Eve. Know that challenged people are humans, too."

"You *are* a perfect woman."

"Till another 'chick' comes along. Pandora, now me."

"I didn't kill anyone!"

"I fancy professional men. I prize upright career men, too. No—"

"That's a good start."

"But you behave like an alien among your colleagues."

He pointed to his chest. "I'm growing inside."

His faithful friend licked his fingers, jumped the steps, and bolted ahead.

They entered the hotel. On a red-carpeted platform, a pianist in a tuxedo played Tchaikovsky's *Nutcracker Suite*. The music offered Chandler relief from the quarrel outside.

Baraka jogged in and zipped under the tables. Like kings and queens at a royal ball, the diners mumbled at the creature's presence.

"I'm atop the world," he said.

"You're on top of something else," Michelle retorted.

"Michelle!"

The restaurant resembled a palace. It had red velvet carpet, a frescoed ceiling, and crystal chandeliers. He still had no courage to ask Michelle about the suspicious phone call.

They didn't speak. He tapped his fingers.

His dog popped up with a man's extra-large black shoe.

"Even your canine companion is behaving queerly."

He strained his voice. "Baraka, take that back."

Baraka yowled like a slave unwilling to serve his master.

Chandler yanked the shoe off the dog's snout. He grimaced at the shoe's odor and hid it below the table. "Leave it there." His voice became harsh. "The hotel will put us out."

"Maître d'!"

"No!" He gave her a level stare.

The man came. "I'll keep him safe in a special room for visitors' pets." He took Baraka away.

"Al, I'm now a sick woman." She swallowed air. "One hour, and we leave."

"Dinner takes two to three hours. I recognize your condition. Three quarters of an hour will do."

"I'm angry at my life."

"You have me."

"Oh, good God!"

"You embarrass me." He lost his tongue, and then he managed to say, "My existence, and our lives. Oh, your well being, too."

"At twenty-eight, what a life! Falconer and others worry about us. You like me. You hate my people. I work with them because of the pharmacies." She folded and refolded the cloth napkin.

He crossed his arms. "I created a problem on the island. The experience has made me a new man. I'm turning over a new leaf."

She turned a cold eye on him.

They ordered Cristal champagne and Châteauneuf-du-Pape red wine. By accident, he hit his glass. It fell and spilled the bubbly liquid on the table. Michelle uttered a sarcastic laugh. The kitchen helper came to their rescue and cleaned up.

She studied the gold-trimmed napkin. "I'll skip the appetizer."

He passed his fingers over his bearded chin.

"I'm not like you. I can change my mind anytime." She studied the menu. "Stuffed mushrooms, turkey-and-broccoli-filled lasagna squares, and crisp breadsticks."

"I'll go for marinated prime ribs. I'll have it with horseradish sauce, steamed asparagus, orzo, and dinner rolls. Enough to shoot up my testosterone."

"Oh, merciful God!" Michelle averted her eyes.

Chandler raised his crystal glass. "Here's to the most divine woman in the universe." Champagne spilled on his shirtsleeve.

She smirked and shook her head. "I want to believe you, Al Chandler." She glared at her glass flute. "I'm quitting."

"Please don't."

Her eyes took on a wounded look.

"You could be Miss Universe," he told her.

The piped-in music changed to *An Affair to Remember.*

"Maître d', how's my pet doing in the holding room?" he demanded.

"He's just fine. He was whining. Very clever for a dog. He unlatched his cage, and emerged. He's so playful. He's licking Falconer's rabbit."

Chandler focused on his food and ate. Michelle dawdled with hers. For dessert, he ordered tiramisu. She took crème brûlée.

"That's just to unburden myself." An icy expression chiseled her face. "It's too bland and watery." She scowled at her plate. "Now, Al, this is hard for *me*. The nonsense you're involved in is spinning your head." She glanced at her watch. "I did say an hour. Time's up, almost. You're even declaring war on my Papa's business."

"I believe in doing no harm. I'm sure health for all is the answer to Atlantic Isle's dream."

"Now my earthly idol is dead." She jerked her face away from him. "You're mauling everybody and fooling yourself that it's over. You'll kill out the population with this crazy healthcare nonsense." Her eyes narrowed in disgust.

The flutist stopped at the table. He played a rendition of *I Love You for Sentimental Reasons.*

Chandler ordered Port wine. He ate his dessert and buried his head in his plate. She wasn't eating.

He went for another bite. "The medical community, the board, the pharmaceutical industry, and the political dogs gave me a lemon. I splashed lime juice into their faces." He sipped his wine, the liquor reducing the pressure of the explosive vacuum inside him. "It's my gig, but someone is squeezing me in a vise, Michelle."

"I figure so."

"You can blame me. We've achieved much. I've had enough."

"Or Atlantic Isle has had enough of you."

The red wine burned his stomach. "I bought two tickets for a two-week Caribbean cruise." He dreaded her response.

Her lisp grew stronger. "I'm sorry Bridgette Ford is dead. You two—"

"Who?" He belched acid wine.

She pushed back her chair, jumped up, and glared at him.

"*You* shamed *me*!"

He looked in front and behind. "Careful, people are observing."

"The world's watching you!"

"Ease down back to your seat, please."

She dropped to her chair with a sigh. "Attacking my father, shaming yourself in the medical world, and playing hero!" Frenzy filled her voice. "I'm also referring to my stepsister. Bridgette. We have different fathers. Got another sister in San Francisco from my father's side, Margo, but—"

The revelation blinded him. "You-you-you never told me. Brigitte was your—?"

"And Al Chandler's playmate!"

He toned his voice down. "Leave the gossip aside."

Her voice turned icy. "You fool around like this and you die long before me. Maybe I'll celebrate."

"Forget the rumor. The cruise is for us. We'll talk."

"You have the world ahead of you!"

He stretched his hands over the table to hold hers, but she pulled away. "Let's while the time away. You and I."

"You go wherever you want. I'll-I'll safeguard Baraka." She blinked. "I'll-I'll redo my new office, and reorganize my legacy, and ... I'll reestablish contacts with Atlantic Isle Chemicals and other pharmaceutical companies abroad. I'll speak to the doctors to revamp the pharmacies. Your health plan is getting in the way. You're talking government control—"

"State and private."

"What the hell?"

"You're a businesswoman. You and I—"

"I'll lobby with the political boys to keep the business going. It's my duty. They were once Papa's."

Chandler developed a throbbing headache. He visualized America. He focused on President King's offer, which he had refused. He was a mess. A mistake created a domino effect and made his life a living hell. "I blame you," he heard his mother's voice telling him.

His eyes stung. He flinched and shut them tight. They burnt like fire. Sweet, acid liquid drenched his face. He rubbed his eyelids. Port wine seeped into his mouth. He sniffed it. Like lava, it seeped deep into his nostrils and scalded his nose. He covered his mouth and sneezed.

Something liquid soaked his shirt. He looked down in horror, his vision blurred. A red substance stained his clothes. He groped for his handkerchief and wiped his eyes. They blazed like fire, and he squeezed them again. He forced them open with the help of his fingers. He looked across the table and around the restaurant. Michelle had vanished. He grabbed ice-cold water, leaned forward, and splashed it into his eyes to irrigate them. It made him shiver. "Shit, Michelle! Why did you—?"

The maître d' brought a cordless phone to him. "A call for you."

He wiped his wet shirt collar.

"One Dr. Arnold Kennedy." He whispered, "Your dog mutilated the rabbit."

"Oh my God!" Chandler grabbed the phone. "Arnold?" He could no longer suppress his tears. He gulped air. "She walked out on me."

"I'll tell you what to do. It works every time I'm stressed out."

He pressed the phone to his ear. "Go ahead."

"Swallow port wine and act pixilated. Go stark bananas! Act nutty as a fruitcake."

"They'll take their eyes and pass me."

"Daddy-o! The board fired me."

Chandler cringed and shook his head.

"*We end your services* is all, in essence, the letter says. The Board's Acting Chairman signed it."

"So who's now—?"

"Dr. Falconer is."

"Murder in the courtyard!"

"Al, Vanessa and I parted. She said she's now bunking with Falconer."

"Jesus!"

"She says it guarantees her job."

"The Viking strikes!" Chandler clicked off.

The maître d' approached a familiar face and whispered into his ear. It favored Falconer. He was not sure, but the man looked shocked.

Chandler called the maître d'. "Could you call the wine steward?"

He bowed. "The dinner and drinks are compliments of Dr. Falconer. Says he's celebrating a new position on a board."

Chandler's breath caught in his throat.

The steward came.

"Port, a bottle of it, please."

In a minute, he returned. He poured an ounce or so into a crystal snap glass and handed it to Chandler.

Chandler shoved the glass back to him and grabbed the bottle. He put it to his mouth and downed the wine until his stomach gurgled. His mind raced. He slammed the bottle on the table. His eyes dimmed, and he hiccupped. "I have a complimentary dinner. Michelle's gone. Let's drink and celebrate."

A demon took over Chandler. He stood, clapped for attention, and addressed the diners. "To keep my character intact, I'll goddamn roam the world. Alone. I'll bear my cross." He hiccupped twice. "I'll do nobody any harm. Never in my sound mind. I'll transport healthcare reform elsewhere."

Clearly startled, the diners murmured to one another.

He had an idea. He stooped under the table and grabbed the shoe. In his dismay, he fancied he was declaring World War III. He peered at the shoe sole: OCMSFS14 ½. He mumbled, "Jesus fuckin' Christ!" Pandora's killer sat among them. He held the shoe high above his head.

He scanned the crowd. Doctors, politicians, lobbyists, pharmacists, and opulent patients regaled and sipped wine. Dr. Falconer and his M&M boys dined in an alcove. Gray was there. He picked out the Atlantic Isle Chemicals Chairperson and the high rollers.

"I feel inches taller from my American heritage and my Kenyan genetic makeup. I'm proud to have an orphan background. I got to America and enjoyed the best healthcare in the world. Do I favor the evildoers?"

A brittle silence needled the air.

Falconer sprang up. "Holy friggin' Jah!"

Chandler reviewed the ID again on the sole. OCMSFS14 ½. The O stood for Obi. The F for Falconer. What's CMS? Chandler poured wine into the shoe and dropped it onto the table. He thought about Michelle. A tunnel in his chest roared with hot wind and baked his rib cage. His legs wobbled.

"Mr. Prime Minister," Adolph clamored, "get him locked up! Besides, his stupid dog beheaded my brother's rabbit."

"Oops! You're here. Mind your P's and Q's." Chandler maintained his self-confidence.

Adolph left the restaurant.

Gray stood and raised his finger at Chandler. "Chandler's got thousands of union ignoramuses following him."

From across the room, Ivanov chimed in. "Leave Chandler alone. Election campaigning is coming up soon. Be diplomats in the field. We'll pin him when the time is right."

Chandler crouched like a wounded gladiator, a lost soul. "Adversity is hard. It's hardening me. Pandora's death is still fresh in me. I visited the Seaside Massage Parlor. Obi Falconer and Adolph Falconer appeared on the shop register. The Falconers bribed the receptionist to put the names in the book. Why would the Falconers bribe?"

Everyone kept silent.

"About my parents: A surgeon wrote deadly prescriptions, and they died. The doctor blamed his confidant, who, according to hospital administration was on a one-day sick leave. The sick physician wasn't at work. The prescription records disappeared. The companion carries a .22-caliber automatic gun to protect his master. He is a sharpshooter, and so is the other doctor, who visits the rifle club. The villain collaborated with his boss's brother to practice shooting a human target. That's the gossip there. Isn't it interesting? Now, who would want to shoot whom? I understand most of the doctors of a certain hospital belong to the gun society. They feel the need to experiment with a living man. 'Bull's-eye' rifle targets are getting boring, they say." Chandler turned to the maître d'. "Get me my dog please. I'm leaving."

A gun fired in another room.

The headwaiter blazed up to Chandler. "Your pet is dead."

Chandler pictured Adolph leaving the room earlier. Sudden grief grew like a cancer in Chandler's head: *My treasure's dead. My canine friend has gone to rest. Baraka's in Abraham's bosom.*

The ensuing day, another shock hit him.

"Darling!"

His head throbbed with a splitting headache. He shuffled to the kitchen and searched for Baraka. Grief hit him again. He called out.

"Michelle! Michelle! She left me. She didn't come home from the restaurant."

He sipped coffee.

"It's bitter!"

He added sugar and stirred the drink. His eyes burned and his eyesight dimmed. He hurled the hot drink against the wall. Down the stairs he went to say good morning to his children. Abraham and Abigail possessed his life. Michelle was gone. His little ones became his existence. *I'll educate them to university level. They'll marry decent partners. I'll have a large family. What great joy!*

He knocked on the children's door downstairs. No one answered. Still sleeping. *Angels at rest.*

He would come back later. He turned to go, but decided to make sure they were asleep and not busy on their laptops. He cracked the door open.

"Good day, children!"

Joy washed over him. They slept on the floor, electronic devices switched on. *They sat up all night playing with their computers. Now, knocked out.*

"Abraham!" he called. "Abigail! Get into bed."

I'll protect my children for the rest of my life. If anything happened to his beloved son and daughter, he would go berserk. He ran up and tapped them on the cheeks.

"Come on, sweethearts, get up."

They could pass for cherubs. His little angels were his life. He agitated them again.

"A-a-ah! Dead!"

He held on tight to them.

"Why? Why am I left alone to mourn? No-o-o-o-o!"

His body numbed, his fingers trembled, and his sight went blank. With a throbbing pain his head exploded.

"Abraham! Abigail!" *Someone lynched my true possessions.*

He heard Michelle's voice. "I did it."

The words were only in his head. "Jesus flippin' Christ!" Tears welled in his eyes, and he convulsed.

Chandler used the USB storage devices and recorded the pictures. He'd pin his enemies. He hugged the children, kissed them, and cried, delirious with grief.

"How come? Why didn't the vipers end my life instead? Give me the reason?"

Someone behind him scared him. "Oh, we will."

"Uh?" He twisted around. He was hearing his own voice. What he saw in the room made him schizophrenic.

CHAPTER 19

"I'll avenge you, my children." He called the pigs. They came, interrogated Chandler, and snapped photos. Porters carried the bodies away in bags. Chandler retched. *No more trust funds for my loved ones to inherit.* He wept again. With trembling lips, he mumbled, "Farewell, my angels."

Falconer, Adolph, Michelle, and Chandler were at the police station. Detectives interrogated them in private rooms.

The struggle within Chandler was making him sick. The police superintendent knitted his eyebrows.

"I'd like to show you the crime scene pictures on your computer."

Falconer wore a cynical smile.

Adolph glowered at him. "Arrest him, sir. He killed his children!"

Michelle shot up and stomped around the room. "In the name of justice, let's watch the webcam videos."

"I'll allow it." The superintendent nodded.

Chandler pulled out the memory sticks from his pocket and inserted them into the computer. The crime scene flashed before their eyes. One of the windows was ajar a fraction of an inch. The laptops were running, and the webcams were connected. The children's computers showed vivid video pictures. A yellow tube ran from the window.

Chandler yelled, "A Trojan horse gassed my kids!"

The pictures showed Adolph coming through the window. He had a handkerchief over his nostrils, but his face was visible. He checked the pulse and the eyes of the children. Dead. Adolph giggled.

Anger cracked Chandler's skull. "You shortened my little angels' lives, Adolph! Falconer's plan worked! I will eat you people alive!"

"Stop the masquerade!" Falconer shouted. "Chandler doctored the webcam pictures. After the restaurant, Adolph and I had two hookers with us on my yacht. I'm not ashamed to say it. Adolph was not at your house. We even took photos."

"Alibi?" Chandler's self-respect was still in play. "How dare you!"

Falconer huffed, "Superintendent, I have one of the photographs here."

They passed it around. Chandler studied it. It was a flash Polaroid photo.

Chandler pinpointed the answer. "Examine the picture again. Falconer and his people stand together, and they face the camera squarely. The flash brightens the right side of the faces."

"So we used a flash, stupid," mumbled Falconer.

"Adolph was present at the crime scene. All the faces are bright on the right. Adolph's face is dark on that side. This means we're dealing with a composite picture. A good photographer used computer technology and inserted Adolph into the picture from another snapshot."

The room was dead silent. The police arrested Adolph.

Chandler left the building alone. Later, at a preliminary inquiry the court heard the defense and prosecution evidence. The magistrate pronounced, "The court finds there is insufficient evidence to order a trial." *If you suppose I'm finished with you wiseacres, think again.*

CHAPTER 20

Kennedy scratched his chin. "Michelle will call."

"She's not mine anymore." Delirious with grief, Chandler sat in the den and drank beer. Kennedy kept him company.

The telephone rang. Chandler's tone was low as he answered.

"Dr. Chandler, the hospital's calling. This is an emergency."

Chandler inhaled sharply.

The voice on the phone said, "Michelle Lang's in ER. The doctor diagnosed renal failure. She's in a deep coma. I'm only a nurse." The phone clicked off.

"Michelle's critical. Let's hurry," Chandler blurted.

He dashed outside. Kennedy ran behind him, but saw a note on a slate on the concrete floor. He picked it up. "Daddy-o, I have a love letter for you."

Chandler grabbed it. "Look, the Blazer's outside. Someone smashed it. Damn! What the hell! My adversaries are killing me."

"Shit! The Ferrari is yours and mine. You can drive it."

They raced to the hospital. "Stay alive, love." Seventy miles an hour. "She won't." The gauge went up to eighty.

The wrecked Blazer flashed before his eyes. Up to eighty-five miles per hour.

They reached the hospital and stormed into the crowded ER.

A nurse jumped up from her desk. "Dr. Chandler, down to Unit Seven. Hurry! She won't live."

His knees going weak, he hastened to the unit. What he perceived shocked the hell out of him. The nurses were wrapping up a body.

Kennedy bumped into him. "Oh my God! May-may-may her soul rest in peace."

Chandler plummeted to his knees. His face fell into his open hands, and he convulsed with tears.

Kennedy touched him on the shoulder. "You have me."

"Oh, my gracious God!" He whimpered. "G-gone, but not forgotten. F-forgive me all my t-trespasses."

Kennedy stared at the dead body. "That's a toddler, Daddy-o."

"Nurse, my fiancée. Michelle Lang. Where is—?"

"One unit down. This is Unit Eight."

They ran to the right unit.

She lay comatose. An examination lamp shone by her side. Tubes attached to her nostrils, mouth, abdomen, and hands. She was on oxygen.

An Indian physician switched off the light and turned on his penlight. He examined her pupils.

"I'm Al Chandler." He shook the man's hand.

"I'm Dr. Jahlall Singh, Fellow of the Royal College of Physicians, England, yes? I'm the new ER chief, yes?"

"I worked here as that."

"Nice thing the chief of staff did to employ me. He's a fine man. Michelle Lang is on abdominal dialysis. I specialize in kidney diseases and transplants, yes? Her blood tests, scans, and MRI show damaged kidneys."

Fed up with Singh, he shook his head, but said nothing to annoy him.

"A slim chance to save her, yes?"

"No!"

"The chief of staff was here and he expressed the same opinion. He advised not to waste more medicine on her. He's right."

"Dr. Singh, death may have its sting, but life abounds with venom."

"My big chief's blood has no poison. He offered a decent doctor like me a pretty good position here. Michelle has lupus. This lupus disease I study. I wrote my thesis on lupus—systemic lupus erythematosus, to give you the full name. No plaything, yes?" He shook his head. "We'll keep her on dialysis. It will do an amicable job for the kidneys. I'll speak to Dr. Falconer. You see—"

"For heaven's sake, hush!" Chandler tried hard to maintain his self-worth. "Keep him far away from this."

"I've done a million such operations in India, yes? Dr. Falconer—"

Chandler pondered for a mind-prickling moment. "Her mother is dead and so is her stepsister. Her father passed away. She has an aunt at National Insurance. She's sickly."

"No kidney, no chance, yes? Dr. Falconer—"

"Cut out that name off your tongue, please!" He licked his parched lips. "Michelle's my fiancée."

"The lymphocyte-mediated immune reaction opposing transplantation antigens is the big thing against acute rejection."

"Enough!"

"She might just have seventy-two hours to live, yes?"

Ivanov and Falconer stomped in. Falconer looked haggard.

Chandler held his throbbing temples. He was downcast. His voice waxed into a hoarse tone. "Arnold, let's go." His legs remained rooted to the floor.

The boss walked off and came back, tapping his chest. "Michelle was an employee here. She's entitled to free medical treatment. Can you imagine how many thousands of dollars we're wasting? She'll eventually die of kidney failure. I advise terminating her."

"Friggin' asshole!" Chandler lunged forward to grab Falconer's white coat. "Stop!" echoed his parents' voices in his head.

Kennedy held him back. "Al, no!"

"You hinder her in any way, and I'll pull the plug from your ass!" He was steaming inside.

"Nonsense!" Falconer back-stepped and his eyes shifted, a worried look on his face. "I'm exiting."

"Exit from Michelle's life. I'm leaving. You touch her, and you die." He walked out.

Outside, the sun attacked him. He was beginning to hate it and everything around. He slid into the Ferrari. Hot air radiated inside the car and irritated his senses. "Three days to live!" He sniffled hard. Life would not be the same without her. "So many questions; no answers."

Kennedy reached over and turned the ignition for Chandler. "That's called a crisis, Daddy-o."

Something nagged at his brain. "Arnold, I can recall Michelle's words at the restaurant." He whistled as if discovering something. That light at the end of the tunnel again.

"She said she had a stepsister." Chandler's eyes brightened. "Her name was Margo."

From rooster crowings at dawn to beetle dronings at dusk, Chandler was on the phone. He interviewed every Margo Lang in the Internet directory. He was ready to die. Life was cruel. Falconer was unfair. He and Michelle would go to heaven. One day was gone. Two more days to go.

Luck struck.

"Yes!" he shouted with joy.

"I'm Margo Lang. I call mother, and she say father move to Atlantic Isle. His name Larry Lang. I love to—"

"I'll reserve your return passage to San Francisco. You'll stay in a hotel and I'll take you to view your Papa's resting place. Ten thousand dollars I'll give you, and I'll try to get you permanent residence if you like." Hope coursed through Chandler's veins.

She hesitated a moment. "I burn inside to help my sister. I come soon. That's plenty money! You can take two kidneys, or three."

Margo arrived the day after they spoke. She was shorter than Michelle by a foot, and chubby. She fanned her face. The heat flushed it. Strong Giorgio perfume preceded her.

One more day to go.

Falconer was not God. Chandler was all smiles as he took her to her hotel. He was hanging on to hope and was already descrying the horizon.

"I want you to know Michelle can die on the table," said Singh. "Happens, yes?"

After a barrage of blood analyses, the doctors cleared Margo for the transplant. Singh let Chandler be in the theater. Michelle suffered a cardiac arrest. The anesthesiologist revived her. Singh worked hard on her, and in the end the operation was an astounding success.

Margo recovered in ten days, and stayed at the hotel. Michelle settled in with Chandler and recuperated.

"Michelle, I treasure you." Chandler admired the moonlit sky through the window one night. He bent and hugged her. "You're worth fighting for, for life." He released his hold on her. "We'll clean up the garbage in our lives soon."

She buried her face against his chest. "Easy."

"Not anymore." He wiped her tears with a handkerchief. "Our souls are well. We worry about the cronies."

The following day he dropped off Kennedy at the inn, where his pal planned to deliver a bouquet of roses, fruits, and champagne to Margo.

He hit his fists on the steering wheel. "That's too much, Arnold."

"She'll fall for me."

She liked him. They drank the bubbles to excess, giggled, and kissed. He told Chandler about the date.

"Arnold!"

"We can be one family, Daddy-o."

He burst out laughing. "Indeed, I sense a change of consciousness. I'm not yet at the peak of the mountain.

"Conflict rekindles my spirit. You'll see."

CHAPTER 21

"Nature at its best." Chandler perched on a garden bench. He looked up at Pandora's castle. He liked life in the servants' quarters. The sun warmed his skin. Birds twittered from a Poinciana tree.

"What a paradise!"

He pondered the merit of following matters on the Isle.

"Not worth the trouble."

Hunters trapped turtles and collected turtle eggs on the beach.

"Hey, you! Leave them alone!" *They are as cruel as Falconer extorting money.*

Chandler hired a lawyer. He fought his medical licensure and won, and so, he broke another link in his chain of freedom. He encouraged an ER doctor to front for him. He was opening a private clinic.

He received an urgent call. "This is Abdul Ali."

"Who?" Chandler asked. "You have the wrong number." He shook his head in disgust.

"No, no, no. D'you remember Noelle?"

"Noelle?"

"She was asthmatic."

"I'm not there anymore."

"That's why I'm calling."

"I'm on another line."

"I'm grateful for all you've done for Noelle. I understand the problems. I would like to give a million dollars toward the new clinic."

"I-I-I—"

"I'll ask my lawyers to speed up the transaction."

He and Kennedy worked with other physicians. They came from Falconer General Hospital ER. Chandler was the clinic's medal malpractice consultant. He offered services to the public. He focused on healthcare reform and a proactive lifestyle.

One day, in his office, he scoured the media and looked for concrete loopholes in Falconer's management. He thought he found a case.

"It's judgment time."

Falconer had to pay for his wicked deeds. Chandler had to get him away from the evil he perpetuated. He would prepare for change in health. Chandler had to clear the water of the carcasses: Falconer, his consultants, and others. He had to act. His time was running out fast. He called his assistants.

They researched the case before them. Chandler volunteered his services. The report read, in part:

THE GOVERNOR EVACUATED. Florida governor William Carter complained of acute right hip pain. He suffered a hip fracture at the craps table. He screamed with agony and dropped to the floor. Casino Royale evacuated him to Jackson Memorial Hospital, Miami.

Chandler smelled victory. His staff helping, he made hundreds of phone calls to Governor Carter. The fax machine spat volumes of documents. He was getting somewhere. The scale of justice was tipping in his favor. Maybe.

"I'm prepared," he affirmed. "I smell the cheese. We're ready to kick Falconer's butt."

His battle gear was a black T-shirt, a tiger-striped bandanna, and red rope sandals. He was preparing for Falconer's death. He and two junior female doctors took a seat in Falconer's office. Kennedy nodded to him and made an O with his thumb and index finger.

Falconer barged in. A team of doctors followed him.

"Let's begin." Chandler shuffled documents. "Physicians in the States requested a second opinion on a case. It's about Florida governor Carter and Dr. Singh."

"You're wasting my time," blurted Falconer.

"Then don't waste mine." He stood and stated the case against Singh. "Dr. Singh, do you recall treating the governor at Casino Royale?"

"Dr. Falconer requested a house call to consult Carter."

"His American lawyers, through a local attorney, filed a suit against Falconer General."

"Ridiculous!" thundered Falconer.

He leaned forward. Ivanov's cheeks reddened.

"You even gave him not one, but *two* cortisone shots, the second a long-acting one!"

"It's an emergency procedure." Singh's face paled, and he chewed on his lip.

"He was already taking heavy doses of steroid tablets for his asthma. You overloaded him."

Singh fumbled with his answer. "I—"

"I respect your medical intelligence. The preparation has serious complications. Did you tell him to change to a newer nonsteroid antiasthmatic drug?"

"I had no time—"

"Answer the question, Doctor."

"I didn't, yes?"

"Please forgive me. Is that a yes?"

"No."

"Doctor, did you warn him alcohol interacts with the medication?"

"I-I-I—"

Chandler's voice waxed into a razor-sharp tone. "He stated in his letter that you didn't warn him. You never asked him if he was willing to continue steroids, despite the horrific side effects. You acted without his permission. Think before you talk now, Doctor."

"I cautioned him about the problems."

Chandler glanced at the wall clock. "He said you never did."

"Singh's word against the governor's," objected Falconer.

The Russian doctor folder his arms and clenched his fists.

Chandler presented photocopies of Carter's medical files to Falconer. "They reflect nothing. No consent given!"

Falconer's dour lips thinned as he scanned the chart.

His confidant fixed a level stare. "Someone tampered with them."

Chandler jumped on Ivanov's words.

Falconer's voice lowered. "I'll check."

"I read the full report." Chandler was winning a lottery. "Within five days, he contracted a right hip fracture."

The Indian doctor looked shocked. "I hinted to him about the treatment."

Ivanov nodded several times and affected a brief smile.

"He claimed you didn't."

"Untrue."

"Your ER nurses and paramedics put in affidavits. They insisted you said nothing." He gave the documents to Falconer.

"Lies! I advised him, yes?"

"You aggravated the sick man's condition!" Chandler left his desk and strode up to Singh. "Something strange happened: You wrote the prescription for more steroid tablets. You added to his complications. Hippocrates said, 'Do no harm,' Doctor."

Falconer shook his head in dismay. "Chandler, we need to prepare more evidence."

Kennedy cut in, "The hour has passed for that."

Chandler offered a hint of a smile. "I've done the reviewing and the preparation for you."

Singh said, "I may have suggested."

Chandler stepped back.

"I did everything right," the Indian doctor snapped. "I'm leaving this country!"

He walked back to his desk and read Carter's documents from Florida. "Governor Carter developed necrosis and pathological fracture of the neck of his femur. The drug prednisone caused it." He presented the document to Falconer. "Overdose of steroids. The thighbone rotted and broke at the hip."

"I did not break his hip."

Falconer eased himself up. "Chandler, Singh works for me in a reputable institution. He comes fully qualified from one of the most prestigious medical schools in England. He has a specialist degree in medicine and emergency care. Behind his name, he has subspecialties."

Their reaction tickled Chandler. "Fine."

Falconer continued, "His knowledge has rescued many on the island."

Chandler teased him. "Those lives aren't in question."

"He even saved the life of Chandler's fiancée." Falconer offered a bleak, tight-lipped smile.

Kennedy threw his hands up. "Irrelevant."

"No way would he commit the mistakes Chandler alluded to." Falconer bit his lip. "I suggest we quash the case and restore the hospital's good name. Tell the local law chambers to back off my doctors."

Kennedy took out a DVD and gave it to Chandler.

He was going for the kill. "Allow me to present to you this DVD recording."

"I object to that," cried out Falconer.

Chandler held the DVD up high. "It's relevant to the case."

Ivanov hesitated, "Let's watch it."

Chandler's assistants unveiled a DVD player.

Chandler nodded to the assistant. "Casino Royale's surveillance team shot the scene as a routine round-the-clock security procedure."

Falconer slapped his hands on the desk. "Let's watch the DVD and get it over with."

The assistants started the DVD. A casino hum pervaded, but voices rose above it. Tourists gambled and laughed.

He pointed at the screen. "Note the unfortunate scene. Singh in action. The governor in inaction." He played the emergency scenario to the end. "This is fair evidence, Dr. Singh, that you gave the drugs. You didn't warn the patient."

Falconer dropped to his seat. He was dumbfounded.

Chandler mustered a small, tentative smile. "Dr. Singh is censured for failure of consent and causation. He caused the governor to end up with complications. Singh works for your institution, under contract. You're responsible for his performance."

Ivanov whispered something to his boss, who jumped up. "Ridiculous!"

Their anger made Chandler chuckle. "Singh was negligent in his duties. He caused bodily and emotional harm to Carter. The governor came to our shores to enjoy a holiday. Gray invited him. Carter's lawyers are asking for a hundred thousand dollars in damages. That includes all expenses. In addition, compensation to him of five million, legal costs to the plaintiff. Punitive damage of ten million, which I'm sure this hospital will cover. National radio and TV paid witnesses and staff to comment. The news flew from here to America to elsewhere." *Life hurts,* he thought, *but has its payday.*

"I quit, yes?" Singh responded.

Chandler heard another chain link popping. He was beginning to sense the richness of his soul. He had much more to come. Victory was a sweet itch.

The crowd scattered. Falconer brushed by him and mumbled, "Stupid man! I corrected my computer account. Every spyware has a greater spyware."

CHAPTER 22

The local judges dreaded Falconer and Gray. Chandler's lawyers found a foreign Supreme Court judge to preside.

In court, the judge summed up. "Never, in my native Australia or on this island, has anyone committed such an odious crime."

Sunrise brought heartbreak, and sunset fetched a harrowing experience. The full moon gave him a macabre feeling. His existence was melting his brain.

Kennedy touched him on the shoulder. "Easy."

"They were innocent orphans."

The judge sentenced Adolph to life in prison.

The following day, at teatime, Chandler tried to relax with the doctors. In the TV office lounge, they celebrated young Dr. May Maynard's birthday. The group sang "Happy Birthday." His voice was the loudest.

She coughed in her falsetto voice. "Thanks a million."

Something on TV caught his attention. "Anaphylaxis is a deadly reaction to a drug."

He turned up the volume.

The male anchor made an announcement. "Irene Lyford, an American tourist, died of anaphylactic shock. A doctor at Falconer General had treated her for sand fly bites. Dr. Allan Smith, the ER second in charge, consulted seventy-five-year-old Lyford. Smith prescribed triamcinolone, a steroid, but a young graduate nurse gave Penadur by mistake. Penadur is a slow-release penicillin antibiotic, to which Lyford was deadly allergic. The specialist failed to check the vial of medication before the nurse injected the drug."

Chandler called Falconer and discussed the Lyford dilemma.

"I'm a citizen of this country. I handled malpractice in the state of Florida for years. I'll help to correct the wrong."

"What wrong? We do no wrong."

"The report indicates gross neglect. The doctor is guilty of negligence. He neglected to check the vial prior to the nurse infusing the drug."

"Ambulance chaser! Our lawyers have already reviewed the case. The doctor will lose his license to practice. Goodbye!"

"New York is willing to exact retribution out of court for ten million, which includes punitive damages."

"Absurd!"

"The local and foreign media had a field day. They paid you, the chief of staff, for interviews. You received thousands of dollars. I researched the case. I can save you the time. I can detail all the damages, frustration, emotional trauma, and public embarrassment."

"You're a sucker."

"Should the court decide?"

"You're a madman. Tell them ten million. Now, get off my back."

He eased the phone down. *I will drain Falconer's pocket—and cripple him.*

CHAPTER 23

"You're unable to manage because you're monkeying around."

"Michelle, I'm asking you to consider taking over the union." Chandler had too much on his hands.

"I'll accept the position." Her lisp hardened.

"I worship freedom."

"You behave like a star player of the underworld," she retorted.

He changed the phone to his other ear. "I'll continue to dig deep. I'll better understand, and correct, your glorious world."

"Here's the deal. You quit irking the chief of staff and the hospital," she demanded.

At a union meeting, the members had elected Michelle Lang president.

She nodded. "I'm the president. You're now a friend of the present health system."

She betrayed me, thought Chandler.

The morning after, the phone rang in his office. He grabbed it.

"Hi, Michelle here at work. Al, I reconsidered what I asked of you."

"Why the sudden change?"

"Dr. Falconer—"

"I'm listening."

"Push for the cause. I'm with you all the way."

"I'm on yours."

"Al, someone needs advice."

"I'm yours to command any day."

"A Nurse Brown and a patient named Yvonia King are here.

She's a Jamaican nurse working with the ENT Russian doctor, Alex Ivanov. Her mother is a union member."

"Ivanov!" His voice was cold.

Michelle's lisp grew pronounced as she spoke. "Brown made a report. During a local anesthetic tonsillectomy on twenty-five-year-old Yvonia King, Ivanov yelled at the nurse. An instrument had fallen off her hand by mistake. He cursed her in Russian. "*Yup ... yup*" something."

"Seems like a curse. I'll research the phrase." He pressed the phone to his ear. "If the words are what I imagine, the Medical Workers Union takes offence. It's also bad for prestige."

"She wants to sue."

He weighed the pros and cons. "For the sake of peace, let's try to settle with the hospital board first."

"She's asking for your help."

He sensed the subtle challenge. "I'll set up my team and find out. I'm getting hungry. Lunch?"

"I have another thought."

He swiveled in his chair. "Speak your mind."

"Brown has a second tale to tell."

The sun hit his face.

"We'll talk at lunch. Sales reps are coming in for talks."

"I don't care," he said.

"Al! You're still the same."

He hung up and paced the floor in his office. He was a lucky man. Michelle phoned back. "Sorry, Al, something came up. Have to cancel lunch. A-a strange person called. He-he threatened to take me away."

"What d'you mean?" he demanded.

"Like kidnap me and maybe terminate Margo. Didn't get the voice."

"Check the caller ID," he told her.

"It says *unknown*. Al, please do something!" Michelle cried.

"Calm down, sweetheart. I'll manage everything. Leave it to me." He clicked off.

He had to act. He called in his staff. "I crave your support. It's about me, Michelle, Kennedy, and Margo. That's the woman who gave a kidney to Michelle."

May Maynard showed concern.

"Check into the best home security company."

Kennedy and the kidney donor moved in with the Chandlers. After work, Chandler oversaw the security installation. The company fitted the house with alarms, which communicated by phone to the network. They assigned Margo a bodyguard.

She was in a fit of temper.

"They're not the police." Kennedy held her shoulders.

Chandler touched her hand. "We'll protect you."

"We're safe now," added Michelle.

Margo wrung her hands.

"We live in trying times." Chandler squeezed her hand.

Margo shuddered and cried.

The bodyguard introduced himself. He was a short muscular bald man, about forty. No smile.

"My skin clammy." Margo rubbed her arms.

"He'll be observing the houses, and you won't know. He'll monitor you whenever you go out."

Her eyes twitched, and her lips trembled. "No flowers from him; never!"

The following day, Chandler had a crowded clinic. He dialed a number. "Hello, Dr. Falconer. Do you know the Russian phrase 'Yuppa twaya matta?' Fuck's the word Ivanov used on Brown. Only in Russian."

"It means motherfucker. The Russian doctor is a gentleman."

"Nurse Brown and a patient, Yvonia King, don't think he is."

"You've done enough siphoning from our treasury. They have our apologies."

He moved the phone to his other ear.

"I'm the chairperson of the board. You'll never get a hearing."

"We'll let them sue," Chandler countered.

"Fuck! I'll give you a hundred thousand dollars. I'll get you whores. Transform your life, for heaven's sake!"

Chandler inched to the edge of his seat. "Just so you know; I record my phone conversations."

"Oh, Mighty Jah! I'll put the matter into the agenda for next month's regular meeting. I scheduled a long list of operations and events for the month."

Chandler took off his bandanna and smiled. "Cancel your plans. Do you realize Ivanov embarrassed Brown? He upset her in the presence of the cleaners. He belittled her under the eyes of nursing students. My research shows that he's used the Russian expletive before." He inhaled sharply. "His behavior caught the attention of the newspapers and the radio. With Google, Facebook, and Twitter, news flies. It even gets to Russia. You shamed Nurse Brown before the nation."

"Nonsense!"

"Good morning, Dr. Falconer. You're responsible for Ivanov and his actions." He slammed a fist on the desk. "Brown walks around the hospital, and nurses hail her as the '*yup twaya mat* nurse.'"

"Lie!"

"People call her the '*yup twaya mat* nurse!'"

"You made up a story," Falconer charged.

"She told me she cringes every time they tease her. She recoils from society and is becoming agoraphobic. She stays in her house and stares at the four walls all day long. King suffers psychological trauma and endured bouts of anxiety attacks and suicidal depression. She even lost her job and her fiancé because of this. I have the reports."

Falconer sucked his teeth. "Name your stupid settlement. I'll give ten grand, gold digger."

"That reminds me, ENT patient Yvonia King came in to Ivanov for a tonsillectomy. She signed for general anesthesia. Ivanov gave the cheap local, much to Yvonia's discomfort."

"You make me sick, Chandler."

"Ivanov made Yvonia sicker. She now suffers from chronic TMJ syndrome—pain in her jaws from the mouth gag Ivanov used. I have the pathology report on the tonsils. No evidence of pathology." He smiled faintly, sensing victory. "Ivanov performed three hundred and one tonsillectomies during the past year."

"I-I-yes. But—"

"Our office checked with National Insurance."

"Who asked you?"

He waited until Falconer's breathing slowed down before raising his voice. "The records show Ivanov filed claims for twenty-three hundred operations at ten thousand dollars each. You permitted it. You signed it. Quite a slave your Russian doctor is!"

Falconer snapped, "Sounds like the wrong statistics."

"I'll send you photocopies of the insurance records. Ivanov kept his tonsillectomy patients in the hospital for seven days. Post-tonsillectomy stay is two to three."

"False!" Falconer yowled.

"I'll send you certified Xerox prints of the lab reports. They showed normal tonsil biopsies. You slapped National Insurance an invoice for millions instead of thousands."

"The report stinks and damages my reputation and the name of my hospital."

"My client seeks a settlement of half of what the ENT Department billed National Insurance for."

"Nine million dollars?"

The amount cracked him up. He kept his calm. "You beat me to the game. Thank you!" He plunged on. "We would accept the amount. Put Ivanov on one-year probation for his cruelty and conspiracy to defraud National Insurance. Your man must pay, too. Collusion is two minds with a single crime." He put his hands on his hips. He was enjoying the challenge. *Sorry to cut down on your baccarat money, Falconer.*

Adolph Falconer released from prison.

That evening, Chandler lounged in his den and read the newspapers headline.

Although under pressure in prison, Adolph claimed responsibility for attempting to kill Dr. Chandler with shepherd's pie, claiming he entered the house through an open door. He also said he killed a woman named Brigitte Ford. He's out of jail. The sub-line read, *Today Is the Prime Minister's Annual Pardon Day.*

Pandora wasn't around to advise the PM. A vise squeezed his consciousness and took away the freedom and change he was experiencing.

"No way!"

At sunrise, a newsflash hit the airways. "Prime Minister Gray just died in a helicopter crash. Deputy Prime Minister John will act as the chief executive."

Chandler heard a knocking on the front door. He ran down and opened it.

Michelle looked exhausted. Stress lines filled her forehead. "Did you listen to the news?"

"About the nation? Come in, please." They went upstairs.

"John was a foreign student at the university I attended."

"Oh!"

"The wheel will spin."

She looked away. Tears flowed from her eyes. They ran up to each other and hugged.

He whispered into her ear, "Come back to me."

She kissed him and rubbed her nose on his. "Adolph is out." She pressed hard against him.

"We'll watch him like an eagle would."

CHAPTER 24

In his study, Chandler sipped Campari and grapefruit juice. "I have to cool my temper." He was running through the *Sip-Sip* gossip rag. An article about the richest three men in the country caught his attention.

The Atlantic Isle Chemicals CEO, $1 billion; Prime Minister Gray, $2 billion; Dr. Obi Falconer, $0 billion. Falconer makes money, but he is a high-roller gambler ... and he might be hiding it somewhere.

Someone knocked on the front door.

He dropped the *Sip-Sip* news and tied the sash of his blue Rasta hoodie. He ran downstairs and pulled open the curtain.

The man stooped. "I'm a hospital messenger."

Chandler opened the door an inch and shaded his eyes against the sun.

The man slipped him an envelope. "From Dr. Falconer, sir."

"Take it back," Chandler ordered.

"It's for Michelle Lang."

Chandler dashed up the stairs. The chrome kettle was whistling and steam gushed from the nozzle. He prepared a mug of honey chamomile tea for Michelle. She stepped out in a white silk bathrobe and perched on a stool.

"Thanks." She tasted the tea. "The pharmacy business is booming.

Close to lucky seven." Her eyes narrowed. "With this trend, we can build a Caribbean conglomerate."

"We?"

"I've spoken to the architects and the builders."

"Tell me more."

"I'll build a home for the hearing, speech, and sight impaired."

"I appreciate your style."

"It's a three-story structure. It can house the Lupus Foundation."

"What about funds?"

"I collected enough to cover the project. I've placed an order for materials from the US."

"You fascinate me. You're my chick." He brewed Cuban coffee and sipped it. "The hospital messenger brought you something."

She glanced at the envelope. "From the god of the netherworld?" She ripped it open. "*We cherished the bond we had with your father and you. Gray owned part of Atlantic Isle Chemicals, which I front. The company and my hospital will quit doing business with you.*" She bit her lower lip. "*With Prime Minister Gray's death, his estate—and mine—ended ties with Atlantic Isle Chemicals. I'll withdraw our forty-nine percent shares in your pharmaceutical business.*"

He doubted Michelle could singlehandedly support her new building for the physically challenged and the union. He didn't want her to aggravate her lupus. "Let your giant doctor imagine me an eagle."

She held his arm.

"Leave me alone."

"Be careful. The chief will pin you," she warned.

"I'm just pondering his words in the letter. He's trying to get at me by spiting you," he said.

She hugged him.

His voice trembled. "I try to change. His scourge traps me."

"I fear for you, Al. Just ease off."

"I'll rock his mountain."

Over the next few days, Chandler relaxed in his home office. He read the *Atlantic Isle News*. He had to stay abreast of Falconer's continued abuses of the health system. Another storm was brewing.

The doctors sat on black leather chairs in the chief of staff's office. Falconer's cold eyes sniped at Chandler.

"I'm a citizen of this country. I'm exercising my rights."

"You're still American."

Chandler looked behind and to his side. "Where's Ivanov? Gone back to Russia?"

Eyes blinking, Falconer snapped, "His mother passed away."

"That's one down." The ringing phone interrupted his thoughts.

Falconer took the call. "Yes?" He listened and covered the mouthpiece. "It's for you, Chandler."

He hesitated then took the phone.

"I'm still waiting for you." It was Michelle.

His heart skipped a beat. "Refresh my memory, Michelle."

"Al! The Lupus and Disabled Children fundraising tea party."

He held his forehead. His tone of voice turned apologetic. "Mercy, I forgot. I'm attending an important meeting here."

"Our deputy prime minister is coming."

"Would you please give him my regards and my apologies?"

Michelle assumed a harsh tone. "So, you're not coming!"

"I'm with you in thought."

"My butt! He called me. The governor-general swore him in as the acting prime minister until election day."

"Please congratulate him."

"You'll wish him luck yourself. He thinks—get this—Arnold looks promising for a political career."

"Don't make me laugh!" The phone died in his hand. "I'm sorry, folks."

Falconer crossed his legs. "State your case and scram. You're wasting my time."

Chandler intended to crumble more cookies. He studied Dr. Nda Amoono, the heavyset African gynecologist. "Dr. Amoono, do you remember twenty-five-year-old Gloria Hunt?"

He gave a hoarse *no*.

Chandler showed him a photo of Hunt.

"I'm diabetic. I'm poor at remembering faces."

He produced facsimiles of her medical records with Amoono's signature. "You molested her." He threw Hunt's sworn statement at him and slid a copy to his boss.

"Rubbish!"

He shared copies of a petition with over a thousand signatures.

"Carry on with your garbage." Falconer flapped his hand.

"Hunt's Pap smear came out average and was normal three times. Amoono repeated the Pap."

Amoono's face glowed with rage. "You're no expert in women's health."

"I have the results." He slid the forms on Falconer's desk. "Here are some more reports." He addressed Amoono. "How often should a woman do a Pap smear?"

"Oh my bother! Once every two years if all's well with her."

"How many Pap smears do you do a day?"

"I'd say about twenty."

Chandler regarded Falconer with contempt. "The reports show Amoono invoiced National Insurance for forty a day."

"I never did."

"Our census and Births and Deaths Office documented no record of many of these patients."

"Nonsense!" Falconer was sweating.

"That's a case by itself. Your hospital bears the blame of double billing. I can help to set up a class action suit against Amoono for sexual molestation."

"Rot!" Amoono's eyes blazed.

Falconer was miffed. "Give me a figure."

"You're caring, sir." He savored the triumph.

"Jah! Spit out a charity."

"The Lupus Foundation, the Disabled Organization, and the Humane Society."

"Done! But shut up!"

"Ask the board to fire Amoono."

"You got it!"

"What?" Amoono stomped to the door. "A wife and ten children are waiting for me in Ghana."

Chandler empathized with him. "I'll give $10,000 to Amoono and his family. He'll live like a king." His wits sharpened. He eyed Dr. Pierre, the

Haitian pediatrician. "Dr. Sam Pierre, our private inquiry into your records indicates for the year you treated fifty patients daily. That's for seven days a week, three hundred and sixty days. You look God-fearing, Dr. Pierre."

"*Merci.*" His accented baritone trembled. "I'm Seventh-Day Adventist." He ran his fingers over high cheekbones and lantern jaw. "I acknowledge the Sabbath."

"Your records show you were off-duty fifty days within the year, *excluding* the Sabbaths. How often do you examine a child with a simple virus?"

"I'll check."

"I've spared you the trouble. Children returned to you three times a week for the common cold. These are children without any adverse medical history." He turned to the chief. "Probing fraud on anybody's behalf is legal. I'm not prying into your attempt to get Pierre citizenship, am I?"

"You knew that?"

Chandler handed out a bundle of papers. "Many complained, Pierre, and I'll show you the signed letters."

Falconer rose and stomped to the door. "Fed up!"

"You insisted on patients returning for the same uncomplicated condition. All the while, you were defrauding the insurance. It's against the law under Section 500A of the Medical and Insurance Act."

Falconer stepped back. "Who told you how many times a doctor needs to consult a patient?"

A faint smile touched Chandler's lips; he felt it. "That's a good point. Dr. Pierre, your contract expires in a year?"

"*Oui*, oh, yes."

Falconer cut in. "I'll propose his renewal."

"Even if he fondled a three-year-old girl?"

Falconer dropped to his seat.

Pierre bowed in shame. "Oh, *mon Dieu*! Oh my God!"

"I'll invite the lawyers working on the case to come in."

"You're relieved of your duties!" Falconer glared at Pierre and snapped, "I'll speak to the Board."

Pierre shuffled out. "*Mon Dieu, mon Dieu!*"

"Let the record show you recommend the firing." *Satan,* Chandler thought.

From the hospital, Chandler cell-phoned his staff. He asked them to arrange an appointment for him with the National Insurance Board.

A staff member called back.

He phoned the Medical Council. A woman answered.

"This is Al Chandler. I'd like to make an appointment with the chairperson."

"The chair is unavailable, sir."

He called Milton. "Congratulations on your appointment. I apologize for not being able to come to the fund-raiser." He joked about their university days.

"Al, people speak of your heroic deeds at the hospital. They do the same at the union and in the community. I'm recommending you for a Queen's honor."

"I'm American."

"And you're Kenyan."

"You're a magician to know that."

"I check on my friends. You're also a citizen of this island. You adapt well. We are still in the British Commonwealth. The Queen will knight you. We'll call you Sir Al Chandler."

"My heavenly kingdom!"

Just as he was through talking to his old school chum, he returned to the meeting. He was feeling revived and ready to charge. A wall television was on. They saw him and turned it off.

The telephone signaled a call. Falconer picked it up. He looked sideways at Chandler. "Crap! It's Michelle again."

Chandler gripped the cordless phone. "Hi!"

Michelle sounded hysterical. "I just got a call from Arnold. He said he called the house."

"Go ahead."

"No one's home. Margo never goes anywhere without calling."

"Stop worrying, love. She's somewhere."

"Milton spoke well of you, me, and Arnold."

"That's a good start. He has to control the National Insurance and the Medical Council."

He looked up from the phone. Falconer slit his eyes and shot him a wicked smile.

"We've made $255,000 in pledges."

"You amaze me, dear. I'll be home soon." He gave the phone back to Falconer, stood, and looked around.

"Where's Dr. Kristos Demos?"

"Our eye specialist?" The brass hat laughed. "His island wife divorced him and robbed him of his three-million-dollar house."

"My soul goes out to him."

"He's busy working again to fly to Greece and marry a Greek woman."

Bespectacled Demos entered. Chandler rose to stretch his legs. He stood well above the eye doctor, who was only about five feet tall, with a blubbery abdomen. Chandler stared down on his bald pate.

"Dr. Demos, I'm sure you're a hip eye doctor."

"The pay is good, and tax-free."

Chandler walked off to the desk and returned. "Hundreds of people have filed suits against you. Dr. Demos, Grandmother Rolle had a cataract operation. Four of her sons and ten of her thirty grandchildren had the same procedure."

Demos stared back at him blankly.

"You followed a similar pattern with the Johnsons and the Bethels." He grabbed the patients' biopsy results and took them over to Demos. "The reports indicate only the grandparents had cataracts."

Demos faked a smile. "Stupid!"

Chandler rushed back to his seat. He obtained another report and addressed Falconer. "You countersigned the insurance claims. You, the high command, charged National Insurance millions of dollars for unnecessary operations. Demos was your stooge. He's guilty of collateral lynching."

Falconer slapped his hands on the desk.

"This probe was private. The insurance knows nothing about it. I'm a concerned citizen. I'm the medical doctor for the families. I insist on an answer. Provide compensation for the people," demanded Chandler.

"Squealing is fast becoming your pastime," Falconer noted.

"I visualize the hospital doors locked."

"You're dreaming."

"No patients to treat," Chandler said.

"You're fantasizing."

"And no ambulance sirens. How about fifty million dollars to go to the families that Dr. Demos mutilated?" Chandler demanded.

Falconer spoke up. "You're of unsound mind."

"That's a good out-of-court citizen's settlement."

Falconer sprang to his feet. "Get out of here!"

Chandler gathered his documents. "I will right now."

Demos jumped up. "Let's cut this short. Save the hospital. I'll get the hell out and go to Greece."

"The monetary penalty stands," stated Chandler.

"My man's got to go back to Greece. I blame you. Whistle-blower!" Falconer spat.

"Your godfather Gray is dead. May he rest—"

"We'll cough up the cash." Falconer fell silent, clearly in deep thought.

Chandler raised an eyebrow, surprised at the quick response. He gave the promissory note to Falconer for his signature. "I'm beginning to like you."

Falconer's face turned sour.

Chandler sorted through his papers. "Where's dentist Parco?"

"I told Parco about the meeting. He weighs over two hundred pounds." Falconer chuckled. "Takes him time to shuffle in."

"On record here is an affidavit from a patient." He studied the document. "Elizabeth Darville, twenty-four, consulted Dr. Parco a month ago to clean her teeth. The records show she's healthy with a perfect mouth. Yet the dentist referred her first to consult the internist. Then he sent her to the infectious disease specialist. After him, to the gynecologist. That wasn't all. She had to consult the ophthalmologist. All for no reason."

"My hospital boasts of efficiency." Falconer's voice was still taut.

"Good reasoning, sir. On file are copies of the records, signed for by the patient—a union activist. Our investigators got them." Chandler slipped out documents from his portfolio. "Transcripts of Parco's insurance claims for the past five years bear your seal." He silently thanked the new administrator, Michelle's successor. She was a wonderful woman of Chandler's political persuasion. He praised himself for the little Internet gig he did.

Falconer fumed, "I'm tired of this rigmarole. Parco needs the money.

He raised nine children back in the Philippines. His mother is sick with Alzheimer's disease. Leukemia plagues his wife."

"We checked. He has no family." He was warming up. "A physician sends a patient from one doctor to another. He does so without reason. The chief instructs him to. He and his boss are guilty of 'boomeranging.' For every consultant at fault, fire him and replace him with a trained doctor. I'll get them from the States."

"You're demanding too much."

"The clock's ticking," Chandler said.

"Dr. Chandler!"

"Here's the best part. Compensation of twenty million dollars to all the patients in the suit. These are respectable, hardworking union members. Or ten million and your consultants go."

"Oh, Mighty Jah! No, you can't!" Falconer cried.

Chandler firmed his voice. "Yes, I can."

"Look, I'll pay! I'll take the American doctors!" Falconer shook his head, pain on his face.

A resonant ring stopped them.

"Goddammit, people!" Falconer lifted the phone to his ear. He listened, and dropped his jaw. He held his chest and sighed.

"Someone called to say Parco just hung himself."

The room fell silent.

Chandler bowed and pressed his hand on his face. "May his soul rest in quiescence. Imagine what a doctor has to do to please his master."

The chief lamented, his head down. "No one rests in peace with you around."

Dr. Oliver Jarvis took off his coat and stomped to the door. "Anything is better than working here." His apple-green dewdrop eyes blinked.

Chandler focused on him. "Dr. Jarvis, you're the psychiatrist. I filed a note on you."

His clipped voice sounded dry. "I'm gone."

"Right, considering Falconer's offering you another three-year contract."

Falconer showed surprise. "How do you know?"

"Let's just say we're good at our job." He fished out a pocket recorder from his briefcase and pressed the *on* button:

"Oh, my sweet Oliver!" someone groaned. "You do me so well."

The shrink jumped up. "Stop it!"

The tape continued to roll. "Give me more. Fuck me!"

Chandler stopped the recording.

"You're a regular asshole, darling." Jarvis' eyes bulged from their sockets.

"I repeat, do you recognize it?"

"He's a patient. I'm proud of being gay."

"Freddie Dickson had hypnotherapy for an unresolved crisis. You took advantage of him. Ten times during his days of therapy."

"He's lying."

"He walked in on you once and found you with another Freddie. He squealed on you. That's human nature, I guess."

Chandler turned to the big man. "What say you, master?" Triumph sounded in his head. "Union member Dickson is seeking a million dollars. The hospital caused him embarrassment and psychological trauma." He whistled. He took out an independent psychologist report and shoved it to Falconer.

Jarvis lunged forward and seized the tape recorder. He yanked the cassette free and aimed for the door.

"Keep it." Chandler gave him a bleak, tight-lipped smile. "Freddie made several copies."

Falconer turned his face away and mumbled something.

"Jarvis charged National Insurance for sixty sessions of hypnotherapy for Freddie Dickson alone. You approved it." Chandler brought out scans of the insurance checks. The insurance company wrote them out to the hospital. "Instead of six thousand dollars, the insurance sent checks out for six *hundred* thousand dollars. That's according to your claims."

Falconer hesitated, sweat showing on his forehead. "We'll pay."

"You're a good man! I want the dog show to open for the rich. I demand free access for the poor. Equal rights for island citizens. Americans believe in equality."

Falconer stuttered. "I-I-I totally agree."

He hammered on. "Give up the dog track ownership and offer shares to the public."

Falconer shrieked, "You're gaga!

"I'll buy major shares in the dog arena."

"Not you! You're American, you can't."

"I'm a citizen. Must I?"

"I don't need the goddamn dog sport."

"You're most kind." His voice was courteous but patronizing. "Your specialists are worthless. Invite American doctors to become department heads until our union scholarship doctors return. My president can fix that."

"That's your aim."

"I believe in fair game," Chandler said.

"Listen, Chandler, you caused enough trouble."

"For which I humbly apologize."

"You embarrassed me and drained my pocket. I didn't disappoint you. My consultants did. They were the criminals."

"May I suggest I take your position?"

"You're a madman!" Falconer screamed.

Chandler walked to the door, opened it and knocked once, giving a signal. "Did I tell you Milton John asked me to represent National Insurance? That would cut down on precious time I spend with you." He stepped up to Falconer and planted a quick kiss on his cheek. "I forgive you your sins. I'll say farewell to you."

Three police detectives stomped in. An executive from National Insurance barged in. The head police detective, with the police superintendent, approached Falconer. "Sir!"

Falconer stared with horror. His facial muscles twitched.

The superintendent grabbed his arm. "You're under arrest for fraudulent transactions against National Insurance."

"Shit!"

"Adolph wanted to win the lottery. He wanted to buy an island and grow marijuana." Chandler chuckled with a dry and cynical sound. "He did without winning. He carried out his dream with your bread. The pigs incarcerated him, but he's out. He stoked up your bunk bed."

"W-w-wait a minute, p-people!"

"The wheel will spin, but the hamster will die." Chandler took out the velvet cloth with the pineapple pendant and shoved it into Falconer's pocket. "Welcome to your new world."

The pigs handcuffed Falconer. He struggled. They restrained him. Tears emerged from his eyes and he cried like a baby.

"Mama!"

They marched away with him.

The police siren blared. Chandler rubbed his hands together, washing off the sins of Satan. *God does exist.* Falconer's words to him surfaced. *You belong behind bars.*

The doctors shuffled away without saying a word to Chandler. He stood alone in the room and felt alien. The wall TV kept him company. He raised the volume.

The TV flashed breaking news. *"An unknown assailant shot and killed Margo Kennedy. She was the common law-wife of Dr. Arnold Kennedy."*

"Oh, friggin' heavens!"

"Mrs. Kennedy had a bodyguard hired to protect her," the news anchor announced. *"Our report indicated he didn't show up today. Employees found him dead in his car in the security company's parking lot. He died of a gunshot to his forehead."*

Chandler dropped to his knees. For the first time since his parents died he cried from his heart. Tears ran down his cheeks and into the corners of his mouth. He pondered the evil of men. An echo in his soul played and replayed the words: *You're a trapped superhero.*

He pulled out his cellular phone to call Kennedy. His cell phone rang before he dialed.

"Daddy-o!"

"I was just going to dial you."

Kennedy sobbed and lamented, "She ... Al? She's fuckin' gone!"

"I'm-I'm so, so sorry."

"You destroyed the hospital."

"Arnold!"

"Makes no sense."

"Arnold, I understand your frustration, but—"

"Stop the revenge," Kennedy demanded.

"I can't believe this. Is this Arnold Kennedy?"

"Cease touting healthcare reform, Daddy-o. People want medicine for profit. Let the hospital remain as it is."

"You're my pal. I thought you and I were together on this. We're friends. Don't let—"

"I'll be happy with that."

"And you will be, Arnold."

"Sure, with my Margo now dead. All because—"

Chandler's voice trembled. "I am so-o-o-o sorry, Arnold." He suppressed a tear.

"Soon you'll destroy me."

"Arnold! Never!"

"I don't believe you. We're not friends anymore."

"Oh, no, this isn't happening."

"You bet your sweet ass it is."

"Arnold!"

"You're alone," Kennedy said.

"I can't be."

"I quit the friendship and that's definite. I'll stick to Falconer's way of life. I might even get back my job. It's safer."

The line disconnected in Chandler's trembling hand. His body slumped, and his eyes misted over. He gripped the phone and hurled it against the wall.

"God, help me, please! I can't take this anymore."

The cell phone rang. Chandler jumped on the table for it. Kennedy was calling, for sure. The caller ID showed Milton John. "Mercy!" He took the call.

"Al, executives of the union are here. I'll recommend we call the union building The Chandler Medical Union."

"Milton, you're the same you." He looked up, thinking. "We'll broaden the membership. Equality for all! Let's better ourselves. Let us show normalcy on the island. The world has changed. I feel the mutation in my bones."

"Keep up the good work, Sir Al."

"'Sir'?"

CHAPTER 25

Chandler raced home. He had to care for Michelle. He fretted over Kennedy. He had to pray for Margo's soul. He would beg for his own.

His new Lexus SUV screeched to a stop in his driveway. He ran to the front door, raced up the stairs, and hugged Michelle. He embraced thin air. She was nowhere.

"Michelle?"

He ran to all the rooms shouting for her.

"Michelle!"

She answered from another room.

"Thank you, God!"

He rushed to it. Michelle was nowhere.

He called work. He dialed the PM's office and left a message. The radiologist shunned him. The agony was driving him crazy. He picked up his cellular phone, and called Kennedy.

"Why are you hailing me?"

"Arnold, Michelle—Michelle—"

"Why is she my problem?"

"Arnold, she disappeared."

"Oh my God! You're paying for your plan."

He switched off the cell. He was going to face his problem alone. Betrayal stung him worse than the fangs of a snake.

"I liked Arnold like a twin brother. I worshipped Michelle. Does a true God exist?"

A knock on the door downstairs numbed him. He raced to it. The pigs must be bringing back his Michelle.

Kennedy leaped inside, sobbing. His face twisted in pain. He hugged Chandler. "I-I'm sorry, Daddy-o. Forgive me. You'll forever be my friend."

He nodded to Kennedy.

"I'm returning from the morgue. Margo's gone!" His eyes were red.

"Arnold, grief has its peace," Chandler said.

"If only we accept the truth," Kennedy added.

"We can't."

"I think I understand. No word so far on Michelle?" Kennedy asked.

"I-I drove around the block," Chandler moaned. "I walked back and forth. No trace of anything."

The phone cut in.

"Al, Milton here," the voice said.

"Milton!"

"I've expressed my sympathy to Dr. Kennedy. If I can do anything—" Milton said.

"Please do something!"

"I've alerted the police commissioner."

"I salute you!" said Chandler.

"Criminal Investigation is on the case."

"May I ask you a favor?"

"Proceed," said Milton.

"Let the police allow Arnold and me to work with them."

"You're not making sense, Al."

Chandler accented his words. "Milton, give us this one last favor."

"Granted."

Chandler called the police chief. "It's Chandler here. D'you mind questioning Dr. Falconer?"

"We-we do, and we have. We're-we're aware of the rage between you two. He affirmed he had nothing to do with it.

Obi Falconer wants you to stop blaming his brother. His lawyers will negotiate. 'Defamation of character and wrongful blame.' Adolph departed when we did, but he kept mumbling something we couldn't decipher."

"Explain more."

"He speaks like someone who knows the hospital."

"I don't understand."

"Be careful, Dr. Chandler, how you accuse prominent citizens."

"That's the wrong word." He had to act fast to find Michelle.

He purchased hourly ads on Atlantic Isle Radio. He put daily center-page ads in the *Atlantic Isle News*. His protégé helped. He printed posters with blown-up pictures of Michelle Lang. He stapled them on telephone posts, notice boards, and in fast-food restaurants. They stood on traffic islands and handed out fliers.

The police superintendent called him at the house. "We have the airport and docks covered. Our detectives and plainclothes police officers are knocking on doors. Working on other leads. Roadblocks erected everywhere."

Obi Falconer was the mastermind. Chandler dialed Milton. "Sorry to disturb you."

"We're old school friends."

"The matter will move faster than the Millennium Falcon. It's left to you."

"I'll direct my minister right away," Milton said.

The phone buzzed fifty-five minutes later. Michelle had to be on the line.

"Hello."

"It's Milton here, again. Al, Falconer admitted his guilt. He's the mastermind."

"Yes! You throw an excellent overhand action."

Milton told him where Michelle was.

"I'll return you the favor, Milton," Chandler promised.

Kennedy barged in from the kitchen. He was chewing something.

Chandler looked around.

"Michelle?"

She was sitting before him. He hugged her.

"Daddy-o. You're hallucinating." Kennedy laid his hand on Chandler's shoulder.

"Michelle's talking to me. She's calling me." Chandler rubbed his temples and pressed on them. "We're going for her."

"You mean the real sweetheart, Michelle?" Kennedy glanced around.

"Just follow me."

Tears emerged from his eyes and he cried like a baby.

"Mama!"

They operated like hunters in the gloom of a moonless night. Chandler and his dwarf friend squeezed into the skiff with the defense officers. The boat radio cracked in. "*We are experiencing a strong tropical depression, with lusty winds and choppy waters.*"

The prime minister's helicopter hovered above six police whaleboats and six defense tenders. Sirens blasted everywhere. The cathedral belfry pealed twelve times.

The choppy inky waters created a nightmare. The boats headed for Falconer's catamaran. They circled it. The yacht tossed and turned. The helicopter droned and focused its searchlight.

Officers took turns to call out on their bullhorns: "Adolph Falconer!"

No one responded.

Chandler expected nothing good from Adolph. Still filled with hope, he snatched an officer's bullhorn. "Michelle!"

No answer came forth.

"Try telepathy," quipped his comedy-karate pal.

"Adolph's a terrorist!"

A distant female sound came from inside the yacht. "Al!"

"Michelle, show yourself," Chandler called.

Her voice squeaked.

"Step out if you can," he called again.

They counted to ten. No sign of Michelle.

"Action!" The superintendent grabbed his gun.

The police chief fired a warning shot.

Chandler heard a voice: "Al!"

Kennedy shouted, "It's Michelle!"

Adolph hailed. His voice was raspy. "I'm coming out, you bastards!"

Chandler cringed. "Release my fiancée!"

The mad waves clapped against the boats. They ventured in closer until they butted the yacht at port and starboard. Giant Adolph emerged on deck. He had Michelle.

"Here is your krugerrand," he spat.

Adolph's coal-black face and bald head appeared, blurred by the mist and the darkness. The searchlight caught his glasses and T-shirt. "I didn't intend to have Margo shot. No intention to harm the kids, but now I have Michelle."

Kennedy sprang to his feet. "You sonofabitch! I'll smite you dead!"

Michelle's face was a mask of terror. Her lips trembled. Her hands were tied behind her back. The gust rocked the boat. Her hair was bound back.

Adolph pressed a gun to her ear. He kept pushing the gun until her head almost touched her shoulder. "I'll shoot if—"

"Listen to me, dude! I advised the pigs to hold their fire, and we will not press charges. I'll speak to Milton John. We're friends."

"Bullshit!"

"I'll beg him to pardon you."

"Lie! Lie!" Adolph pressed the gun harder to her head.

"Adolph! I swear to God, Adolph!"

Adolph didn't budge.

"I'll count to ten." Chandler was on edge. "Release her, or we'll fire."

"Drop the gun," the police chief demanded.

Chandler counted to a nervous ten.

Adolph hurled the weapon into the stormy onyx-black sea.

The police scaled the starboard rails. Chandler and Kennedy followed. They ran in. Adolph bolted into the yacht's hull.

"Al!" Michelle shook her head.

Kennedy plummeted into the patrol skiff and collected her from the rails. She whimpered, and her eyes took on a wounded look.

On board Adolph's yacht, the police czar spoke over the bullhorn. "Adolph, exit now!" He repeated the command three times. No reply came.

"Let's crash." Chandler saw something he had seen on the children's webcam recordings: yellow tubing. Next to the tubes was a gas cylinder with an imprinted label: CYANIDE. "Merciful Father!"

"Come on, attack mode."

They slipped Chandler a pistol and filed in. Guns drawn, the police charged.

Wind whistled through the portholes. A gun went off. The police boss succumbed. Chandler twisted around. He fired at Adolph.

"I'll work for you," moaned Adolph, gripping his right leg in agony. He spat at Chandler.

Chandler shot him below the waist. Three officers swooped on Adolph behind the door. Bleeding, Adolph uttered his last words. "Oh, friggin' God!" They lugged him out on the wet deck.

Chandler pounced on Adolph and kicked him.

Adolph grinned and flashed a crazed look. "You whoring motherfucker!"

He zeroed in on Adolph's mouth. No rotten teeth. "Have mercy!"

"I-I-I am Obi Falconer."

"Dude! You bloody fucker!"

Chandler remembered his words: *I didn't intend to have Margo shot*. He didn't say, *I didn't mean to shoot Margo*. Adolph would use those words.

He visualized the jail scene. The police chief had said *Adolph departed when we did. He talks like he knows the hospital*. He'd switched with Adolph!

"It's Obi Falconer!" Chandler cried.

Falconer held his head and shook it. "T-Truce! I-I'll end with a truce."

They jumped off the yacht into the pigs' boat. Chandler secured his pistol in his waist.

"Falconer abused you."

The yacht swayed in the waves and the wind. Falconer slid off the deck and dropped into the wild black waters. "I received my reward."

Chandler tossed his head and eyed the boat. It leaned on one side and started to sink. Wads of paper money floated on the waves. He grabbed one. *Hundred dollar bills by the millions. Easy come, and, as simple as one, two, three it goes. Sometimes life takes over from man and solves problems.*

They motored back to shore and approached the main port. A woman stood by a dock pole. She was white, tall, and chubby. Her fair hair was blowing.

"What the fuck!"

Michelle hugged Chandler. "Easy. You're stressed out."

The woman on the dock opened her arms. Chandler shrugged in mock resignation.

Kennedy stared saucer-eyed. "It's a ghost."

"I'm for real. I am Pandora. I never died, and it's not likely I will. The fake corpse was a life-like dummy. Paid thousands of dollars to make it resemble me. The same for the cadaver the police dragged from the sea. I had to escape from you. Remember the skeleton in your closet. I had to break loose and go. The PM, my brother, arranged it. I lived in Zurich, Switzerland."

"Holy God Almighty! I now understand Falconer's frequent visits to Switzerland. Area code 41."

"I ran Falconer General and the entire estate from there. My hospital, my dog show, and the track are part of the Gray property."

"Jesus fuckin' Christ!"

"Obi was our cat's paw. I exploited him for sex. I used him big time for business."

"Merciful fuckin' Father!"

"The donations he gave were all my honest cash and my idea. I used the consultants for sex and enterprise. The bastards thought they were using me. So glad you destroyed them for you and me. The loot you got was my precious wealth. A pittance."

She breathed in spasms. "I broke into the orphans' computers and forwarded child pornography. I was messing with my husband's brain."

"I'll kill you!"

"You already did. I employed Falconer to keep you astir. He brought me my money to Switzerland. All he wanted was a piece of my body. Oh, men—you fools!" She closed her eyes. "You got away with so much loot." Her eyes opened wide. "I intercepted your $100,000 and deposited it into my bank account. Little token payback. I read you."

Chandler remained speechless.

"We use the same Fort Knox. The wax mannequin of me by the pond fooled you. An old puppet artist—your patient—did a perfect job. Money does anything. It can fake reality. I made an ass of you."

"Damn!" He slammed his fist on his breastbone.

"Men are fools anyway. I inquired about your case. The good news is I located Astrid Wagner. A yacht here was from Switzerland." Pandora's face hardened, and her voice turned husky. "Her parents were on board. Astrid was busy with you. They took her back to Switzerland. I met her. I also met a boy. He's a teenager. He's a picture of you. His name is Al Chandler."

"Oh, Almighty Father!"

"I already dealt with Adolph."

He spoke fast. "What d'you mean?"

"I shot him. Adolph took care of my yacht. I have no use for him. He's in the morgue." Pandora flipped out a pistol. "Falconer was my sex slave and I fooled him big time. He loved ritzy items. I got him custom-made shoes from Switzerland. My brother and I did. Good to have a relative as the chief executive." She pointed the pistol at the boat.

"Pandora! This is a dream. It's a holy, fuckin' nightmare!"

He envisaged the shoes. In a flash, he solved the puzzle: OCMSFS14 ½. CMS stood for Custom Made Switzerland. ACMSFS14 ½. The A is for Adolph.

"Don't work up a sweat. You have my close friend Michelle to warm you up under her skirt. Al—at no time did I love you. I enjoyed your emails and chats—all cyberspace bull. A false sense of reality. I had to dispose of me to expend you. You're a fighter and a survivor. I arranged the will to relocate you into the servants' quarters. I had another title deed. My mansion is now yours—yours and mine. My Porsche, too, is yours and mine. Just don't ditch it into any mud pond anymore."

"I want nothing. I don't need you. I have Michelle."

"From now on, you're defunct. *Hasta la vista*, baby." She fired a shot.

"Al!" Michelle cried out. "Oh, my arm!"

Chandler snatched her and plunged into the sea. He took off his shirt and tied her arm to stop the bleeding. The waves rose and fell. Kennedy huffed and dove into the ocean. To drown together, like friends forever.

The mourners sang the hymn *City of Gold*.

Rain drizzled at the cemetery, but the sun fought against it. *Good conquering evil.*

Dressed in black, Chandler held Michelle to his right and Kennedy at his left. She sobbed and trembled. Tears filled Kennedy's eyes. John stood next to them, his head down.

The priest spoke of grief.

Chandler delivered his speech. "We extend our deepest sympathy to our friend, Arnold. Margo departed, but she's here in spirit. She's not dead, but alive in us. Her kidney dwells in Michelle Lang. The love she gave me and Arnold lives on in us forever. She showed affection to all who crossed her path."

As the casket descended, mourners laid wreaths on it. The priest quoted a hymn. *"It's all right, for I am in my Savior's care. It's all right now. My Savior answers prayers. He'll walk beside me, till I climb the heavenly stair, and everything is all right now."*

Chandler, Kennedy, and Michelle hugged and lamented until a shower came down and drenched them. "Pandora behaved like a wild animal. I grabbed the pistol and secured it in my belt. From the ocean I shot her."

Kennedy said, "She fell into the blustery waters. Dead meat for sharks."

Michelle exhaled. "My wound was slight. The bullet scraped my arm. Thank, thank ..." She shuddered and collapsed, eyes rolling up. He started CPR. "Call an ambulance right away!"

She hissed, convulsed, and turned pale. Chandler touched her cheeks. "You'll make it, baby."

The siren blared. The attendants whisked her off to Falconer General. Chandler went along. She was slipping away.

"Do not leave me, Michelle!"

The next day, Chandler sat by her bedside. She looked well.

The male hospital messenger brought him a letter. "From Acting P.M. Milton John."

He opened it and read it loud enough for Michelle to hear:

"I'm pleased to let you know government has taken over Falconer General. The Health Minister, the Medical Council, the Attorney General, and I concur. I appoint you, Al Chandler, Doctor-in-Charge of Falconer General."

He stretched over the bed. He buried his face in her neck and breathed a kiss.

"Congratulations!"

"I'll change the color of the hospital from pink to blue. It means 'Do No Harm.' I vow to uphold the oath of Hippocrates. President King promised to cut healthcare costs in America, guarantee choice, and ensure quality care for all. We will do that, too, here, starting today."

"I promise, when I'm well, I'll make you a favorite meal. New York steak with baby potatoes and butter."

"This is the beginning of a magnificent friendship. Remember I told you I had a secret?"

"Keep it in your bosom."

"I'll tell."

She swayed her head and rolled her eyes. His voice was distant and flat as he recounted his lore.

ooo

A few days later, Chandler walked into his new hospital office. He obtained the *Atlantic Isle News*, and read the headline. *Attorney Bootle's Firm Files Bankruptcy for Obi Falconer Posthumously*. Chandler's heart soared. Below was an article with the caption *New American-Trained Consultants Have Arrived*. The sub headline stated, *Blessings of US President*. He scanned the first few lines. *Union Scholarship Specialists to Replace Them When They Graduate*.

He prepared papers to buy government shares for citizens in the hundred million-dollar hospital. Milton John advised renaming the hospital Chandler Healthcare Hospital.

"The world must speak of us," said Chandler. "The universe will copy us. The planet will be better than I found it."

Dr. Ralph Ranfurly, a new American consultant, helped. Chandler cared for Michelle. They put her on daily abdominal dialysis for kidney failure. The doctors let her rest in bed in a private ward.

One day, a dog woofed in the corridor. A German shepherd, identical with his Baraka, sauntered in.

He sidled up to the frisky canine and sang, "*How much is the doggie in the window* ..." He stooped and kissed him. The dog licked his hand and his face. A note around the collar read: *Congratulations on your achievements. I'm most grateful for all your help. Always yours, Michelle.*

In the morning, Chandler stepped onto the hospital dining room's sunny deck. He gave Michelle a slow kiss. "Close your eyes. It's a surprise."

He took out a little box from his pocket. He eased out a diamond ring. To the tip of her ring finger, he held it. "Michelle Lang, will you marry me?"

She flipped her eyes open and blinked with wonder. "Yes! Wow! That's w-w-worth about a hundred thousand dollars!"

"I worked for it, remember? I recovered the money from Pandora's account. You deserve this, sweetheart."

John, the consultants, and Kennedy joined them. Union members, Michelle's old staff, and pharmacists crowded the patio. She gawked in disbelief.

The priest moseyed in. "Will you take Al Chandler to be your husband?"

"Yes!"

He repeated the same questions to Chandler. "In sickness and in health?"

"Yes! Yes!" He knelt on the floor and slid the ring onto her index finger. "I cannot live without my twin soul—and you are! With this ring, I you wed."

The new dog barked and strolled in. He had a band on a ribbon around his neck. Chandler retrieved the wedding band and slipped it onto the finger. He choked back a cry, a cry of joy. The crowd applauded. Someone walked in and the clapping stopped.

"Congratulations!" The US president clapped. Everyone put his hands together and made noise.

"Arnold, Milton suggested you enter politics."

Chandler's midget chum moved in full time. He sat with him in the kitchen and drank coffee.

"We're on the opposite side of the government, Daddy-o."

"Milton told me he's been an opposition Working Class Party man. He's resigning from office and wants you to take his place."

"Really? When I catch hell—"

"You're the expert in political science," Chandler said. "I'll throw in the little I grasped from King's campaign."

"So, got to kill the porno movie habit?" Kennedy made a karate punch. "Then I wasted years practicing medicine."

"Nothing goes to waste. Everything is a plan."

"I'll erect a karate school and comedy clubs all over the island. Make people laugh."

"Keep talking to me," Chandler said.

"I'll build you a new radiology clinic. A mobile units I'll set up to reach the poor."

"Now you're speaking fine politics."

"Let's buy a bottle of Campari and two six-packs and celebrate."

Chandler felt energized.

"I'll spike your liquor well."

"Sounds like good politics! I'm dying for a hot, juicy, jumbo American hot dog."

"I'll get a dozen."

Kennedy and Chandler conducted a successful canvassing. On May thirteenth at 11:00 p.m., at campaign headquarters, they chatted with members. The island radio made an announcement. *"National Insurance caps only government and nongovernment workers. Healthcare for all has been a major issue. It covers men, women, and children from the cradle to the grave. The people spoke. Arnold Kennedy won by a landslide."*

"No!" The radiologist-politician jumped up with joy.

Chandler laughed.

"Let it sink in, Daddy-o. Everything takes time."

The party continued at Chandler's house.

Loudspeakers from the roof blasted island music. Ten bars supplied liquor. Six shacks dished out food to thousands of fans that sang and cavorted.

"Al!" Kennedy cried out as he approached him.

Chandler danced next to his politician-crony.

"Al, listen to me!" Kennedy held his arm and shook him. "The hospital called!"

"We'll collect Michelle tomorrow morning."

"She's having a relapse. Hopeless case, the hospital says."

Chandler's future was melting away.

The news spread fast. The music stopped. As silent as a vacant cathedral, the earth stood still. Chandler rushed to the hospital.

She was comatose and was receiving dialysis and intravenous medication. They expressed no hope for recovery.

Chandler touched the palm of her hand. "You'll recuperate." His voice grew tight. He caressed her cheek. "You motivated me to be who I am."

Kennedy saw a note stuck to the clip chart. He read it. "Care to see this?"

> *Michelle will die and perish in hell. Falconer is still alive. We rescued him.*
>
> —*The Great Falconerites*

Chandler summoned a conference. The doctors expressed little hope. He called in the recently employed Chinese-American acupuncturist.

"You helped me come here." He stuck needles into Michelle's comatose body from head to toe.

A tall, muscular doctor sidled by. He stopped, eyed Michelle, and walked away. Chandler recoiled at the man's appearance and spoke to an intern.

"Never saw him before."

He ran after him. "You!"

The doctor turned and ran through the exit door. Chandler rushed after him. The strange man disappeared. Chandler peered down at the concrete pathway. He saw a yellow post-it note: *We the Falconerites are still strong. We support Falconer and Pandora. We dispose of the bastard children. We'll terminate Michelle. Falconer will emerge one day and take back what's his.*

He arranged twenty-four-hour security for Michelle. On the third day, the acupuncturist asked him to do the procedure under his guidance.

Uncertain, he plunged the needles into her skin.

"You're like a pro. You worked in ER, Doctor. You're experienced. Read the tutorial on acupuncture. Continue the treatment for another ten or eleven days."

He studied the CD-ROM and the textbooks in his office. Each night, he spent as much time as he could with Michelle and dropped asleep by her bedside. Daily he lanced needles into her skin.

Nine days passed. He was beginning to lose faith. On the tenth day, he came to visit her. The acupuncturist put needles into her head.

"Glad you're back to help."

The Chinese doctor turned around to face him. He was not the acupuncturist. "What the hell!" He turned to security. "This is an impostor! Arrest him now!"

"Falconer's still in command." He bolted before security got him.

Chandler placed the acupuncture needles into her body. *Sorry, Michelle.*

He spotted something. Her fingers started to move. He squeezed her little finger, then her hand. "I idolize you, babe."

The nurses ran to him.

"She's alive!" He smooched her on both cheeks. Her eyelids trembled. He put his lips to hers.

The acupuncturist checking in on him, Chandler continued the daily acupuncture. Only he could attend to Michelle. She was too precious to be with the Falconerite devils. By the fourteenth day, Michelle was fully conscious.

"Al?"

"She said Al!" He bent down and hugged her.

"I'm in the hospital?" She slid her arms around him. "Thanks for coming."

Chandler introduced food, vitamin and mineral therapy, and bodywork. She received massage and physiotherapy daily. Kidney functions were normal.

In a month, Chandler discharged her and took her home. "Never fight a winner. You are the victor."

Kennedy gripped a box in his arm. He brought in a huge bouquet of tropical flowers he and Chandler had ordered.

"Thanks." She smiled as she reclined in the love seat in the study.

"Open the box."

"A fourteen-day Mediterranean cruise for three! Me, you, and Arnold."

They hugged her.

Chandler said, "Meet Prime Minister Arnold Kennedy."

She raised an eyebrow.

Kennedy opened his arms wide. "Let me introduce you to the new head of Chandler Healthcare facilities."

Shock glazed her face. "You're confusing me."

They explained everything.

"We just couldn't afford more of the same." Chandler swept his arms open and raised them high. "'Do no harm.' Hippocrates can now repose in his grave." He dropped his hands. "Now, Arnold will take over your project. He'll finish the structure for the disabled."

The dwarf politician nodded. "Michelle, we'll name the building after you. I'm thinking of making Al my health minister. Healthcare falls under his portfolio. National Insurance covers only 65 percent of the population. Al will deal with the entire country."

She had a special hug for Chandler.

"Your cabinet is taking form." Chandler turned to Michelle and kissed her. "I drool over your lisping. You're the first person I'll see in the morning. Nude!"

Michelle winked. "Just keep your pajamas on."

"You're the quintessence of existence to me, Michelle. We'll spread the word of the island's success. We'll do this for you, for us, for the Isle, and for all people. Life just began again."

She ogled him. "Got something to tell you. Close your eyes. I'm pregnant."

His eyes opened wide. "Goodness!"

"More like badness, Al."

He embraced her. "T-t-the baby will have a brother in Switzerland. I'll find him. I'll unite the children. I found Margo for you, right? My world changed, and I'll go with the flow. I'm free at last to enjoy the majestic symphony of life, liberty, and joy."

"That's heavy stuff!" Kennedy opened the lid of the box he brought with him. "Al, got something for you."

He glanced at the gift. "An empty cage?"

"Look at the bottom."

"A boa constrictor!"

Michelle cringed and peered into the box. "A baby one!"

He tapped Kennedy on the back of his shoulders.

The new dog barked. He trotted in, sat on his hind legs, and stared at them. Chandler opened his hands and smiled at his palms. He stooped and patted him on his back. "Let's call him Whistle-blower."

The following day, Kennedy phoned from the prime minister's office. "Al, remember Pandora's will to strip you of the mansion and the car."

"Go on, Prime Minister Kennedy."

"The document was a fake. I checked it. You can move over to the house. The house and the car are yours exclusively."

"I know."

About seven in the morning, the phone woke him up. "Hello, Al Chandler speaking."

Michelle was still sleeping. He pulled himself up on a pillow. He squeezed his eyes and squinted against the morning sun through the window.

"It's Abraham King. I have a security briefing soon. I read about the great job you accomplished on the island. It's been six months. Your deadline. I still admire your charisma. The United Nations is boasting about it. You created an impression on the world."

"President King, I'm just a doctor."

"You are still a US citizen. I researched you. You kept saying you were an orphan. We found your real parents."

"Y-you're pulling my leg."

"They worked at an American embassy in Indonesia. Your father was American."

Chandler grew patriotic, and a strange feeling gripped him.

"You were born there. A guerilla group took you and your parents hostage. America rescued you and sent you to an orphanage in Kenya. We dispatched Secretary of State Hailey Clint to Indonesia. She had to negotiate your parents' release. They're in Coral Springs, Florida."

His breath caught in his throat, and he felt numb.

"Al, the rumor is Dr. Falconer is alive. I sent the CIA to Atlantic Isle to check. He's not. Divers found his body. They buried him in Switzerland, alongside Pandora's grave."

He rubbed his chin, exposing his peace symbol tattoo.

"You advocated healthcare reform well in Atlantic Isle."

"Your knowledge is a marvel."

"The American ambassador kept me informed. My health secretary is resigning. I'm offering you the position. Call me and let me know what you decide." The phone went dead.

He shook his wife. "Wake up! Michelle? Oh my God!"

CPSIA information can be obtained at www.ICGtesting.com
Printed in the USA
LVOW082217260112

265661LV00001B/2/P